Praise for the Nationally Bestselling Authors of

# *Finding Amos*

"J. D. Mason's stark portrayals of her characters and their innermost thoughts bring the readers right into the emotional center of the story. Those who enjoy Carl Weber and Eric Jerome Dickey will add Mason to their list of favorites."

—*Booklist*

"J. D. Mason will take your breath away."

—*RT Book Reviews*

"ReShonda Tate Billingsley's engaging voice will keep readers turning the pages and savoring each scandalous revelation."

—*Publishers Weekly* (starred review)

"Billingsley infuses her text with just the right dose of humor to balance the novel's serious events."

—*Library Journal* (starred review)

"Bernice L. McFadden has a wonderful ear for dialogue, and her entertaining prose equally accommodates humor and pathos."

—*The New York Times Book Review*

"Truly a welcomed voice in the literary world."

—Terry McMillan

"Writing in a mystical style . . . McFadden is an imaginative storyteller who mesmerizes readers with her words."

—*Library Journal*

ALSO BY J. D. MASON

*Crazy, Sexy, Revenge*

*Drop Dead, Gorgeous*

*Beautiful, Dirty, Rich*

*Somebody Pick Up My Pieces*


ALSO BY ReSHONDA TATE BILLINGSLEY

*Mama's Boy*

*What's Done in the Dark*

*The Secret She Kept*

*Say Amen, Again*


ALSO BY BERNICE L. McFADDEN

*Loving Donavan*

*Gathering of Waters*

*My Name Is Butterfly*

*Glorious*

# FINDING AMOS

J. D. MASON
ReSHONDA TATE BILLINGSLEY
*and*
BERNICE L. McFADDEN

Gallery Books

New York    London    Toronto    Sydney    New Delhi

Gallery Books
An Imprint of Simon & Schuster, Inc.
1230 Avenue of the Americas
New York, NY 10020

First Gallery Books trade paperback edition October 2015

GALLERY BOOKS and colophon are registered trademarks of Simon & Schuster, Inc.

For information about special discounts for bulk purchases, please contact Simon & Schuster Special Sales at 1-866-506-1949 or business@simonandschuster.com.

The Simon & Schuster Speakers Bureau can bring authors to your live event. For more information or to book an event contact the Simon & Schuster Speakers Bureau at 1-866-248-3049 or visit our website at www.simonspeakers.com.

Designed by Akasha Archer
Cover images © Shutterstock

Manufactured in the United States of America

10  9  8  7  6  5  4  3  2  1

Library of Congress Cataloging-in-Publication Data

Mason, J. D.
    Amos / J. D. Mason, ReShonda Tate Billingsley, and Bernice L. McFadden.—
1st Gallery Books trade paperback ed.
        p.   cm.
    1. African American women—Fiction. 2. African American families—
Fiction.   3. Alzheimer's disease—Patients—Fiction. I. Billingsley, ReShonda Tate.
II. McFadden, Bernice L. III. Title.
PS3613.A817A79 2013
813'.6—dc23
                                                        2012033947

ISBN 978-1-4516-1704-7
ISBN 978-1-4516-1726-9 (ebook)

*To Junior. The first man I ever loved.—JDM*

*To Bruce. I'll always be a daddy's girl.—RTB*

*For my daddy.—BLM*

# Amos

*H*e was barreling down the dirty road leading toward Tupelo, Mississippi, in his copper-brown 1969 Cadillac Eldorado. Amos was returning for the first time since he'd walked down the same road twelve years ago, determined to leave his childhood home forever. Yet he remembered every curve, every crook in that old road.

He'd promised never to set foot in that small country town again. Amos had been seventeen then, with seventy-eight dollars in his pockets that he'd saved from too many summers of picking cotton. He swore he would not grow old in a place like this, the way his daddy was doing. And he sure as hell wasn't dying down here.

When he left, he'd headed north. Amos hopped on a bus to Detroit and never looked back. The only reason he was returning now was to show his old man that he'd been wrong about his son. Amos tapped his fingers on the steering wheel, listening to the sound of his own voice playing through the speakers. He bobbed his head and sang along to lyrics he'd written. It was his first single release, and he didn't doubt that there would be many more to come.

"You made a fool outta me, baby!" he sang. "But I'll gladly be the fool ova you!"

All he'd ever wanted to do was to sing and make music. He was born with a melody in his head so strong that it dared him to chase after it all the way to Motown.

*His daddy never believed he could do it. He said Amos should stay on the farm like all the other boys were doing.*

*"Ya play that piano and sang to have a good time, boy. Good-time party, hoopin' and hollerin' like you ain't got nothing betta to do. But a real man works. He goes out into the world and puts in his time."*

*Amos used to sit on the top step of the porch at his daddy's feet.* A real man. *His daddy used to throw those words around for Amos's benefit.* A real man works. A real man's hands got calluses. A real man's got a crooked back from being bent over all the damn time workin' in them fields. *Nah. As often as he had to listen to his daddy telling him that, he never bought into it. Real men were cool. They sat on top of barstools, with guitars straddling their knees, singing out into audiences filled with fine women made up pretty and smelling nice, nodding their heads and swaying their round hips to the sounds of soulful music.*

*Amos was tired of listening to his daddy complain about what kind of man he should be. And that afternoon, sitting on those steps, he knew that the next words to come out of his mouth would be the words to seal his fate—and finally set him free—or get him killed.*

*"What about Bo Carter, Robert Johnson, 'Papa Charlie' McCoy, Otis Redding, Chuck Berry, Little Richard?"*

*His daddy cut his eyes at him. "What 'bout 'em?"*

*"They make music. Music you listen to all the time. You mean to tell me that you don't think what they do is work? You mean to say that they ain't real men?"*

*Southern boys knew better than ever to challenge their daddies. Amos knew better, too, but more than that, he knew what he wanted and what he didn't want. He didn't want to become the man his daddy was.*

*His daddy's gaze sliced right through him. "You ain't Bo Carter. You ain't Robert Johnson or Otis Redding."*

"But I could be," Amos protested, standing up to his old man in a way that he had never had the courage to before. "You don't know."

His daddy leaned forward and balanced his elbows on his knees. "Yo momma done filled yo head with nonsense, son. Ain't nothin' special 'bout you or what you wanna do. All I know is what I know. You stay here, you work 'long side me out there." He pointed to the fields across the dirt road.

Amos swallowed and felt his heart racing in his chest. "I ain't workin' myself to death in them fields, Daddy."

His father slowly stood up and adjusted his pants. Amos thought for sure his old man was getting ready to take off his belt and beat the mess out of him, but the old man just huffed.

"I 'spect you to be gone by mornin'" was the last thing he said to Amos before going back inside the house.

When his momma passed away, Amos hadn't even come back for the funeral. But he was going home now to show that old man that Amos's so-called foolish notions had gotten him a new Cadillac and a record deal with Atlantic Records. His first single was hot like fire, baby!

Wide-open, lush green fields on either side of that road stretched along for about forever. They sure had more trees in Tupelo than they did in Detroit. Amos pushed his foot down hard on the gas.

"Show me whatchu workin' with, baby!" he shouted, enthralled by the purr of the engine.

"Slow down 'fore you run us off this road," the pretty woman sitting next to him said. She'd been staring out of her window the whole time he'd been driving. Amos wanted so badly to see her face, but she never turned away from the window. She looked good, though. He could tell just by the way she was built—thick, shapely, wearing that pretty dress she always wore, the one with the flowers and the buttons that went all the way down the front. She'd crossed one luscious thigh over the other one, and that dress split nearly up to her hips.

"*Why don't you lean over here and give me some sugah?*" he coaxed.

*She just shook her head.*

*Wait until his daddy saw this fine thing right here! He didn't think Amos would amount to nothing. He'd been wrong. And Amos was about to show him how wrong he was.*

*He turned his head to one side and saw the vast delta spread out like a blanket, but when he turned his head back, the pretty woman sitting next to him was gone. That was strange. How could she be gone? Ahead of him, through the windshield, he saw tall buildings mixing in with the trees. They didn't have buildings like that in the country. The sound of his music coming from the radio started to fade and mix over to another man's voice.*

"*In an effort to win over evangelical voters, GOP candidate Mitt Romney emphasized in a commencement speech to university graduates his opposition to President Obama's support of gay marriage, by stating that he believes the sanctity of marriage should be between . . .*"

*Something wasn't right. The world was shifting by the second. Amos watched with growing bafflement as the narrow road leading him home transformed like magic in front of his eyes. That old pot-holed road turned into a ribbon of black asphalt. He wasn't alone, no sir. Traffic was coming straight at him, horns honking. "Watch out, old man!"*

*Amos glanced up at his rearview mirror and was startled by the reflection of the person staring back at him. It was his face, but not the face he had expected to see. Gray hair sprinkled his head and beard. He glanced at his hands, old man hands, gripping the steering wheel. This wasn't his prized Cadillac. He was driving the old beater he'd bought secondhand from his old bass guitarist.*

Panic took over where confusion left off, and Amos swerved at the last moment to avoid hitting an oncoming SUV. He realized he was driving the wrong way down a one-way street and careened crazily onto the sidewalk and into a streetlight, then felt a massive jolt amid the crashing metal and splintering glass . . . and then nothing.

# Cass

## Fall 2011

"We found your name and number written on the back of a drugstore receipt in his wallet," the nurse explained. Her nameplate read IRIS, and she'd been the one Cass had spoken to over the phone.

Cass Edwards followed the nurse down the long hospital corridor lined with rooms. She'd been catering a fiftieth wedding anniversary party when she got the call that her "father" had been involved in a car accident. She'd left in the middle of the job to come here.

"He was driving the wrong way down a one-way street. The police said he swerved to avoid a collision with another vehicle and crashed into a pole. He has a severe concussion, a broken hip, some swelling around his spinal cord, and a fractured ankle. He's lucky to be alive."

"The doctor said he had something wrong with his heart and that his liver was bad?" Cass probed, concerned.

"He has some blockage in one of the arteries," Iris said solemnly, stopping in the hallway. "We're monitoring him closely, and the doctor believes he'll have to have surgery eventually." She almost seemed to be apologizing for Amos's condition. "There's evidence that your father's already had several heart attacks, Ms. Edwards. Were you aware of that?"

"He's not my father," Cass clarified.

The nurse was caught off guard. "I'm sorry. I just assumed—"

"He's my stepfather," she said, letting Iris off the hook.

The nurse scratched her head, looking puzzled. "You're the only next of kin we could locate," she explained, pushing open the door to Amos's room.

On most days, the image she had of Amos had been constant through the years: a dark and handsome man who had a head full of hair, gold chains around his neck, and rings on nearly every finger, sitting at the kitchen table with the yellow Formica top. But looking at him lying there, a gray-haired, broken old man with deep lines etched in his face, Cass became painfully aware of how many years had passed since she'd last laid eyes on the only father she'd ever known. Amos had come into her life when she was just a toddler, barely walking and still in diapers. She barely knew her biological father, and as far as she was concerned, especially as a kid, that didn't matter because she had Amos. She'd had Amos Davis—until she didn't.

He'd been her first love. She stood there, looking down at him and thinking that most girls probably felt that way about their father. He didn't know it, but he'd left a void in her that seemed impossible to fill. Early in her life Cass had established a pattern of falling for the wrong guy that she still hadn't been able to remedy. At sixteen she'd gotten pregnant by her boyfriend, Ricky, and she'd convinced herself that she was in love and that the two of them needed to spend their lives together. It wasn't until after they were finally able to legally get married that she realized she and Ricky were not meant to be together. And a few years later, Ricky had decided that dying was better than living and took his own life. Cass was startled by the vibration of her cell phone in her purse. She pulled it out and read the text sent by her son.

*Ma— Can U spot a brotha a 20? I need some gas.*

She rolled her eyes and shoved the phone back into her purse.

"He's been sleeping a lot," Iris explained. "But you're more than welcome to stay."

Cass waited for the nurse to leave and then quietly pulled a chair over next to Amos's bed. She didn't know what surprised her most: the fact that he was carrying her phone number around in his wallet, or her reaction to seeing him again after all these years. She'd tried to keep in contact with him after he left. But Amos had made promises he either never intended to honor or just didn't know how to keep.

*"All you got to do is say the word, Li'l Mama Cass."* Amos laughed, pulled her close, and kissed her head. *"You know I'm always here for you, girl."*

Cass had been ten when Amos left her mother. When he left her, too.

"Men like Amos leave and don't look back," her mother told her once before she passed away. No matter how many years passed, her mother never shed the anger she felt toward him. *"He's a liar and a fool, Cass. You might as well believe in Santa Claus or the Tooth Fairy if you're goin' to put your faith in him. Don't fret about Amos, Cassandra. You leave him alone, and keep it movin'. If he ain't taught you nothin' else, he sure as hell should've taught you that."*

Cass's mother had passed away from cancer eight years ago. Cass had no brothers or sisters, and at the sight of Amos now, lying there asleep, looking worn-out and frail, she realized that, besides her son, RJ, Amos was the closest thing to family she had left. She hadn't spoken to him in years, and at times she had assumed he was dead. Leave it to Amos to live forever, she thought, smiling despite her conflicting feelings.

She hated him. She loved him. He was a walking, talking, breathing contradiction, and it was impossible for anybody to feel mildly about him. His kisses could be as biting as his temper. His love stung almost as much as his curses. But Amos always managed to balance the opposites of himself in such a way as to leave a person second-guessing herself until she didn't know whether she loved him or hated him. That's what happened to Cass's mother. She finally said, Enough!

*"I'm tired, Amos!"*

Seeing her mother cry was gut-wrenching, and it was not hard for young Cass to hate the person making her cry.

*"It ain't me makin' you tired, Linda," he said, defending himself.*

He sounded as if her crying didn't matter. But it broke Cass's heart.

*"Of course it's you! It's always you! You doin' whatever the hell you want when you want! You actin' like you love me when you here, then forgettin' my name as soon as you walk out that door! You want me to sit here and act like it don't bother me! You got all these women and I'm just supposed to . . . to be cool with all that?"*

*The expression on her face showed how badly she was falling apart, and he didn't seem to care one way or another. He just tossed his things carelessly into the suitcase on the bed.*

*"You out there makin' babies with other women! Layin' up with them, then comin' home to me, and you got the nerve to get pissed when I say somethin'! You can't see how wrong that is? Are you that damn selfish that you can't see how much this hurts me?"*

*That's when he stopped and looked at her, really looked at her for the first time since he'd walked through the door.* "Course I see you hurtin', Linda," *he said, unemotionally.* "I see it. I hear it. Hell! I can even taste it! That's some bitter shit, but no matter what I do, I can't change it. We been at this too damn long and that's how it is, how it's always gonna be."

*Her mother looked so defeated and worn.* "I love you," *she said, sadly.* "I thought you loved me, too."

*He went back to packing.* "There you go again." *He shook his head. Amos sounded sad himself, as if this was something he had no control over.* "Love is a four-letter word. Most times, that's all it ever amounts to."

Her mother had never been able to compete with his true love, Cass concluded, watching him now, all these years later. The only thing Amos really loved was music, black soul music that paid homage to broken souls and broken hearts. Back then she remembered how confused and hurt she had felt when he made her mother cry. Amos had been honest in his own way. He had loved Linda the best he could, which was nowhere near good enough. Without realizing it, that man had set a precedent for Cass. He had taught her that a man loved the best he could, leaving a woman to cry herself to sleep every night until she came to her senses and let him go.

His eyes fluttered until they finally opened. Cass sat up in her chair, suddenly aware that she, too, had changed so much since he had last seen her. Amos blinked, focused on the ceiling of the hospital room. She stood up and hovered over him. As a little girl, she had called him Daddy.

"Amos," she said softly.

He turned his head slightly and stared at her.

That vivid sparkle he'd had in his eyes when she was growing up had grown dull. He'd been so full of fire the last time she'd seen him. Cass had been in her twenties back then. Her mother had been diagnosed with cancer, and she looked him up and asked if she could stop by. She needed to talk to him, to tell him how scared she was that she was losing her mother. She needed for him to try to step in—even after all the time that had passed—and try to take away the fear, the loneliness that she knew losing her mother would leave behind.

*"You still playing?" she asked, sitting in a chair across from Amos on his couch.*

*His face lit up. "You know me, Li'l Mama Cass." He beamed. "I'ma play till my fingers fall off and I can't raise my arms."*

That was the first time she realized that any passion he ever had for her or her mother could never be matched by the passion he had for his music. And she felt sorry for any woman who thought she could take its place. She was no different. Cass left his apartment feeling emptier than she had before she walked in.

The old man blinked. "Do you know where you are, Amos?" she asked quietly, as she hovered over him.

His eyes darted around the room, and he cleared his throat. "Hos-hospital?"

She nodded. The nurse said that the doctors suspect that he had Alzheimer's. "Do you remember me?"

His blank stare alarmed her for a second, but soon recognition filled his eyes, and Amos managed to smile. "Course I do," he said sluggishly. "Li'l Mama Cass."

Cass couldn't help but smile. She hadn't heard her name said like that in years. She studied his ravaged face, wondering how or where he might've ended up. They said she'd been the only one they could locate. But she wasn't Amos's biological daughter. She knew he had other children. Maybe he'd even managed to settle down and get married.

"I need to call your family, Amos," she told him. "Let them know where you are and that you're all right."

Amos looked at her as if she were speaking a foreign language.

"Who can I contact? Who else needs to know you're here?"

Emptiness filled his eyes, but Amos smiled again. "Li'l Mama Cass," he repeated. "How you been, baby?"

Lonely, Amos, she thought but didn't say. And sometimes lost. Staring into his eyes, she suddenly realized that maybe Amos was just as lonely and just as lost as she was. "Fine," she lied. "I'm fine, Amos."

# *Toya*

Euphoric sighs filled the room, and Toya McCann exhaled in relief. She'd done good. Real good if she judged by the look of contentment on Max's face. The unadulterated look of happiness that danced in his eyes gave her hope. Finally, he would realize that she was everything that he needed *and* wanted.

"Ummm, you want more?" Toya asked, rolling over in her queen-size bed, which took up most of the space in her tiny bedroom. She used her index finger to draw a *T* on his chest. "Are you ready for round three?"

"Girl, you're like a dog in heat," Max joked as he gently pushed her aside and sat up. "But I got to get going." He leaned over and picked up his cell phone. "My wife has called me twenty times." He sighed. "I'm really gonna hear it when I get home tonight."

His wife. Toya was so sick of Max's wife, she didn't know what to do. "Even more reason for you to stay the night with me," she cooed.

He had the nerve to laugh as if she'd said something really funny. "Come on, babe. You know I can't do that."

Toya was about to protest when Max flipped open his phone, punched some numbers in the keypad, then put the phone to his ear.

"Hey, honey," Max said, his voice lively and warm, "sorry I missed your call." He paused, and then nodded like his wife could actually see him. "I know, babe. I tell you, this old phone of mine won't hold a charge." Another pause. "I know. Sorry, I'll get a new one tomorrow. Anyway, I got held up at the office." He sounded like he was lying, and Toya couldn't believe Max's wife was falling for any of that. "We're getting ready for the strategy meeting tomorrow, and my part of the presentation is a mess," Max continued. "I tried to call you, but this phone kept acting up. Anyway, I'm on my way home now. Try to—" He abruptly disconnected the call.

Toya stared at him in disbelief. He could lie so easily to his wife.

"What? Gotta make her think the battery is dead." Max leaned over and lightly kissed Toya on the lips. "I need to get going. It's only so long that battery excuse is gonna fly."

Toya was speechless. Max had done some low-down dirty things in the course of their six-month relationship, but this one was outright bold. He used to at least respect her enough to make his phone calls to his wife in the bathroom. Now he didn't even bother. That wasn't a development that augured well for the future.

Clueless as to her mood, Max nibbled her neck and Toya pulled away. He leaned back, surprised at her reaction. "What's wrong with you?"

"What do you think is wrong with me?" she replied, feeling her blood starting to boil. She took a deep breath, trying to calm herself, and decided to try another route. "I don't want you to go," she gently said.

He squeezed her exposed breast, then stood up. "Trust, I

don't wanna go. But I have to. You know how Jewel gets to trippin'."

Jewel, Jewel, Jewel. He was always worried about Jewel. Toya wanted to scream, *When are my feelings going to matter?* Instead, she just said, "Max—"

"Let me jump in the shower real quick," Max said, cutting her off as he darted into the bathroom.

Left alone, Toya grabbed the comforter to cover her naked body, then pulled herself up against the headboard. She desperately fought back tears as she wondered why she couldn't find a man of her own to love.

*Because you blew any decent chances at love,* she reminded herself. *Because you're just like your mother.*

*Like mother, like daughter.*

Her mother's words from earlier in the week rang in her head. Only Melba Jean McCann had said them as if they were a compliment.

"You're just like me, sweet pea," Melba had said when Toya lamented her relationship with Max. "We love different from most folks. Like mother, like daughter."

But Toya didn't want to be anything like her mother—-bitter after being left with a lifetime of broken hearts and shattered dreams. She had been that way for as long as Toya could remember, so she couldn't understand why Toya expected the men in her life to be any different. They were always leaving—just like her father.

*"If a man stay planted too long, weeds grow underneath his feet."*

Toya didn't know why that line popped into her head. She'd heard Amos say it when she was a child.

*"You haven't been givin' my sugah away, have you?"* Five-year-old

*Toya giggled as her father tickled her chin. "I told you, that sugah only belongs to me."*

*"I wish I could hear you say the same thing about me," Melba Jean muttered from the kitchen, where she was putting up dishes. She'd cooked a delicious meal of fried chicken, corn casserole, turnip greens, and corn bread. Toya knew after a meal like that, her dad would spend all evening with them.*

*Amos cut his eyes at Melba Jean, then turned back to Toya without saying a word. "And on that note, baby girl, time for me to go."*

*He hadn't been around for long, but she had loved having him there. Amos had never been more than a fantasy for her growing up, but for that short period of time, he'd been real. She stuck out her bottom lip and frowned at her mother. If Toya were brave enough, she would've asked her mother why she was always doing stuff to run her daddy off. The way she nagged, fussed, and complained, it was no wonder Amos never wanted to stay at home.*

*Shoot, if she could've, Toya would've left with him. In fact, she'd asked him on more than one occasion if she could go with him, and his reply always was, "Who's gonna be here to take care of yo momma if you run off with me? Besides—pretty, young thangs like you don't need to be running the streets with an old man like me."*

*That would be followed by some quip from Melba Jean like, "Unless that pretty young thang is a thirty-six double-D."*

*Toya didn't know what that meant, but it always brought a chuckle from her father. But never enough to make him change his mind and stay home.*

*"Man stay planted too long, weeds grow underneath his feet," he said, placing his big, brown hat on his head as he exited out the front door.*

Toya shook off the memory. She'd been determined not

to nag, or complain, or fuss like her mother. She didn't want to run her man off as well. But her strategy of niceness didn't seem like it was working.

*Like mother, like daughter.*

Max came out of the bathroom, drying himself with an oversize towel. She admired his nakedness as the water glistened on his body. He had a rock-hard physique, complete with abs that looked like they had been carved by Michelangelo himself. He was blue-black, as her mother used to say about dark-skinned men, and was the sexiest man Toya had ever seen.

He half smiled when he noticed her taking him in. "You like what you see?" he said, dropping the towel.

She did. Very much. Then a voice reminded her that he had just cleaned himself up to go home to his wife.

"Max, where is this going?" Toya asked, deciding to toss aside her no-nagging rule. "I'm tired of making love to you, only to have you leave me and go home to your wife." Max was the fifth married man she'd been with, and Toya was determined he would be the last.

He let out a heavy sigh as he walked over to pick up his clothes. "Can we please not have this argument?" he said as he slipped his legs in his underwear, then slid on his pants.

Toya fought back the sick feeling rising in her stomach. The last time he'd left her, she'd cried herself to sleep and vowed to put an end to the affair. But the next time he'd called, speaking to her with that suave, debonair voice of his, he'd convinced her to let him back in.

But now Toya told herself she *really* was going to end it.

"I can't do this," she whispered with resolve.

He slid his shirt over his head. "Yeah, I know," he said indifferently, slipping his feet into his shoes. He leaned over and kissed her. "I'll call you tomorrow. Love you, babe."

He hadn't heard one word she'd said, and if he had heard her, he hadn't cared. Like a businessman on the run, he hurried out of the door. Toya wanted to cry, but honestly, she didn't have any more tears left. She snuggled into her pillow and said a silent prayer that God would give her strength to ignore that call tomorrow—and every day thereafter.

# Tomiko

Tomiko stared at the bright white document on her computer screen. Four black words were staring back at her: "I can't do this." She'd typed that line more than an hour ago. It was what she did whenever she was blocked. She'd type those words and read them enough times until a voice in her head would say, "Of course you can." Then the words she really needed—the ones to start the next project—would finally come. But not today. Today she really couldn't do it. For the first time in a long time she was experiencing the dreaded writer's block, which she didn't really believe in, but the page was still blank.

Annoyed, Tomiko pushed away from the desk and walked over to the large picture window that looked out onto her spacious backyard. Weeks earlier, winter had waved its frigid wand, and magically everything green and vibrant had turned brown. The family of squirrels leaping from one naked tree limb to the next didn't seem to mind the chill, or the baleful lack of color, but the season was bringing Tomiko down.

"What's wrong with you?" she uttered aloud to the empty room. "It can't just be the winter blues. It must be something else, so what is it?"

The walls remained mute.

"Okay, I guess I'm still not over him," she said with a bitter laugh.

Desmond Pilgrim. What a name! And what a love affair she'd had with her chiseled state trooper. Tomiko had come from nothing but had reached the upper echelon. She favored fine restaurants and the theater and wanted to travel the world. Desmond, well, he preferred takeout and was fond of saying, "The world will still be there when I retire. That's when I plan on traveling."

When they met, Tomiko was just turning twenty-nine and he was thirty-five. Did he really think she would wait two decades to apply for a passport? He did, and she convinced herself that she could.

The beginning was heavenly. His British accent, the stylish car he drove, and the way he walked on ahead, parting the crowd and making way for her passage, made her feel like a queen. Tomiko was dazzled. But not dazzled enough to accept his marriage proposal. In four years of dating he'd asked her to marry him three times, and each time she'd turned him down. "I love you, Desmond, but my career is just starting to take off," or "I just found out that my publisher wants to send me on a thirty-city book tour, so let's talk about it when I get back," or "I've got so much on my plate now with this new series I'm working on. I'm already two months late on the deadline, and it's really hard to focus."

He wasn't a bad guy. The time they had been able to spend together was magical, and she supposed that's why she felt his absence so strongly. Perhaps, she mused as she once again took her seat in front of her computer, it was the same reason why, decades later, she felt the same void whenever she thought about her father. Oh, Lord. Was she really about to go *there*?

She hadn't thought about her dad, Amos, in a long time. Not even holidays or birthdays conjured her memories of him anymore, but lonliness could do it, sometimes. That little girl in her still clung to him, despite Tomiko's misgivings about it. She'd let him go from her thoughts and her heart, at least, that's what she'd tell herself. But time spent with him had been magical, too magical and too temporary.

When Tomiko was born, her mother, Ruby, wanted to name her Elaine, after a favorite great-aunt. Even though she had died long ago, she had left an indelible impression on Ruby's heart. Aunt Elaine had always been the one to tell her that she was beautiful and that she could be anything in the world. Ruby's own mother had never told her that. But Ruby had told her stories about her father, Amos, and Tomiko had loved hearing them. Not all were good, though. Some of those stories stole her breath and broke her heart.

*Amos didn't favor that name at all. When Ruby woke up the day after giving birth, she found him standing at the foot of the hospital bed. His eyes were bloodshot, and whiskey was seeping from his pores. It was just after seven on a Sunday morning, and Amos had come straight to the hospital after playing at two different clubs.*

*He shook his head. "Nah, baby, we ain't gonna name her no damn Elaine."*

*The baby was swaddled in a hospital-issue pink blanket, sleeping contentedly on Ruby's chest. When Amos just stood there fidgeting, Ruby asked, "Well, don't you wanna see her?"*

*Of course he did. That was why he had come. He wanted to see his brand-new baby. So why couldn't he will himself to move closer?*

*"Come on, Amos, hold the baby," Ruby urged sweetly.*

*Amos sauntered over and sat down on the side of the bed. Ruby gently poured the baby into his arms.*

*"I think we should name her Tomiko," he said, smiling down at his daughter.*

*Ruby blinked. "Toe-mee-who?"*

*"Tomiko."*

*"What kinda name is that?"*

*"Japanese."*

*"This baby ain't Japanese, Amos. She black!"*

*Laughter from the other new mother filtered through the white privacy curtain.*

*"It means child of wealth."*

*Ruby cocked her head to one side and said, "Child of wealth?"*

*They didn't have a dime. They were about the poorest people she knew. Ruby was sure that she would be bringing her baby girl home to a dark house because the final notice from the electric company had been sitting unopened on the kitchen table for days.*

*"Child of wealth?" she repeated dryly.*

*Amos shrugged his shoulders and said, with a little too much humor, "You know me, baby. I dream of things that could be, not things that are."*

*"That was his problem,"* her mother had told her. *"He spent more time dreaming than anything else."*

But that's why Tomiko's mother had loved him. Amos had a way of talking sometimes that held people hostage. It wasn't so much *what* he said as how he said it. He could look you in the eyes and make you believe that you could fly to the moon and back, and he could make you believe that he was the sun.

Ruby and Amos met at Vaughn's, a small blues club in downtown Detroit. Patrons would come to Vaughn's for some of the best rhythm and blues, fried catfish, smoked pig tails, and potato salad within one hundred miles. Just thinking about food like that made Tomiko's blood pressure soar.

Vaughn was Ruby's uncle, and all of the family members had worked at the club at one time or another. When Amos started playing there, Ruby was just twenty-two years old. She had been waitressing for exactly four months. Amos was forty.

She was a beauty. Curvaceous, with chocolaty smooth skin. The men knew she was off-limits 'cause she was Vaughn's kin, but occasionally some drunk would forget the rules and Vaughn would have to bust him in the head with the butt of the .45 he kept behind the bar and then send him off with the warning:

"Next time, it'll be a bullet in your ass!"

When Ruby first laid eyes on Amos, she was saving up to attend beauty culture school and had plans to open up her very own hair salon.

"You goin' places, girl!" the older waitresses declared when she shared her dreams with them.

Ruby would just nod and sway that big ass between the tables. Yes, she was going somewhere, and nobody and nothing was going to change her plans, not even that fine-ass piano player named Amos, who was the one and only man to walk into Vaughn's and not give her a second look.

Who in the world did he think he was—God's gift? Ultimately, to Ruby, that's exactly what he became.

Tomiko did not welcome remembering her father. It always led her down a sorrowful road, and that road always ended with her opening a bottle of wine and putting on the *Aretha*

*Franklin Greatest Hits* CD. Tomiko would drink and sing until the tears came. By the time the bottle was done, the CD would be on its fourth play and Tomiko would have fallen into a wine-soaked slumber.

This trip down memory lane was not doing her writing a bit of good. She hit the Delete button on the keyboard, and the offensive statement disappeared. She gave her head a hard shake. "Come on, girl, you have a contract to fulfill!"

The cursor just sat there. She watched its monotonous repetition, feeling that it was somehow a metaphor for the time that was ticking away while she stared at the stupid screen. Her mother's stories about Tomiko's father always held a hint of sadness. Recalling them, even those parts that didn't include Tomiko, resonated with that impending unhappy ending that she had always hoped to avoid in her own life. Time marched on, and with it, so did that hollow feeling she'd tried to ignore, still wanting, still needing something that she was beginning to doubt anyone or anything could ever fill.

"Tomorrow is another day." She sighed as she rose from the chair and headed out of her office toward the kitchen, where the wine was stored.

# Amos

Damn! When the hell did he get old? Or rather, when did he get old enough to end up in a joint like this? An orderly pushed Amos through the long corridors of the Sunnyview Assisted Living Center, headed to the cafeteria. Amos rode past decrepit old fossils who didn't look a day under a hundred. One guy crept around the corner, balanced on a walker, looking like that dude from that TV show *Tales from the Crypt*. Amos was mature, but he wasn't their kind of old. He was seventy-one, and most of these people looked old enough to have raised him.

"Wanna try the oatmeal this morning, Amos?" that dumb orderly asked, pushing him up to an empty table near a window.

Amos looked at him in astonishment. Oatmeal? He hadn't eaten oatmeal since he was a boy back in Mississippi. Grown men didn't eat oatmeal, at least, not grown men who still had teeth in their head. Was that the kind of mess they fed these people here? No wonder they looked miserable.

The young cat smiled and disappeared across the room. A few minutes later, he came back with a bowl of oatmeal, wheat toast, a side of fresh fruit, and a glass of orange juice. He looked so damn proud of himself, like he'd just found the cure for cancer.

"Enjoy." He drummed the table lightly with his fingers and left.

Amos stared out at the naked trees and the dead garden just outside the window. The reason they'd put him here was because they thought he was crazy. Told him he had Alzheimer's and he couldn't take care of himself anymore. Crashing up his car, all while recalling cotton fields, had proven that to them. Sometimes Amos talked too damn much, and he cursed himself for even mentioning that nonsense to these people.

"Is there someone you could stay with, Amos? A family member, perhaps—someone who could help look after you?"

Cass had asked him that silly-ass question, and he had stared at her like she was from Mars. Hell, wasn't she family? Couldn't she look after him? But before he had a chance to say that to her, a chord of truth struck him down in his gut. He hadn't seen that girl in years, hadn't spoken to her or even called her. He had meant to. He'd had her phone number for a long time. Linda had given it to him before she passed. Even if he had called her, though, he wouldn't have known what to say. Amos was lousy at keeping in touch. He was so much better at holding on to memories, especially the good ones. At least he was until he caught this damn Alzheimer's. Now he was probably gonna forget to have memories, at least on purpose—memories of all the fine people and places he'd known—and the thought didn't sit well with him. Not at all.

He saw the reflection of his face in the window, and it didn't please him. He looked old. Amos looked sloppy and raggedy. Had he forgotten how to shave or get a damn haircut?

*"A man's 'fro is his crown. It's his glory. It's his righteousness,"* he used to say.

*"People ain't wearin' 'fros no more, Amos,"* Linda said, sounding

bitter. "*And how long you gon' stand in front of that mirror pattin' your hair?*" Linda stood behind him, looking annoyed, like he was patting her head instead of his own.

"*Just makin' sure I'm put together, darlin',*" he said proudly. "*You love me for my good looks.*"

"*And you talk about me always primping in the mirror,*" she said, giving him an ugly look like she couldn't stand him, but she wasn't fooling anybody but herself. She didn't want him to go because she knew he looked good, and she knew that somebody else was gonna know it, too. "*You spend more time up in the mirror than I ever did.*"

Linda was skinny with big hips and bony legs. She was cute, though. At least, she was cute when she wasn't wearing a head full of pink rollers and a bad attitude. Her titties were smaller than he normally preferred, but her hips made up for what she lacked on the top half.

"*Why don't you get dressed and come check me out tonight, baby?*" He met up with her in the doorway.

The trick was to say it like he meant it and to make her believe it. That was all it took.

"*You know I don't have a babysitter,*" she said, looking pitiful. Yeah, he knew. "*I wish I could, though.*"

The next trick was to look as disappointed as she felt. So he held her pretty brown face in his hands. "*It ain't gonna be the same without you.*"

She melted. "*I know.*" Linda stood on her toes and wrapped her arms around his neck. "*I hate that I can't be there to support you.*"

*Bless her heart*, he thought warmly. "*Me, too, baby. Me, too.*"

Amos always did have a way with the ladies. The fact that he played music didn't hurt none, either. They told him all the time how much he reminded them of Marvin Gaye or Sam Cooke. If he needed to remind them of Marvin or Sam, then so be it. Amos let it be what it was and never failed to reap the benefits from the comparisons, either.

"Awwww . . . sooky, sooky!"

Man! The sound of her little high-pitched voice was music to his ears. Amos looked over Linda's shoulder and grinned back at the cutest brown pie-face he'd ever laid eyes on in his life.

"Where you get them threads?" Li'l Mama Cass propped her hand on her narrow hip and gave him the once-over like she was grown.

Jive talk coming from the mouths of babes messed him up every time, and before Amos knew what was happening, he'd dropped his arms from around her momma and pimped over to his little darling. Four years old, his little Hershey's Kiss, this one here was cute as a kitten with her big brown eyes and cornrows with every color barrette ever made dangling off the ends.

"What's happenin', Li'l Mama Cass?" he'd say, holding his hand in front of her with the palm facing up. "Gimme some skin, baby."

Linda brushed past him. "People don't say 'skin' anymore, Amos," she said, annoyed.

Little Bit slid her small hand across his with all the finesse of a brotha who's been sliding skin for forty years.

"That's a bad suit." She circled him like a baby vulture, checking out a brotha's threads, a khaki leisure suit with white stitching around the edges and a big-ass winged collar.

"You know me, young blood," he said to that child, like he was talking to one of his band members. Her mother just shook her head and rolled her eyes. "I got to look good. You dig?"

"Course I do," she said, with attitude. "It's copestetic."

She meant "copacetic" but made a mess of the word as usual. Shit, he couldn't help it. It was just funny, and Amos chuckled.

She wasn't his biologically, but she was his in spirit. She'd been

*two when Amos and Linda had gotten together. Cassandra, her mother*
*called her, but Amos called her Li'l Mama Cass, because she was sassy*
*and cute and liked to eat. A woman after his own heart. Truth be*
*known, Cass was the love of his life. Most times, the best Linda could*
*do was a close second.*

Now here he was staring into a sorry-assed bowl of oatmeal
with his stomach growling like a beast. He didn't want to eat it,
but hell—he was hungry.

Cass was the one who'd signed him up for this gig. She'd
pushed him in the wheelchair while the woman in charge gave
them the thirty-cent tour of this place.

"There are plenty of activities available to help keep our
residents busy," the cardboard woman said. "You can watch
TV here, play chess or checkers, join the knitting or bowling
clubs. We encourage everyone to get involved, and constant
monitoring and supervision ensures our residents' safety and
well-being."

Sounded like jail to Amos.

"That's wonderful," Cass declared.

He didn't want to be here. He didn't have to stay with Cass,
but he didn't have to be here, either. Amos had been taking
care of himself just fine. He'd just had a little accident.

In the week since he'd arrived, Amos hadn't bowled one
game or knitted one stitch. He spent most of his time out in
the sun room, trying to remember what was so good about his
life before he ended up here. For all the money in the world,
he couldn't recall a damn thing. Amos lived alone in a small
house on the Southside. He ate, drank a little, slept a lot. And
he wasted days away, living in the recesses of his best memories.

His life hadn't been much, but but it was a whole lot better than this. After he'd finished breakfast another orderly showed up, wheeled him outside, parked him in the sun room, and left.

The weather was good today, but it was starting to get cold. He didn't know what the hell he was going to do now that winter finally set in. Maybe he would end up taking a knitting class after all and make himself a sweater or something. Amos chuckled at the thought.

"Will you please move?" an old woman asked him irritably.

Amos grimaced at that old fool, and then followed her gaze over to what she was looking at. When he saw it, all that oatmeal he'd just eaten threatened to come back up. Damn! That woman had to be at least ninety, wearing dark shades almost as big as her head. Her hair was pure white and cut short, almost like a man's. She had more wrinkles than a prune and had the nerve to spread pink lipstick across the space where her lips should've been. The woman had on a tank top and shorts. It was pure nonsense, but then again, she was ancient. He'd always been a firm believer that old folks had certain inalienable rights that the rest of the world didn't possess, so if she wanted to dress like a hoochie at ninety, then more power to her.

"You blockin' my view," the other woman said impatiently, waving him out of her way.

"Come on over here by me," another old woman said to Amos. A black woman, with gray-streaked hair and a floral muumuu, smiled sweetly at him. If he didn't know better, he'd have thought that she was flirting. He managed to roll himself over to where she was.

"Don't mind Beverly," the woman said, leaning close to him.

Amos glanced at old Beverly. "Ain't she a little old to be wearin' that?"

"She ain't but eighty-seven," the black woman said. She motioned to some prehistoric dude slowly making his way across the grass, using two canes. "Martin's comin'. She just wants to make sure he sees her. That's all."

"What?"

The old woman shrugged. "She likes him."

That man was a hundred if he was a day, traveling at a snail's pace, but gradually, he turned his head in Blondie's direction, stopped, and nodded. The old girl struck a pose, pretended to look away, and muttered something that Amos couldn't make out. That old dude started walking again.

"What the hell just happened?" Amos asked, confused.

The woman next to him thought about it before answering. "Foreplay." She studied him. "You new?"

"Yes, I guess you could say that," he admitted reluctantly.

"Why you say it like that?" She frowned.

"Like what?"

"Like you embarrassed or somethin'." The old woman rolled her eyes. "It is what it is, and when you get our age, you end up where you end up."

Giving her another once-over, Amos quickly surmised that he wasn't her age. The woman had at least ten good years on him.

"I'm Jennie," she announced proudly. "Jennie V. Cookson."

"Amos," he said simply.

Jennie waited and then finally asked, "Amos who?"

Amos none-of-her-nosy-damn-business! he'd wanted to say. *That's* who. But Amos had been raised better than that. He'd been raised to respect his elders, even the ones who didn't deserve it.

"Davis," he shot back eventually. "Amos Davis."

All of a sudden her eyes stretched wide, and Jennie V. Cookson leaned back to get a good, long look at him.

"Amos Davis? The singer Amos Davis?"

She'd heard of him? "Yeah, that's me."

All of a sudden, Jennie V. Cookson laughed out loud and slapped her hand on her knee. *"You made a fool outta me, but I'ma be a fool ova you,"* she sang off-key, pointing her finger at him. "Boy, my old man got me pregnant with my third child to that song!" She laughed again. "That there was some good love-makin' music back in the day."

Amos found himself sitting up a little straighter in his chair. A sly grin crept across his lips. "I'd like to think so," he said proudly.

"Fool Over You" had been his biggest hit song. Radio stations across the country played it so much it got on his nerves. It was the record that was supposed to launch his career and put him right up there with Marvin Gaye, Bobby "Blue" Bland, and Otis Redding.

"How come you didn't make no more records?" Jennie V. Cookson asked bluntly.

Amos had made plenty of records after that, but none of them had taken off the way "Fool Over You" did, and one day, all of a sudden, he was a one-hit wonder. He didn't bother answering her question.

"Can you still play the piano?" she asked slyly, leaning in his direction.

"Course I still play," he said defensively. Why the hell wouldn't he still play? He still had fingers on his hands.

"They got a piano here in the dancin' room." She grinned, winking.

He hadn't been to the dancing room.

"You play that piano and sing that song for me, and I'll put a coupla dollars in the jar," she joked.

Amos wondered if she was making fun of him and shook his head. "Ah . . . I don't know," he said hesitantly.

"Come on, Amos," she coaxed. "I ain't heard that song in way too long, and I never did get to see you sing it in person." Jennie V. Cookson was already shifting in her seat, preparing to get up. "You the only star I ever met," she continued.

*Star?* Is that what she thought of him? Amos couldn't help but smile. When was the last time somebody called him a star? When was the last time he had felt like one?

"Do an old woman a favor and play that song for me. I sho would 'preciate it."

Maybe he would appreciate it, too. It had been years since Amos had sung that song. He doubted he'd even remember the words, but if she was asking . . .

He nodded. "Tomorrow?" he asked her.

The old woman relaxed and sat back. "That'll be fine. Lord willing we'll both still be here."

He frowned. What the hell did she mean by that?

# Cass

H e's going to need someone to take care of him."

Cass had sat across from the doctor's desk, staring blankly at the brunette, knowing what she was going to say. Amos had been staying in that nursing home for a few weeks, and he had called Cass nearly every day since they'd first brought him in.

"Your father is . . ."

How many times did she have to tell these people that Amos wasn't her father? Cass let that truth burn the back of her throat. She wasn't in the mood to repeat herself again.

". . . unable to look after himself, Cassandra," the doctor explained earnestly. "I know he seems fine right now, mentally, but he's really not. Alzheimer's is a disease that can strike without warning and leave an individual feeling lost and confused. He'll need round-the-clock supervision."

The way Cass saw it, Amos was a stray puppy and she was like the Humane Society. It was her job to make sure he had a home and somebody to look after him because, of course, she couldn't possibly take on the burden of caring for that old man herself. She was his stepdaughter, at best, depending on which rumor she chose to believe.

Some people said he had been married to her mother,

Linda, and others said he hadn't been. Through the years, Linda's version of the truth changed with her moods. If her memories of them together were good, then he was her *man,* her *husband.* If they weren't, then he was that *sonofabitch,* that *mothafucka,* and *hell naw, I ain't never been dumb enough to marry that fool!*

Cass's only option had been to admit him into a nursing home, at least until she could locate an actual family member. Maybe one of his other children could look after him or hire a nurse to do it.

She had no idea where to start except with a name her mother took in vain over and over again throughout the years, a woman who had lived with Amos: Melba Jean McCann.

Her name was tattooed on Cass's brain because those three little words had pretty much driven her mother crazy when she was alive. Years after Amos left, Cass's mother still spat that woman's name like venom long after she should've put to rest any business that had taken place between Amos and good old Melba Jean.

Melba had a little girl named Toya. He claimed she wasn't his, but Cass's mother had never believed him.

*"She said she got a baby by you, Amos! Tell me she lyin'! Please! Oh, Lord."* Her *mother sobbed, covering her face with her hands and falling back onto the sofa.*

*"I told you like I told her, Linda! It ain't my baby!"*

Cass had heard that Amos had several children scattered from city to city. He was good at making them and even better at leaving them. Maybe he hadn't left them all, though. Maybe the old man had sprouted a conscience and reached out to one of them. In any case, he wasn't Cass's responsibility.

Seated at her kitchen table, while her cake baked in the

oven, Cass began searching the Internet for an address for Melba McCann in Michigan. She found a Melba J. McCann living in Flint and decided that it was as good a place to start as any. If this was the same woman her mother had loathed all those years, she might have a daughter who was Amos's daughter. Maybe Amos knew her and he just didn't remember. Cass thought about calling, but considering the history of bad blood between her mother and Melba Jean, she thought better of it. She decided to write a letter instead. That was neutral enough. Melba and her child just needed to know where he was. That's all. And Cass could walk away from him the same way he'd walked away from her.

Oddly enough, Cass didn't entertain the idea of Melba Jean and Amos as a couple. If he'd had a woman in his life, his wallet had showed no evidence of one—except for Cass, whose number was the only one they could find inside it. Thinking about that just made her sad all over.

She stared at the blank screen of her laptop, wondering how to start a letter like the one she was about to write.

*Dear Toya,*

*I know you don't know me, but our mothers knew and hated each other deeply.*

She frowned, hit the *BACKSPACE* button, erasing every letter, and decided to try again.

*Toya,*

*You don't know me, but my name is Cass. Amos wasn't my real daddy but he was yours. He's in the Sunnyview nursing*

*home and you should probably go check on him because, like I*
*said, he's not my daddy.*

"That's just immature," she muttered, deleting the letter
again.

She did care about what happened to Amos. Of course she
did. Amos had helped to raise her when she was a kid. He'd let
her be Gladys while he was her one and only Pip. He'd taught
her the James Brown shuffle in the kitchen of their small
apartment. But those old memories didn't offset the fact that
she hadn't seen or heard from him in years. Now all of a sudden here he was back again, acting almost as if he'd never left.

Half an hour later, by the time she had finished typing the
letter and printing it out, another name came to mind. Amos
had another daughter whom she knew about. She remembered because the name was so odd. Cass had stopped at a
nightclub one night on her way home from catering a cor-
porate Christmas party. She sat in the back of the room that
night, away from the stage, tossing back rum and Cokes and
mourning Ricky, who had killed himself on Christmas Day,
two years into their marriage. That time of year was always
hard for Cass, and that night, while sitting in the back of that
bar, she'd heard Amos's voice. She almost couldn't believe it,
but there he was, sitting on stage. It was like that with the two
of them sometimes. He passed through her life like a shadow,
close enough to see but not touch.

*"I'm dedicating this last song to my little girl Tamika,"* Amos said
*proudly.* Tamika? Taritha? Cass couldn't remember the name
he'd said.

*"She ain't here tonight, but she in my heart and that's where she*
*gon' stay. Daddy loves you, baby girl."*

Cass sat in the back of that bar, sipping on her drink and listening to him lazily sing songs that reminded her of life growing up with Amos in the house. He sang all the time and back then, music was everything to her. Cass left without saying a word to him.

Tamika or Taritha Davis might as well have been Jane Smith. Cass searched for hours, and even made a few phone calls only to come up empty. None of them knew Amos Davis.

"Why do we love you so much, old man?" she muttered, staring at the envelope addressed to Melba Jean. That was the million-dollar question, and if anybody ever came along who could answer it for her, she'd gladly hand over the loot.

She folded the letter, inserted it into the envelope, and laid it on the table, feeling glad that she was doing the right thing for Amos and, even more so, for herself. She didn't need him in her life anymore. And she didn't want him in it either.

"Whatchu cookin'?" RJ—Ricky Jr., her twenty-four-year-old son—burst into the kitchen, swung open the refrigerator door, and buried the whole top half of his body inside, without even giving Cass a sideways glance.

That boy looked just like his daddy, she thought dismally, staring at his narrow behind hanging out of her refrigerator.

"Don't you have a girlfriend and an apartment to go home to?" she asked.

The boy emerged with a fried chicken leg between his teeth. "We ain't got nothin' to eat."

Cass had gotten pregnant with the boy right after she'd turned sixteen. Ricky, his daddy, had been her first, last, and everything back then. When Linda found out she was pregnant, she gave Cass an ultimatum: "Get rid of it, or go move in with that boy," which she did. They got married two years later, as soon as she was old enough, and stayed married long enough for Ricky to realize that no one or nothing in this world could save him from the depression he was drowning in. Cass came home from work one evening and found RJ slumped over his father's body, which was spread across the bed with half the head blown off. She'd never forgiven Ricky for that. He'd taken the easy way out and had left her and RJ behind to deal with everything he couldn't.

Cass got up from the table, pulled a paper towel off the roll, and handed it to the boy.

"Wipe your mouth," she said.

He smirked, and then leaned in and gave her a greasy peck on the cheek.

"RJ! That's just nasty!" Yet he smiled broadly, and she couldn't help joining in. The father had been a mess, but he had given her a semi-wonderful son.

Cass went back to the business of preparing the most ambitious wedding cake she'd ever tried to make. Her masterpiece—and the one that would catapult her to the ranks of the most elite wedding cake artists in Detroit—would be the centerpiece of an elaborate, over-the-top, all-out production of a wedding the following afternoon. Maybe if she and Ricky had had a wedding like that instead of the one they did have (the two of them standing at the justice of the peace, with Cass holding on to two-year-old RJ's hand and Ricky with that weird look on his face that he had until the day she told him she wanted a divorce), maybe they'd still be married, she thought remorsefully. She pondered that for a moment and then shrugged it off. What she needed to do right now was prepare for a wedding that would hopefully lead to a lot of other weddings.

The next day, Cass and her cake were at the biggest, fanciest reception she'd ever seen. The ballroom was filled with nearly three hundred people, all celebrating the elegant nuptials of Cynthia and Marvin Paris. Cass's cake sat atop a beautifully decorated table; it was the grand, ornate centerpiece of the room. Cass stood back proudly, admiring her masterpiece, protectively guarding it as droves of people, drunk and sober, broke into a massive rendition of the Electric Slide.

Half an hour later, *he* took the stage, dashing and looking like a dream—her dream. And as he started to sing, Cass's imagination suddenly swept her away from this reception and dropped her smack dab in the middle of her own lovely fantasy, starring just the two of them.

*Darryl Styles was playing that song again, which meant that he knew she was close by. Cass chuckled as she strolled across the empty, expansive dance floor in his direction. Darryl glanced at her out of the corner of his eye and continued doing what he did best, making beautiful music, without missing a beat.*

*"There's a spark of magic in your eyes," he sang softly, just for her benefit.*

*Cass blushed, and when she was close enough, she leaned seductively against his piano, balanced her chin in her hand, and swayed slowly with the melody.*

*He wore the black suit she loved so much, along with a crisp white button-down with an open collar. In one earlobe a small diamond glistened against his dark skin. It reminded her of a star shining against the night sky. Darryl was so tall that, even sitting down, he was almost able to look her in the eye. Cass had spent the afternoon shopping for just the right dress to wear for this occasion, and from the look in those warm dark eyes of his, he approved.*

"Betcha by golly wow," *he continued, staring dreamily at her.* "You're the one that I've been waiting for . . ."

*She mouthed the last word: "Forever."*

*A delicious grin spread his thick lips. Electricity shot down her spine, and she hoped he hadn't noticed. Yet the gleam in his eye told her that he had.*

*"You know my weaknesses," she said, taking a deep breath. "And I'll never forgive you for using them against me."*

*He laughed, toying with the piano keys and experimenting with the familiar melody, making it even more personal between them.*

*"It's called fighting fire with fire," he explained. "If I use your weaknesses against you, it's only because you are my weakness." He smiled again and winked. "And I believe a man needs every advantage he can get in matters of the heart."*

*"You know how much I love you?" she asked, sliding on the bench next to him.*

*He continued playing, unabated. Darryl nodded. "And I am blessed, sweetheart. Beyond my wildest dreams."*

"Cass?"

*Cass chuckled and then leaned into him for a kiss. "You might just get lucky tonight, talking like that."*

"Excuse me, Cass?"

Not until Cass felt a hand on her shoulder did she snap out of her fantasy. She had it bad for the man. Too bad she didn't have the guts to tell him.

"I'm so sorry."

Cass turned to face Vivian O'Neal, the mother of the bride.

The woman pasted on a tight smile. "I didn't mean to startle you."

"No," Cass responded quickly. "I was just . . . What a beautiful reception," she added nervously.

"Thank you," Mrs. O'Neal responded coolly.

Cass had never liked this woman, but she'd insisted on the most expensive cake Cass could make because *"nothing was too good"* for her daughter. The six-tier red velvet cake featured a delicate lacelike pattern, silver-coated sugar balls, and ribbons and gossamer strands made of pulled sugar Cass had had to make on-site because pulled sugar decorations were too delicate to transport.

Mrs. O'Neal stared down her narrow nose at Cass, the way she always did. Cass tried not to take it personally because the woman towered over her by almost a foot.

"The cake is absolutely breathtaking," Mrs. O'Neal said passionately.

"Thank you so much."

"It's almost too beautiful to cut into." She laughed.

Almost? No, it *was* too beautiful to cut into, but that was Cass's opinion.

Mrs. O'Neal gently took hold of Cass by the elbow. "We really appreciate all of your hard work."

"So bring your good times and your laughter tooooo! We're gonna celebrate your party with you . . ." *Darryl's voice touched that private place in her soul.*

Mrs. O'Neal tugged at Cass's arm. "A friend of mine has a son who is planning on getting married next spring. I'll certainly recommend you to her. She's here tonight, as a matter of fact, and if you had more time, I'd introduce you."

The exit sign was getting closer with each step. Obviously, Mrs. O'Neal wanted her gone.

"I have your information, and I'll try to remember to pass it along to her tonight before she leaves."

Mrs. O'Neal pasted on that frosty smile one last time as she held open the door and waved her hand dismissively at Cass as the door closed behind her. Cass was left standing outside in the dark parking lot.

"G'night, Darryl," Cass said softly. She was forty years old, and the best relationship she'd ever had with a man had been with him, and it was all in her head.

# Toya

G irl, I know you ain't sheddin' no tears over some man."
Toya closed her eyes and inhaled. She didn't know
what in the world she was thinking. She must've been crazy
even to attempt to hold a serious conversation with her
mother about love.

"I just thought this time would be different," Toya found
herself saying anyway.

"Different? Honey chile, please." Melba cackled as she
added seasoning to the pot of chili she was cooking. They were
standing in the small kitchen of Melba's two-bedroom house,
where she had lived ever since they'd moved to Flint, Michigan,
twenty years ago. Melba's robust frame filled out her signature
baby-blue housecoat. Her long sandy-brown hair was braided
and pulled up, making her look a lot older than her sixty-four
years. "You ain't doin' nothin' but wastin' tears and time," Melba
continued. "They all the same—low-down dirty dogs." She put
a lid on the pot and turned to face her daughter. "That's why
I've been telling you all your life, you get what you can, when
you can, because it's just a matter of time before they get what
they can and move on," she said, wagging the giant wooden
spoon Toya's way.

Toya knew her mother was referring to all men, but her

venom was directed at one man in particular: Amos Davis. At the slightest mention Melba would break into a diatribe about how men were simply no good, and Toya's father was the "chief of the no-good tribe." Toya knew very little about her father except that he'd been her mother's one true love. The problem was that Melba had been the woman on the side.

When Melba popped up pregnant, she'd been all but sure that Amos would be with her. But not only did he not leave his other woman for the first five years after Toya was born, she barely even saw her father. Back in the day Melba had been a beautiful woman, with smooth cinnamon-colored skin; long, thick hair; and a body that turned heads everywhere she went. She could've had any man she wanted—except the man she really loved. Sure, Melba dated other men, paraded a host of "uncles" through the door, but her heart remained with Amos. And the fact that he wouldn't give mother or daughter any real time tore at Melba's core. Toya was sure that played a large part in making her mother the bitter, cantankerous woman she was now.

Her mother turned morose, and Toya was relieved. That meant her mother would remain silent for a while. Toya, seated at the kitchen table, was reminded of Amos's presence. She remembered one of the few times that she'd gone to see her dad, back when they were still living in Detroit. They'd shown up at some club downtown. Melba had ignored the looks of patrons who undoubtedly were wondering what she was doing bringing a child to a nightclub.

*"Miss, miss," the bouncer had said, chasing behind Melba after she burst through the front door of the club like a raging winter storm. "I'm sorry, you can't bring that child up in here."*

*Melba pointed to a poster by the door, with the words* Appearing Tonight *over a photo of a handsome man in a black tuxedo.* "You see that right there?" *she spat.*

"Yes, that's our headliner, Amos Davis. What does he have to do with anything?" *the stocky, bald-headed man replied.*

"That's her daddy!" *Melba screamed, jabbing her finger in Toya's direction.*

*The man's eyes narrowed, and his voice took on a firm tone.* "I don't care if Jesus Christ himself is her daddy. She don't need to be up in here."

"Whatever," *Melba said, trying to push her way past him. He grabbed her arm, and Melba released a string of curse words as she tried to break free. The ruckus drew a small crowd. Suddenly, a tall, handsome, chocolate-skinned man broke through the people. Toya looked closely. He was the man from the picture that was hidden under her mother's mattress. The man her mother had said was her daddy.*

"Melba, what in the hell are you doing here?" *he bellowed.*

*Melba's hands went to her hips as she glared at the man.* "You don't want to come see us, so we *comin' to see you!*"

"Woman, are you crazy? This here is my job. You can't come up here with this mess."

"I told you I wasn't playing with you, Amos. It's Christmastime and my baby ain't got nothing and I'm sick of it."

*Toya wondered why her mother was going off. It was okay if her father wouldn't help. Santa would bring her gifts. She wanted to remind her mother of that, but the fury in Melba's face made her keep her mouth closed.*

"Now you need to do right by us."

"Fine, Melba Jean," *he shot back, coolly.* "I'll do right by you and *that little girl right after I finish this set. Now take your ass home and let me do what I do."*

*"I didn't lay down and make this kid on my own! Your own flesh and blood is sufferin' while you sittin' up there taking care of some other man's child! You have lost your mind if you think I'm gonna let you get away with not taking care of your own flesh and blood!"*

*Suddenly, big-hipped Linda showed up like a magic trick. "Amos, what is going on?"*

*Melba turned up her nose at the woman. "This here ain't none of your business."*

*"First of all, anything to do with my man is my business," the woman said, not backing down. "Second, why are you still sniffing around? He didn't want you then, and he don't want you now."*

*Melba pointed her index finger at the woman. "Trust me, if I wanted your man again—I'd have him," she slowly said. "All I want now is for him to do right by his child."*

*The woman glared at Toya with disdain. "We don't even know that that is his child."*

*"Oh, he know it." Melba folded her arms across her chest. "This here is his blood. Ain't that right, Amos?"*

*"Y'all gonna have to take this family feud down the street," the bouncer interjected.*

*"Come on, you gots to go," Amos said, grabbing Melba's arm and pulling her down the sidewalk.*

*Melba jerked free, then hauled off and whacked Amos on the side of the head. Instinctively, Amos grabbed her and pushed her against the wall. "Take yo' ass home, Melba Jean! This ain't the time or place for this mess!"*

*"You wanna hit me? Come on, you bad, do it!" Melba shouted. "Show everyone what a big man you are, Amos Davis!"*

*"Momma, let's go," Toya whimpered, tugging on her mother's dress.*

*Amos stepped back. It was obvious that he was trying to calm down.*

*"You heard your daughter," the other woman added. "You need to leave!"*

*"Heffa, ain't nobody talkin' to you," Melba snapped.*

*"Oh, I'm about sick of you," the woman said, taking a step toward Melba. "I told you the next time you came around causin' trouble, it was gon' be me and you!"*

*"Stop talkin' about doin' somethin' and just do somethin' if you bad!"*

*Toya didn't remember much after that. The woman and her mother had gotten into a huge fight that ended with Toya and her mom literally being separated by two bouncers and watching that other woman disappear into that club.*

". . . just like the last time you called yourself falling in love."

Toya didn't know how long ago she had tuned her mother out. She just knew this conversation was getting her nowhere. She had real issues with Max, and talking to her mother wasn't going to help.

"Well, I can see you ain't even botherin' to listen no more," her mother said as she started chopping up onions. "Go run out there and get my mail. I'm waitin' on my disability check."

Toya welcomed the reprieve as she scooted back from the kitchen table. Maybe she should just keep walking, Toya thought as she pushed past the front door and headed down the walkway to the curbside mailbox. She'd just explain to her mother that something came up. She quickly shook off that thought. As much as her mother worked her nerves, they only had each other, so it was hard for Toya to turn her back.

But as she reached in the mailbox to retrieve the mail,

Toya knew she had to escape. She needed someone to talk sensibly to her, someone who could help her understand why she couldn't find the love she deserved, and since Amos Davis had walked out of Melba Jean's life, she was definitely not the woman Toya needed to be turning to for advice about men.

# Tomiko

Tomiko didn't think *lonely* was exactly the right word to describe what she was feeling. And *empty* didn't quite encapsulate it, either. But her best friend, Marjorie, had tossed out both of those words just as the waiter set down their plates of food.

Hers was seared salmon served on a bed of quinoa with a side of spring vegetables tossed in olive oil and garlic. Tomiko inhaled the heavenly scent and then reached for her wineglass.

"Shall we toast?"

Marjorie smirked. "Don't think you're going to skirt the subject," she said as she raised her water glass into the air, "but okay. Here's to love."

"To friendship," Tomiko added as their glasses came together with a resounding clink. Tomiko took a sip of the Chardonnay, swirled it around in her mouth, and swallowed. "Mmmm," she moaned.

"So," Marjorie purred, "do you want to meet Greg or not?"

Greg Miller. Six feet three, milk chocolate, almost-went-pro-basketball Greg Miller. He had busted up his knee in a car wreck, and there went his pro-ball aspirations. With the help of intense physical therapy, his momma's love, and her old-fashioned chicken soup (according to Marjorie)—combined with the prayers that poured in from both strangers and friends—he recovered and eventually became one of the most successful entrepreneurs in the city.

Greg Miller owned Laundromats, car dealerships, and a string of rental properties. Yet not all of his successes were professional. He attended church, volunteered at homeless shelters, and sponsored orphans in third-world countries. He had never been married and did not have any children floating around, Tomiko had learned. By all accounts, he seemed to be not just the perfect man but also an ideal human being. He was Barack Obama flawless, and that alone scared the hell out of Tomiko because she knew she was no Michelle.

"Well?" Marjorie pressed.

Tomiko took another sip of her wine and then focused her attention on Marjorie's intent expression. "I really wish you were drinking. You're so much more fun when you have a little alcohol in your system."

Marjorie laughed, leaned back into the chair, and smoothed her hands over her pregnant stomach. "You're changing the subject again."

Tomiko sighed. "He sounds just a little too perfect."

"Since when is perfection a bad thing?"

"Since you and I both know that nobody's perfect."

Marjorie's expression turned bland. "Why don't you feel you deserve a good man in your life?"

Marjorie was a psychoanalyst, and she tended to lapse into psycho-speak without being fully aware of it. Tomiko didn't have that problem, though. She stoutly resisted being shrunk by a friend of hers.

Tomiko answered dryly, "Dr. Rand, please save that psychobabble bullshit for your paying customers. Not every woman needs a man to validate her," she explained. "I'm one of those women."

"But we both know that you want someone, Miko. And you're right. It's not about validation, but it is about love and partnership."

Tomiko had meant for this conversation to be humorous, but it was beginning to get a little intense. The silence stretched out between them. Marjorie shifted in her chair and dropped her gaze. Tomiko sighed, knowing that, once again, she had been too prickly on the subject of men for her own good.

"Look," Tomiko began tenderly, "I just don't have good luck with the opposite sex. I'm tired of falling in and out of love. It saps my energy and my creativity. Not everyone is as lucky as you are. Dwight is an angel sent from heaven, and the two of you—well, you guys are the exception to the rule."

It was true. Marjorie and Dwight had met during their senior year in college and had been inseparable ever since. Dwight had put off going to law school to support Marjorie while she attended medical school and completed her residency. He'd taken jobs Tomiko didn't even know existed:

Drawbridge tender
Jelly donut filler
Eyeglass buffer
Note taker for college students

And others that made her stomach churn:

Abattoir worker
Noodler
Porta potty cleaner

Now if that ain't love, what is?

The men whom Tomiko had dated, had fallen in love with, had almost considered marrying . . . well they weren't Dwight.

"Your problem," Marjorie said pointedly, "is that your expectations for what a man should be are unrealistically unobtainable. I've put a lot of thought into this, and my guess is you're looking for a man like your father. A lot of women have very idealistic views of their father that other men can't possibly live up to."

Tomiko's mouth dropped open. "My father," she squealed in surprise as she pressed the pad of her index finger to her chest. "My. Father?"

Marjorie nodded.

Tomiko laughed and extended her hand across the table to her friend. "I don't think we've met. I'm Tomiko Davis, and my father walked out on my mother and me when I was barely potty trained. I thought I'd mentioned that in my drunken state at your bachelorette party, somewhere between strippers."

Marjorie laughed. "You know what I mean, Tomiko."

Tomiko withdrew her hand and dropped it into her lap. "No, I really don't, so please tell me."

"I'm going to go out on a limb here. So, Daddy was a cad, but maybe that's it. Maybe deep down you're afraid that all men are cads and that the moment you commit to one, he'll walk out on you, too. I still stand by my original prognosis, good or bad, right or wrong. You're still holding all men to his standard, and you won't let it go."

Tomiko frowned. "People actually pay you to do this?"

"Yes, they do," Marjorie said smugly, "because I'm good."

"No, you're overthinking this. I just haven't found the right guy. No big deal. It happens."

Marjorie rested her elbows on the table and folded her hands beneath her chin. "Because of your abandonment issues. I get that," she said placatingly.

Tomiko pressed her lips together. "You get nothing but the bill for my food for that piss-poor and way-off-the-mark diagnosis."

Piss-poor diagnosis or not, Tomiko couldn't shake some of the things Marjorie had said. What if Marjorie was right and Tomiko was guilty of holding other men hostage to the regard she had for her father? Amos wasn't exactly father of the year, but Tomiko had always placed him on a pedestal, deserved or not.

Tomiko's fondest memory of her father was of his sitting at his beloved piano, tickling the ebony and ivory keys.

*He was dressed in slacks and a sleeveless T-shirt. A salt-and-pepper six o'clock shadow covered his cheeks. A cigarette dangled from the corner of his mouth.*

*The midday summer breeze was streaming through the open windows, rustling the cream-colored curtains. Outside, the neighborhood children were running up and down the sidewalk, screaming, "Hot peas and butter, come and get your supper!"*

*"Come here, Tomiko."*

*He lifted the four-year-old into his lap, kissed her on her forehead, and asked, "How's my favorite girl?"*

*"Good."*

*"You wanna play?"*

*"Yes, Daddy."*

*He guided her through "Twinkle, Twinkle, Little Star," and by the fourth time Tomiko was playing it solo.*

That was the first time Tomiko could remember ever touching piano keys, even though she'd seen Polaroids of herself at seven months, one year, and two years old, balanced on her father's knee, her fingers pressed against the keys. She didn't remember any of those times. But that summer day, and the days and years that followed, would remain with her until she was old and gray.

Her parents argued about stupid things, and the more they argued, the longer he'd stay gone afterward. Amos wasn't home often, not because he couldn't find work in Detroit—there was more than enough to go around—but because he and Ruby couldn't stand breathing the same air or looking at each other. Tomiko's father and mother weren't the same kind of people. Even as a little girl she could see that. Hell! Stevie Wonder could've seen it.

If he said that the grass was green, she'd argue and say that it was blue. If she said that the sky was up, he'd swear on his mother's grave that it was down.

*"This here music thing has been cute and all, but you gonna have to go out and find yourself a real job."*

*"Real?"* Tomiko remembered him asking. *"What exactly constitutes real in your opinion?"*

*"Ain't no milk in the house, Amos. What this baby supposed to drink? A real man would make sure there was milk in the house!"*

Tomiko's father was an artist. Tomiko was an artist. Having no milk in the house just wasn't a pressing issue for Amos. Tomiko understood. Besides, she had never even liked milk.

All Amos ever really loved was his music. *"I'll get a damn real job, Ruby, and as soon as I get paid, I'll buy the damn milk!"*

Her mother never seemed to notice his pain, but even as young as she was, Tomiko felt it. Going to work like everybody else was a sin for a man like him. It went against the natural order of Amos.

"Your feelings are deep-seated," Marjorie said meaningfully. "You try to convince yourself that it's not the case, but it is."

What's not the case? Tomiko had stopped listening to her friend a long time ago. She swallowed the dry pocket of air that had filled her mouth. Her hand reached out for the wineglass, but when she saw Marjorie's eyebrows arch, she redirected it to the water glass.

"I told you," Tomiko hissed through her teeth. "I am not one of your patients."

Marjorie casually tossed one of her snakelike dreadlocks over her shoulder. "No, but you're my friend and I care about you, Miko. Everything I say, I say from love."

Tomiko set the water glass down and then, without any qualms, reached for the wineglass and proceeded to drain that as well. When she was done, she raised the glass into the air. Her head swiveled on her neck as she tried to locate their waiter. She was going to need a lot of wine to get through this therapy session masquerading as a lunch.

"Stop being so damn dramatic, Miko." Marjorie laughed. "Deep down, you know I'm right, and I'm probably not telling you anything you don't already know."

The waiter appeared. "Ma'am?"

"More wine," Tomiko ordered. "And this time, fill my glass to the brim, please."

The two women picked over their food until the waiter reappeared and carefully set down a full glass of Chardonnay alongside Tomiko's plate. All of a sudden, she felt less smarmy and more rational. Marjorie was one of the smartest people she knew. And despite her best efforts never to let on, she did appreciate her friend's insight and even her advice. The longer she put off meeting Marjorie's friend, the more the woman would harp on it, so Tomiko decided then and there that it was in her best interest to concede defeat.

"Okay, okay, Dr. Rand." Tomiko sighed. "If I say I'll meet your Mr. Wonderful, could we move off of my fucked-up life and dive into some tawdry gossip?"

Marjorie's eyes popped. "Really?"

"Yes, really."

Finally, a plan Tomiko could get with.

# Amos

*T*hey had a couple of hours before the club opened. Eddie, the owner, was real good about letting them come in early to warm up, catch up, and everything else but drink up. Amos was late as usual, but this time it was for a reason and a damn good one, too. His dream was finally coming true. All of his hard work and praying had finally paid off, but not in the way he thought it would. Telling the fellas wasn't going to be easy, but the longer he waited, the harder it was going to be.

Amos walked into the joint to the sound of Boss Man Jones's laugh, Brotha Luke's guitar strumming, and Ike Preston pushing out drumbeats with his mouth. The four of them had been kids when they decided to put together this group. Amos often laughed at the names they'd played under: the Four Units, Soul Force, Kool Kings of Soul, and a few others he couldn't remember. The name of their group changed all the time, but the four of them had been constants—until this morning, when he'd gotten a call from a producer who wanted him for a solo project.

"Well if it ain't Aretha Franklin, the Queen of Soul, dragging her ass in here all fashionably late," Boss Man teased. "We didn't think you was coming, man."

Amos laughed nervously, and sat down at the piano. "You should be bowing when I walk into a room, man," he joked.

They each took turns tossing a few more jabs in his direction, which gave him time to think about how he was going to break the news to them. No matter how he said it, it wasn't going to come out right.

"Y'all know we tight," he said. "We started this thing together, and we gonna ride this train together all the way to the end."

"We ain't riding this train nowhere if we don't get this last song down," Ike chimed in, taking his seat behind the drums. "That bridge is a mess. If we don't clean it up, they gonna boo us off the stage, man."

"I tried telling y'all we need some horns," Luke fussed. "We could take it out and do something else. That's what I say."

Amos couldn't hold it in any longer. "I got a call this morning from Bobby Jackson at Atlantic Records," he finally said.

Every last one of them stopped and stared at him, because making it big wasn't just his dream, it was the dream they all shared.

"He wants to—" Amos started to say, but he was interrupted before he could finish.

"We got a deal, man?" Boss Man asked, his eyes as wide as saucers. "We got a record deal?"

Every last one of them hooped and hollered and slapped fives around the room.

"No, man, I got a deal," he shouted over their voices. All that excitement he'd felt since that call faded in an instant. "They want me to do a solo deal," he explained.

"Amos?"

Who were these people?

"Amos?" a woman's voice caught his attention. Cold, slender hands rested on his shoulders.

He wasn't at Eddie's club? No. No, he . . .

"Amos, let's go back to your room," the woman coaxed him gently.

He turned to look into her young, big blue eyes.

She smiled. "It's late. I think you're tired."

He turned back to where Boss Man, Luke, and Ike should've been, but all he saw was a table full of old men, staring back at him. Amos was confused. Where was this place? And what happened to his friends?


After telling an orderly he was tired, the young woman had taken Amos back to his room right after supper. How the hell did these people expect a man to live in a place like this? He was supposed to have been in bed, but the light coming into his room from underneath the door kept him awake half the night. Amos had managed to get into his wheelchair and wheel himself over to the window. All them nurses stomping up and down the halls, cackling like hens, running their mouths at all hours didn't help. He just wanted to go home, back to his little apartment on Grove Avenue. It wasn't much, but at least he had a key to his door and he could lock it if he wanted.

He had figured out by now that Cass didn't want to look after him. Amos didn't care that she didn't. He hadn't asked her to. He hadn't asked anybody to take care of him because Amos was a grown-ass man who knew how to take care of himself just fine. Of course, he wasn't going to be able to do the things he used to do, but he had been taking charge of his own affairs for a long time, ever since his last girlfriend, Barbara, had passed—when was it? A year ago? Maybe two. She let that diabetes get to her. It ate away at her like termites eat through wood, taking first one foot, then the other. Then it took her legs, all the way up to her hips. Amos remembered seeing her lying in that hospital bed with her eyes closed. She could've opened them, but he knew she didn't want to. Half of her was gone by the time she died. Amos had always believed she'd died on purpose, that she gave up the fight because she didn't care no more, not about herself and not about him.

Being alone when he was old and gray wasn't something he'd counted on, and being alone and ending up in a place like this, well . . . it was like a bad dream he kept hoping he'd wake up from. People came to places like this to die. Nursing homes were for old, helpless people nobody wanted. Old folks' homes like this were for crazy people who couldn't remember their own names or how to go to the bathroom on their own. Amos forgot things from time to time, but he knew who the hell he was and how to piss without somebody standing over him.

"Dammit!" he growled, banging his hands down on the sides of the wheelchair. The walls of his room were starting to close in around him. Amos stared out through his window. He'd made up his mind that he wasn't staying here. He had a home, a perfectly good house where he could live in peace away from all the nonsense going on in this place.

"There you are."

The sound of that woman's voice grated on his nerves. Amos had been dodging Jennie V. Cookson for days after promising her he'd meet her in the dance room.

"If I didn't know better, I'd think you was avoidin' me, Amos Davis," she said, coming into his room. The short, round woman propped her hand up on one hip and stared down her nose at him. "I thought you said you'd sing me that song."

Amos adjusted his chair to see around her. "I ain't up for it," he grunted angrily.

She cocked her brow. "Ain't up for it? It's just a song, Amos. I ain't asking you to run no marathon."

Amos scowled at the woman. He was through trying to be polite. "You need to leave me alone."

Jennie V. Cookson was nobody to him, and he didn't owe her a damn thing as far as he was concerned.

She crossed her arms across her chest. "Oh, so I guess you must be one of them."

He didn't understand what she meant.

"Think you too good for everybody else because you become this big old singin' star. Forget where you come from and all, and ain't got time to put up with us average folk."

Amos huffed under his breath. He wished like hell he could slap his hands together and squash her like a mosquito buzzing around his head. "You need to get on out of here with that."

"I been waitin' three days, Amos." She held up three bony fingers. "Three days for you to sing me this song like you promised, and I'll be damned if I let you lie to me and get away with it."

"I ain't gotta sing nothin' for you, woman!"

"Like hell you don't!"

Jennie V. Cookson went behind him, grabbed hold of the handles of his wheelchair, and, using every ounce of strength she had, turned his chair around to face the door. All her grunting and his fussing caught the attention of one of the nurses passing by the room.

"What's going on in here?" he asked.

"I need you to help me get him to the dance room, sweetheart," she said sweetly to the man.

"Leave me the hell alone!" Amos complained to both of them.

"He promised to sing to me," she explained. "And I can't leave him alone until he does."

Amos looked up to see the woman batting eyes and smiling at that younger man like she could convince him that she wasn't old enough to be his great-great-great-grandmother. She was embarrassing herself.

"Can you please help me get him to the piano, Mark?"

Mark's fool ass smiled at that old woman, took hold of Amos's chair, and started pushing him out of the room. "Of course I can, Mrs. Cookson. Anything for you."

"I'll be damned," Amos muttered to himself.

Minutes later, Amos sat at that piano, staring down the keys like they'd bite him. Jennie V. sat smack dab in the middle of the room, waiting for him to start.

"If you don't remember how it goes, I can hum it for you," she offered.

"Course I remember," he snapped back. It had just been so long since he'd played that song. He hadn't even listened to it in years.

She began humming anyway. The slow, soulful melody made him uncomfortable at first, and Amos hesitated before putting his fingers on the keys. She left him no choice in the matter. He either had to sing it himself or listen to her butcher the hell out of it.

After a few mishaps, the melody gradually started to come back to him, and the more it did, the quieter Jennie V.'s rendition became. Amos let his eyelids close as he resurrected a sound, his sound, that had been dead too long. Feelings swelled inside him that he had lost; memories came flooding back in waves, high enough to carry him far away from this place; and before he knew it, the sound of his own voice filled that room, older, raspier, but still his.

He was so caught up that he didn't notice the crowd

forming outside the door and spilling into the room. He never noticed the couple slow-dancing over in the corner, or Jennie V. swirling around on the floor like a top, dancing by herself. Amos was back where he belonged, sitting behind a piano, doing the one thing he enjoyed the most. For the first time in a mighty long while, he felt right.

Strangers patted him on the back when he finished. People he didn't know applauded. One of the orderlies offered to take him back to his room, but Amos refused. He just wanted to sit there at that piano and savor the moment. Jennie V. decided to savor it with him.

"It's funny how your mind doesn't grow old but your body does, ain't it?" she said reflectively. "When I listen to that song, in my mind I am still that young, pretty woman who used to love shaking her hips and dancing and drinking until the sun came up." She laughed. "But one of those hips was replaced a long time ago, and I ain't been the same since."

Amos laughed, too.

"I suppose it's all right for me to tell you now, since it don't really matter anymore, but I had quite a crush on you back in the day," she admitted. "Whole bunch of us did. Of course, my husband wasn't too happy about how I gushed over you every time I heard that song."

Plenty of women had husbands who didn't care too much for him back then.

"You ever marry, Amos?"

He shook his head. "Naw. Never did."

"You had to love somebody when you first made that record. A man can't sing a record the way you did unless he feels something for somebody."

Amos sat thoughtfully for several minutes, searching his

memories for the woman he had sung that song for. Her face never came into view because he hadn't sung it for any particular woman. "I can't recall," he finally said.

"You queer?"

He gave her a double take. "What?"

"You like men? It's all right if you do. I mean, I'm a progressive type of woman, and I understand that sometimes men like men and women like women. Ain't no harm in that."

"Naw!" he growled. If she only knew his history, she would never ask him something like that. "I like women just fine."

"But you never married one, you never sang for one, and you never loved one. Don't you think that's strange for a man your age who claims he don't like men?"

A long parade of women, waiting around the edges of so many stages, flashed in his mind. "You crazy woman! Just because I ain't never been married don't mean shit! I've had more than my share of women. Never found the need to marry one. That's all!"

"You got kids?" she asked suddenly.

"I got plenty."

"How come I never see them come visit you?"

That took some of the steam out of his anger. In a less certain voice he asked, "How come you lookin' so hard?"

"How many kids you got, Amos? You even know?"

"Three," he shot back. "Three girls."

"You ever love any of them?"

Amos started to say something, but he pulled up short. He had three girls. Cass wasn't his biological child, but she might as well have been. He'd been the only daddy she knew. Toya was his, but . . . and Tomiko.

"Of course I love them," he said defensively.

He was their daddy, after all. He loved them the best way he knew how.

"But they don't come around," she asked suspiciously. "They know you here?"

Cass knew. Cass knew and . . . he'd seen her only a few times.

"My kids and my grands come to see me every week," she said smugly, standing up to leave and smoothing down her muumuu. "They know I'm here, and they know I always loved them. And because I do, they love me back," she pointed out crisply. "It's a shame, Amos Davis, that a man can write a song like that and not make it for anybody in particular. It's a shame that your girls don't stop by to see you."

She left him sitting there by himself. Amos had had women, and he'd made babies. He'd loved them all as best he could. But old busybody Jennie V. was right. His daughters didn't know he loved them, and that's why none of them ever came to visit.

# *Cass*

Alma Nichols was Cass's business partner. The funny thing was, Cass never asked Alma to be her business partner. The woman just took it upon herself to create an opening in Cass's business and step into it.

"I'm telling you, Cass," Alma said, picking blouses from the rack in the department store and holding them up against Cass. "Vibrant colors"—she pressed a hot-pink satin blouse to Cass's ample chest—"make all the difference." Alma frowned, returned the hot-pink blouse to the rack, then pulled off a shocking electric-yellow one, held it up, and smiled. "They make you come alive," she said, her eyes wide with excitement.

Cass felt her eyes respond in kind, and then she blinked until the wide gaze vanished and she was back to her normal self again. Alma was good at dragging Cass along and making her buy into her ideas. The woman had some kind of mind control that was scary at times, but then at other times she was brilliant. Cass kept her around just for those brilliant moments.

"You'd look so pretty in this," Alma said, shoving the blouse into Cass's arms.

As soon as Alma turned her back, Cass slipped it back on the rack. There was no way in hell she was going to walk around town wearing a shirt that made it look as if the sun had fallen out of the sky.

Alma was everything Cass wasn't: tall; skinny but with a bigger, perfectly round booty; bald-headed; and black. Real black. That lip-licking, perfect kind of black, smooth and silky, without so much as a pimple or scar or scratch on her. The woman looked like some artist had drawn her with a sharp pencil and love.

Cass was at least a foot shorter than Alma and brown—plain, old-fashioned brown. She wore a bob that desperately needed to be shaped, or cut off, or something; glasses; and big, baggy shirts to cover up her baggy body. Cass was round, and when she stood at Alma's side, together, they looked like the number ten.

Alma flitted through the boutique like a butterfly fluttering from flower to flower. She was in her element, loving every minute of it. Cass trailed behind her, scrunching her face at the ridiculously high prices on stuff that cost four times as much as at Walmart.

"So you haven't heard back from any of your stepfather's biological children?" Alma stopped at a rack filled with skinny jeans and flipped through them until she found her size.

Cass couldn't help but notice—size 6. She'd been a size 6 once—6X, back in first grade. That was a while ago.

"Not yet," she answered, holding in her stomach all of a sudden. "I'm starting to wonder if Amos hung around any of his kids long enough for them to care about him."

"As much as I like skinny jeans, all they do is make me look skinnier," Alma said, shaking her head and putting the pants back on the rack.

Cass opened her mouth and started to say, "Yeah, me, too,"

but stopped short when she realized how dumb she'd sound if she said that. She made her mind up, though. As soon as she got home, she was going to get started on Weight Watchers again.

"Well, he certainly can't expect you to take care of him," Alma remarked. "Men like him have it coming, though," she continued, slowly strolling through the store. "They spend their whole lives doing whatever they want, leaving a whole bunch of brokenhearted women and kids who grow up suffering from abandonment issues." She shook her head. "It's a shame."

"Abandonment issues?" Cass balked at being thrown into that category. "I don't have abandonment issues. Amos isn't even my real father."

"I never said you," Alma retorted. "I was talking in general. It wasn't personal, Cass."

Of course it wasn't. Cass was embarrassed at how she'd overreacted. "But I know what you're saying," she said, shrugging. "Amos was just like that. He and Momma used to go at it all the time over all the women he cheated on her with." Cass sucked her teeth. "I doubt if he ever changed, which is probably why his kids don't want nothing to do with him."

"How long did you say he stayed with you and your mother?"

She had to calculate how it had worked out, time-wise. "Amos came to live with us when I was about two, I think."

"And how old were you when he left?"

"I was about ten."

Alma's expression turned introspective, and she nodded. "That's a long time." She slowly walked away, as if she had made her point, even though Cass didn't know what it was.

Cass considered what Alma had just said. It *was* a long time. Cass had only seen and spoken to her real father a half dozen times at the most, and never for more than a few hours. She'd spent an afternoon with him once, along with his girlfriend and her kids. After he dropped her off at home, Cass made a solemn vow that she wouldn't ever spend an afternoon with that man again. She hardly knew him, and he seemed more like those other kids' father than hers.

Amos, on the other hand, never treated her like that. His problem wasn't showing affection to her. When he was around, he filled up the entire apartment with his enthusiasm. He made her feel as if she was the most special girl in the world. He listened to her, like what she said was important to him.

She remembered one time—it really was nothing, but it had stuck in her mind all these years. He had swept through the door like a welcome breeze, planting a smacking kiss on Linda's lips and plopping down on the sofa next to Cass. "Hey, cool cat! What we watchin'?" he asked, nudged up against her, smelling like allspice.

"*The Brady Bunch*," Cass said, half expecting him to tell her to get up and turn the channel.

Amos nodded. "I like *The Brady Bunch*," he said, and the two of them watched that whole episode together. Later on, she found out he didn't care for that show at all. But if she was watching it, he wanted to watch it with her.

"Everybody's got daddy issues, Cass." Alma's voice broke through Cass's reverie. When she focused, she saw the ebony goddess towering over her.

Cass swallowed. "If he was my daddy, maybe I'd have issues with him, Alma, but he's not."

"But he's something like it, right?"

Unexpected tears stung Cass's eyes.

"It's not a big deal, girl. Even women with good daddies got daddy issues." Alma shrugged. "It's the nature of things. He's the first man you ever loved, and then he left. Of course that's gonna mess you up."

"I'm not messed up," she said weakly.

Alma sighed, pulled out her cell phone, and dialed a number. Whoever she called was on speaker so Cass could hear.

"Hello?"

Cass's heart skipped a beat at the sound of the voice, and she glared at Alma.

"Darryl? Hi, this is Alma Nichols. We've been playing phone tag." She chuckled in that way that annoyed the hell out of Cass.

Cass's eyes widened in fear and heartbreak. What the hell was Alma doing calling the love of her life?

"Yes," he said, chuckling. "Finally. It's good to catch up with each other."

Cass wanted to scream.

"So I'm here with my business partner, Cass Edwards." Alma winked at her. "And we'd like to set up a meeting to discuss a possible collaboration for some events we have coming up, and that I'm sure you'd be interested in."

"Yes," he said eagerly.

Cass had not agreed to do any such thing. She shook her head adamantly and mouthed the word no to Alma.

"I think, uh, we should sit down and discuss some opportunities face to face," he said.

"Good. Good. I've checked my schedule," Alma lied, "and

my partner and I are free next Saturday. We could meet to toss around a few ideas."

Cass threw her arms up in disgust. This was not a brilliant idea. How in the hell was she supposed to lose fifty pounds by next Saturday morning? Cass started to wilt like a tiny, delicate flower.

"That would be great! Say, ten thirty at Stewart's?"

"Of course," Alma beamed, ignoring Cass's panicked expression. "Looking forward to it."

Cass was numb after Alma hung up, but she managed to find her voice eventually. "What did you just do?" she asked, appalled.

"Looks like I just made you shit your pants," Alma said, smiling. "But trust me, girl. It's gonna be all right."

# Toya

Toya had been on her way to work when she'd received a frantic call from her mother.

"That disability check should've been here. I sho hope these people ain't playin' around with my money," Melba said as she wiped her hands on her apron. She sat at the kitchen table flipping feverishly through stacks of mail. Melba Jean and her money had an unnatural codependency with each other. She desperately needed to spend it and it desperately needed to be spent. At least, that's how she'd described the relationship to Toya.

After rushing to her mother's house, Toya worked feverishly to calm that woman down before her head blew off her shoulders. She spotted several envelopes sticking out from underneath her mother's sofa cushions, picked them up, and handed them to her. "You need to check your mailbox more than just once a month around check day, Momma."

Relieved, her mother began flipping through a new stack and stopped cold when she got to one envelope in particular. All the color drained from her mother's face as she read the outside of the envelope.

"What is it?" Toya asked, staring at her mother with concern.

"Nothing," Melba finally mumbled, taking the letter and ripping it into pieces before getting up and tossing them into the trash.

"Obviously, it's *something* if it's got you so upset," Toya said.

"I said it was nothing!" Melba snapped, hurrying back over to the table and sifting through her mail again. "Where the hell is my check? Now I got to call these people and act a fool," she mumbled as she stormed out of the kitchen.

Toya waited until her mother had made her exit. Whatever was in that letter definitely had her mother rattled. She knew the old woman wasn't losing her marbles, but it never hurt to be cautious. Toya walked over to the trash can and fished the pieces of the letter out. The fact that her mother had jammed the pieces underneath a discarded Church's Chicken box told her it was something she didn't want anyone to see.

"She probably owes somebody some money," Toya muttered as she shook coffee grinds off some of the pieces. Her mother would run from a bill collector all day long. She was on housing, which was the only reason she'd been able to stay in this house so long, but the rest of her bills were paid only at the last possible moment.

Toya laid the letter pieces on the table and fit them together. It was definitely a personal letter, so that ruled out a bill collector. The puzzle didn't take long to solve since she was working with only four pieces. Yet as she lined up the words to match, she was shocked to see her name.

*Dear Toya,*

*This is Cass. Let me start by saying, I hope this letter reaches you. I had to send it to your mother because I didn't know how else to get in touch with you. I hope that she will pass it on to you, but I can't say that I blame her if she doesn't.*

*Anyway, I'm just writing to let you know that your father, Amos, is in an assisted-living facility here in Detroit. He's in pretty bad shape. He has Alzheimer's and he's slowly losing it. I'm not sure of your relationship with him now, but I'm hoping you can come see him before it's too late. During his life Amos did a lot of things wrong by me and I'm sure by you as well, but he needs family in what could be his last days. I hope you can find some compassion in your heart to come see your daddy. I'm enclosing my number. Please call.*

*Sincerely,*
*Cass*

Toya frowned in confusion. She hadn't thought about Cass in years. Oh, she remembered the name and at least one other whom she knew about—Tomiko. She'd learned about Tomiko from eavesdropping on one of her mother's painful conversations.

"Another child?" Melba Jean muttered to the person on the other end of the phone. "By who?" Toya's mother took a long, slow drag of her cigarette. "Nah, I don't know the woman, but let's hope he do better by that one than he did for this one. Mmmmm . . . ha-ha . . . Tomiko?" She laughed. "He need to stop smoking that reefer. What the hell kind of name is Tomiko?"

Toya read the letter again. Why had Cass written? Was this letter actually saying that her father wanted to see her after nearly thirty years?

"You just had to go and play Nancy Drew, didn't you?"

Toya turned toward her mother's voice. She was standing in the doorway, a cigarette dangling from her fingers. Toya really wished she'd give up those cancer sticks.

"Momma, do you know what is this about?" Toya asked, motioning to the pieces of the letter.

"What does it look like, nosy Rosie? It's a letter from that gal Amos claimed as his own." Melba pushed past her chair as she walked over to the stove to check on her stew. "What does she want?"

"Read it," Toya said as a flurry of mixed emotions ran through her body.

Her mother sat down at the table and read the letter to herself. "Hmph," Melba said. "I guess we supposed to feel sorry for Amos now that he's crazy. Amos can kiss my ass, that's what he can do. I did what I had to do," she said, tearfully. "I raised you by myself and with hardly a dime from his ass, so I care less about what he needs now. Please!" She rolled her eyes. "Just 'cause that fool is senile, we supposed to jump so he can die with dignity? Hell naw," she huffed.

Suddenly, Toya's mind swirled with images. First and foremost was the memory of Amos's denial—she would never forget how much that hurt. He'd been so good to her when they were together, but that night she had learned how he really felt.

*"Hey there, Toya." She'd just come home from school and saw the man sitting on the couch. He looked familiar but . . . "It's me, baby." He held open his arms. "It's your daddy." Toya stared at him in disbelief. She hadn't seen him since she was six years old.*

*She paused before walking near to let him hug her. Amos motioned to some wrapped packages sitting on top of the table. "I* brought you some toys." He laughed as he looked at her. "How old are you now?"

She looked at him. He was her father. Shouldn't he know how old she was? "Thirteen," she answered quietly.

He looked surprised and embarrassed. "Thirteen," he murmured. "Then you probably too old for toys." She shrugged. Amos raised her hands to his lips and kissed them. "Then daddy's gonna have to get you something else." He smiled. "Something for big girls."

To this day, she couldn't remember if he'd ever gotten her something a big girl would like.

He didn't stay long, but he had been there long enough for Toya to start to believe that he might actually stay with them. He came home every evening and sat down at the table for dinner with her and her mother.

"How was school?"

The first time he'd asked her that, Toya's mind went completely blank. "Fine," was all she could say.

He smiled. "Fine? You wastin' your time then if it was just fine, Toya." Amos' eyes filled with something she'd never seen before on anybody. "Good things, important things should be better than just fine, baby. If you love what you do, and somebody asks you that question, you should say, "'It was magnificent.'"

Melba Jean laughed. Toya didn't.

Toya later heard him and her mother talking and Melba's whole mood changed. She sent Toya down the street to play with her friend Reese.

Toya returned home from Reese's that evening to find Amos sitting at the kitchen table, his shirt off, reading the newspaper. Melba was at the stove, frying pork chops and smothering potatoes. The smell of onions wafted through the air, and Melba was humming an Aretha Franklin tune. Toya felt as if they were actually a real family.

Amos had been living with them for two whole weeks, and Toya had never seen her mother happier, which, in turn, made Toya happy. Then, one day, Toya raced home from school to find her mother sitting in front of the TV, drinking a beer and smoking a cigarette. Her eyes were red from crying.

"Hey, Momma," Toya said. When her mother didn't reply, she looked around. "Where's Daddy?"

"He's gone."

"Gone where? When is he coming back?" Toya asked, her heart starting to race.

"He's just gone, Toya," her mother snapped.

"But where did—"

"He's just gone, girl. He left, and this time"—she said, starting to cry—"he ain't coming back."

Three weeks later, Toya was watching television when she saw a commercial on Channel 4 advertising a new music program featuring local talent. She found out the Amos Davis Band would be featured that weekend.

When Toya raced into the living room to tell her mother, Melba Jean had just laughed and told her to keep dreaming. But Toya wasn't dismayed. She convinced herself that her father just had to leave to get ready for his TV show.

A week later, Toya had told all of her friends and invited them over to watch Amos's TV debut. Her friends were so jealous. Laquanta Baker from down the street told everybody that Toya was lying. No way was her daddy going to be on TV. Laquanta said, "She probably don't even know who her daddy is."

They got into a huge fight, and Toya was suspended from school *for three days. But Laquanta would eat her words when they saw her father on television.*

Toya was barely able to contain her excitement on the day of the show. Everyone gathered in her living room, even Laquanta. Toya had invited her just so she could see the look on her face when she realized Toya was telling the truth. She didn't know how she was gonna prove Amos was her daddy, but she hoped something would support her claim.

The show started, and Amos sauntered onto the stage with the swagger of Al Green, the pizzazz of Teddy Pendergrass, and the looks of Marvin Gaye. The six girls gathered around the TV squealed with excitement.

"Oooh, you look just like him," Reese said.

"Girl, I can't believe you know somebody famous," her friend Marissa added.

"He ain't that famous. I ain't never heard of him," Laquanta barked.

Toya cut her eyes at her nemesis but didn't respond. She didn't need to.

"Whatever, Quanta," Reese said. "You can go somewhere with all that negativity."

"Shhhh," Marissa said as the host began introducing the band. "They're about to start singing."

"Ladies and gentlemen, let's give it up for the Amos Davis Band."

The band started with an up-tempo tune before Amos took over on the piano. He played like the keys had been specifically designed for his fingers. The music had the crowd on its feet, and Toya's friends were dancing around the living room like they were at a dance contest. Toya smiled. No one would ever be able to take that joyous moment away from her.

When the host came up onstage after the song, he put the microphone in Amos's face. "That was a powerful performance, my man." He asked some generic music-related questions, then said, "Well, tell our viewers a little about yourself. I know you're from Tupelo. Tell us about your family."

"Well, I'm a proud new papa. Got me little girl," Amos said with a grin.

He was talking about her. Toya's heart raced as she realized that she was the little girl he was talking about. "Told you!" she shouted. "Told you he was my daddy!"

"She's the light of my life. Her name is Tomiko," Amos continued.

The room was silent until Laquanta broke out with, "I told y'all this heffa was lying. That ain't her daddy."

Reese, Marissa, and the other girls looked at Toya, stunned.

Toya's eyes filled with tears. "Yes, he is. He is my daddy."

Laquanta sucked her teeth. "If your name ain't Tomiko, then he ain't talking about you."

"Dang," Marissa said, "we your girls. You ain't gotta lie to us."

"I'm not lying. He is my daddy."

"Mm-hmm, and James Brown is my daddy," one of the other girls said as she started moving across the carpet. "Gonna have a funky good time," she sang playfully.

"Al Green is my daddy," Marissa threw in.

"Lionel Ritchie is my daddy," another girl added.

Everyone busted out laughing—except for Reese, who looked at Toya sympathetically, and Toya herself, who was doing everything in her power to keep from crying.

Toya continued staring at the TV even after Amos was long gone. She accepted that her father had moved on. She was even old enough to understand the drama of his having another family. But she couldn't for the life of her understand how her dad got on TV and didn't even *bother to acknowledge her. It was if she didn't even exist to him. She could forgive a lot of things, but that, Toya thought, she didn't know how she'd ever be able to get over.*

Apparently, her mother couldn't get over it, either. She hadn't seen the TV show, but she'd heard about it because she came home that evening in a rage, crying and cussing and calling Amos everything but a child of God. *"He did it to get back at me, I know he did! I hate that man!"*

Three months later, they'd packed up everything they owned and left Detroit. Toya had actually welcomed the change. Laquanta had already told everyone on the street. Toya knew by Monday everyone at school would be calling her a liar as well. Although she missed Reese something awful, she was grateful that she'd never had to face her friends again.

Toya and her mother started a new life in Flint. They'd had to struggle, but soon Amos Davis became a distant memory to them both.

In the years since, Toya had tried to make excuses for Amos. He'd had a big fight with her mother, and he left Toya's name out just to spite Melba Jean. But that didn't take away the sting, and to protect herself, she learned to bury the awful memory. As she grew up, the time came when it didn't really matter anymore what the reason was. He was gone from her life, gone forever—until today.

# Tomiko

*Here I am again,* Tomiko thought as she sat staring at her computer screen. It was nearly five in the evening, and her rumbling stomach reminded her that she had eaten only two pieces of wheat toast, a cup of yogurt, and a banana, but she was determined not to leave her office without having written at least a paragraph.

"Is one damn paragraph too much to ask for?" she whispered.

Her eyes shifted from the computer screen to the rows of bookshelves that covered most of the wall space in the office. Among the hundreds of books she owned, her own books occupied a prominent space. She had shelved them with their front covers facing out. Even though she was considered a veteran in the industry, Tomiko still got a little thrill whenever she looked at her books. Who knew that keeping a journal would one day land her on the *New York Times* Bestseller List? Life was funny like that.

Tomiko had started keeping a journal when she was twelve years old. She wrote in red quite a bit. Purple ink was used for her happy moments. A black felt pen denoted the times when she thought she would curl into a ball and die. She dedicated some passages to her father, others to the Angel Gabriel.

When she first began to transform the entries into short stories, she didn't quite know. She shared one of the stories with a friend, who thought it was good enough to be published.

Tomiko had laughed and joked, "Friends are supposed to say things like that to each other."

But the idea stayed with her, and the friend kept needling her about it and finally admitted that she knew someone who knew someone in publishing.

"Tomiko, you don't have anything to lose."

Tomiko agreed and finally organized the short stories into a manuscript and sent it over to the friend who knew the editor.

She fully expected a letter or an e-mail from the editor saying, in so many words, thanks but no thanks. But what she got instead was a phone call from a very excited woman with a heavy New York accent saying that she absolutely loved the book and wanted to offer her a publishing deal.

Eight months later, *The Adventures of Li'l Amos* made its debut in bookstores all across the country. Three months after that it was a *New York Times* bestseller. Four more books followed, along with two Caldecott Medals, numerous licensing agreements, and now talk of a movie.

Tomiko had come a long way from the east side of Detroit, but Li'l Amos was stuck there forever, he and his best friend, his guardian angel Gabriel. Throughout the time she was writing, though, she'd felt a troubling undercurrent of despair. She thought the success of the series would offer her solace from those painful feelings, but it didn't. Trapped in a grown woman's body, having stumbled into fame, she was really a little girl missing her daddy and pretending like she didn't care.

Marjorie had, as usual, put a positive spin on the issue. "Okay, so he wasn't around when you were growing up. Things were tough. But look at it this way: he left you with a story that you've spun into gold. You're raking in more money than he ever would have paid in child support!"

Funny how people believe money can make every bad thing good. Tomiko didn't want the money. She wanted that feeling of closeness back, those nights when she would snuggle up next to Amos in bed while he came up with another of his impromptu stories, made up just for her. That longing was shot through every story that she wrote.

Amos's education had come to a halt at the tender age of thirteen, and the schooling he'd received before that had been erratic at best. He was a sharecropper's son, one of six children whose twelve hands were needed for the planting and picking of cotton. He could look at a bale of cotton, bet a nickel on the weight, and win every time. He could look at the sky and tell if the weather was going to turn foul. But when he looked at words, all he saw were letters jumbled together in a way that didn't make a bit of sense to him. And so when his baby girl begged him to read her a bedtime story, he would hem and haw.

"Pleeeeease, Daddy?"

At Tomiko's urging, Amos would take the book from her and thoughtfully flip through the pages before tossing it aside and announcing, "I got a better story."

And so another one of his magical tales would begin:

"Once upon a time there was a little boy named Amos."

"That's your name!"

"Uh-huh ... Amos's best friend was the Angel Gabriel."

He told a story about a little boy named Amos who could play the piano so well that the angels in heaven wept with joy. Amos went around the world, playing the piano for kings and queens who paid him in gold coins.

One day the Angel Gabriel came down from the heavens and invited Amos to play for the king of the universe.

At that point in the story Amos would look at Tomiko and ask, "Do you know who the king of the universe is?"

Tomiko knew because she had heard the story more times than she could count. "I know, I know!" she squealed as she bounced with excitement.

Amos would lean in and whisper, "Who?"

"God."

"Yes, God," Amos agreed, tweaking her nose before continuing. "But if you go to play for the king of the universe, you will never be able to return to earth."

Even though Tomiko had heard the story hundreds of times, she always became anxious when they arrived at that point. And even though she knew the answer to the question, she always asked:

"What did he say, Daddy?"

"Well, Li'l Amos thought about it for some time. He knew that heaven was the greatest stage in all of the universe, and to play before the king of the universe was an honor that not many people—men or women—ever received, and so he figured the right thing to do would be to say yes."

"But what about Li'l Amos's family?"

"Well," Amos would say as he pulled the blanket up to Tomiko's chin. "He would miss his family, but he knew if they really loved him, he would always remain in their hearts."

Amos thumped his chest and then leaned down and kissed Tomiko on her cheek.

"Once somebody is in your heart, they're with you forever."

"Oh."

"So Li'l Amos packed his small suitcase, took hold of the hand of the Angel Gabriel, and the two flew up to heaven."

"But when Li'l Amos's parents came home, where did they think he'd gone off to?"

By then Amos would be staring longingly out the window. His voice would take on a faraway tone.

"Oh, they knew he was with the Angel Gabriel."

"How did they know?"

"Because of the white feather."

Sometimes the white feather would be on the windowsill, on the front porch, or even on Li'l Amos's pillow. But it was always left behind as a sign for the parents not to worry because their little boy was in safe hands.

"When it's really quiet, listen really hard. You'll hear Li'l Amos up there in heaven, tickling those piano keys."

And sometimes, in the middle of the night, when the house was still, Tomiko was sure she could.

Tomiko went over to the bookcase, pulled down three of her books, and hugged them to her chest. Closing her eyes, she could see Amos's face swimming in the darkness behind her lids. He was smiling, just like he did at bedtime. Tomiko felt a smile begin to crest on her own lips. And then she heard a whisper, way deep down in her ears. You can do it, baby, I know you can.

In the next moment, however, all the bitterness of all those years without him washed back over her. Yes, he'd lit a spark.

But she'd had to fan it into a flame on her lonesome. And at times like these when the spark seemed lost forever, she knew one thing for sure: Amos wasn't coming to her rescue.

She placed those books back on the shelf, walked back over to her desk, and sat down behind her computer. "This book isn't going to write itself," she muttered, and started typing.

# Amos

*A thousand women cross in front of me*
*But only one of them will ever be*
*Woman 'nough to make a fool outta me*

My pops used to play this record when I was growing up." The male nurse sat down near the window across from Amos, who was playing his hit record on one of those cell phones. "I didn't know that was you."

Amos smirked. "That was me a long time ago," he told the younger man. Amos recognized his face, but until now he'd never cared one way or another about what his name was. He squinted and read the name tag on his shirt: "Mark Sheridan, LPN."

Mark nodded his head gently to the melody. "Back in the day, though, it was the joint."

Amos eyed Mark curiously. "You weren't even born when I made that record."

He shook his head. "Naw, but I was probably made to it," he laughed. "Like I said, my pops played the mess out of this song. Especially when we took road trips." He laughed. "I remember one year, we drove from Detroit to Mississippi, and he played it the whole way down there, nonstop, and then the whole way back." Mark laughed. "After that, Momma refused to let him play it in the house again."

Amos smiled.

Both men sat and listened until the song came to an end.

"So how long I gotta stay here?" Amos finally asked.

Mark shrugged. "That's up to you and your daughter, I suppose. Cassandra? That her name?"

Amos made a face. "I gotta wait for her to sign me out?"

Mark leaned forward. "Look, man, you need somebody to look after you."

"I ain't gonna have to be pushed around in this wheelchair forever," Amos retorted. "I'm gonna be all right soon. I'm feelin' better, my mind is clear. I'm gonna be able to go home, right? I don't need Cass to sign me out."

"It's not safe for you to be on your own, Amos," Mark explained. "You wander off, man, and . . . that's not good."

"Wander off?" Amos chuckled bitterly. "I ain't no puppy, man! I'm grown, and I don't wander. I go where I go. I do what I want to do. I ain't wanderin'."

"How many times have the police brought you home, Amos?" Mark asked bluntly. "How many times have your neighbors had to pull you off a stoop and take you back inside your house?"

Amos looked confused, like Mark was talking about somebody else.

"Quite a few," Mark told Amos.

"That's bull," Amos said. "I just—"

"You just what?"

"I get a little forgetful sometimes," Amos explained, trying to make sense out of all the times when he was someplace he didn't remember going to. "I'm getting old," he continued. "Hell, old folks forget sometimes."

"Old folks do." Mark nodded. "Young folks do, too. But sometimes the problem is more serious than that. In your case, Amos, it's more than just forgetting sometimes."

Amos refused to concede the point. "So you sayin' I'm crazy," he said defensively.

"Not crazy," Mark replied. "But you need help, and your daughter Cass figured that this was the best solution. It's her way of taking care of you."

A sad feeling washed over him. "She could do better than this," he said, discouraged.

"See, now I'm offended," Mark teased. "We do good work around here, so that's an unfair statement to make, man."

Amos didn't care about hurting this dude's feelings. If putting him away in a nursing home was Cass's idea of taking care of him, then she should've just left his ass out there wandering the streets. He'd have been a whole lot better off.

Amos went back to his room and spent the rest of the afternoon going through some of his private papers that had been brought over from his house, looking for names and numbers of people he knew, anybody who could come get him and drop him off at home.

He came across a slip of paper with a name on it, Ross Cunningham, and a number scrawled underneath it. Ross Cunningham. Ross Cunningham. Amos thought long and hard trying to remember who in the world Ross Cunningham was before it finally came to him.

"Me and some of the fellas, we get together every Thursday night to play poker," Ross Cunningham had told him when they met. He was this cat Amos met at the bar a few blocks away from where he lived. "You welcome to join us, but you can't play if you can't pay, so don't bother comin' if you ain't got no money. We don't extend credit."

Nah, a dude like that wouldn't drive all the way out here to pick Amos up and take him home. So he kept looking. Amos searched through the papers until he came across some photographs that he'd forgotten he'd had. He had one of Cass and her momma, Linda. That girl looked more like that woman than she looked like herself, he thought, shaking his head. Cass needed her behind whupped for bringing him here, so he wasn't feeling too sentimental over her just yet. He tossed those pictures aside and flipped through several others until he came to one that brought a broad smile to his face.

"Tomiko," he said, grinning. "My baby Miko."

She couldn't have been more than five or six in that photo, missing most of her teeth, with hair wild and sticking out all over her head. It was one of those school pictures, and they must have made the mistake of taking it after recess or something. She smiled back at him with eyes just like his, and inside them he saw his spirit—strong and free. She was his little girl, his youngest, and he knew that if anybody would come get him, his baby Miko would.

Amos searched through his papers, looking for a phone number or an address he could use to get in contact with Miko, or even Ruby, her momma. Ruby might've hated him, but Tomiko never could. Amos went through every slip of paper he had, but he came up empty. When was the last time he'd spoken to that girl? He sat and tried to think back. He and Ruby had split up years ago when Tomiko was . . . He couldn't remember how old she'd been when the two of them had parted ways. But the last time he'd spoken to his daughter was . . . He'd meant to call her, so many times. He'd meant to pick her up one weekend and take her to the zoo. He'd meant to . . .

She had been so young when he'd moved out, and the thought had never occurred to him that he'd stay away so long. But one day away from her turned into weeks. Sometimes he'd think about her, wonder what she was doing, where she was. Time just marched on, that's all. In the back of his mind, she was always fine. That's where he kept her, though, never in the front, where he would have remembered to visit or even to call his little girl.

A thick lump swelled up in his throat. Amos had spoiled that girl when she was little. He'd take her to rehearsals with him and let her sit on his lap while he played and sang. Sometimes she'd sing with him. Tomiko loved the music the same way he did. A bitter smile crossed his lips at the thought. Now he was an old man. Amos was about to lose what was left of his mind, and he had no one, not even his little Miko, who had sworn to love him forever.

He lost track of how long he sat alone in his room. Uncomfortable with that thought, he rolled his chair out to the nurses' station to find Mark. "Can I talk to you for a second, brotha?" he asked sheepishly.

Mark followed Amos to a sitting area down the hall. "What's up, man?"

Amos cupped his hands together in his lap to keep them from shaking. He was as nervous as a ho in church, which surprised the hell out of him. But a feeling of panic had set in. Desperation rained down on him, and he felt like he needed to hurry up and do this.

"You know, uh . . . I got other kids besides Cass," he reluctantly admitted.

"Oh yeah?"

Amos nodded. "Yeah. I ain't always been . . . as attentive as I probably should've been." He forced a smile and glanced up at Mark. "My youngest . . . she just like me. She love music, and she plays, too," he said proudly. "She sings like her old man."

"When's the last time you heard her sing?"

Amos stared blankly at the younger man. He couldn't remember. "I'd like to get in touch with her, but I don't know how." He shrugged helplessly.

Mark nodded slowly as if he understood where Amos was coming from. "What's her name?"

"Tomiko," Amos responded hoarsely. He cleared his throat. "Tomiko Davis."

Mark wrote it down on a slip of paper from his pocket and then stood up to leave. "Let me see what I can find out."

Amos returned to his room and stared out of the window at the gardens and sighed deeply. He missed the girl. For the first time in too long, he missed his baby girl.

# Cass

That damn Alma! Cass cursed that woman under her breath up and down every aisle in the market. She had gone ahead and booked a catered ladies' luncheon a week before a college graduation party that Cass had committed to months ago.

"I told you not to book less than two weeks apart," she'd said. Yet Cass could complain all she wanted. She knew that Alma was only going to listen to the parts she wanted to hear. "I can't handle all these events, Alma! It's too much!"

"Let me hire somebody, Cass," Alma shot back over the phone. "I know a woman who can cook her ass off."

Cass sighed and rolled her eyes. "How many times do I have to tell you? The success of an event does not depend on whether we are able to cook the food. Of course I can cook, but I also have to worry about decorating and presentation, too. The food could be mouthwatering, but it won't matter if it's thrown on the table in a heap. I have to prepare a feast for the eyes as well as the stomach and layout is everything so that clients don't have to think about what goes on the plate next, and so that all of it looks so tasty that their eyes get big, and they lick their lips at the thought of eating all of it."

"Cass, seriously, you're making me hungry."

"Because I know how to make you hungry. It's what I do best. Being a good cook comes after that."

"But if we hired some more people, we could double our bookings, Cass," Alma argued, ignoring everything Cass had just said to her. "And you wouldn't have to do all the cooking, presenting, and making folks hungry all by yourself."

"Alma . . ." Cass said wearily. She wasn't in the mood to argue.

"We could make a lot more money, Cassandra."

Thinking about that aspect shut them both up. In the brief interlude Cass's phone buzzed with another incoming call.

"I got a call coming."

"Call me back when you're done," Alma said before hanging up.

"I need you to come pick me up," Amos said as soon as Cass clicked over, before she'd even said hello.

"What?"

"Come get me!" he demanded. "I can't stay in this place. These people are crazy!"

This old man was becoming even more of a burden on an already overburdened life. Cass sighed in frustration, stopped, and rubbed the tension from her forehead. "Amos, what are you talking about? What people?"

"These people here at this nursin' home," he said, sounding as if he didn't want anyone to overhear what he was saying. "They crazy, and I can't stay here! You need to come and get me! I'll give you gas money! Just take me back home."

Amos didn't have gas money. When they found him, he'd had four dollars and twenty-seven cents in his pocket.

"I'm not coming to get you, Amos. If you're having a

problem, then you need to call one of the nurses or orderlies or somebody."

"Who the hell do you think I'm talkin' 'bout?" he said in a loud angry whisper. "Between them crazy doctors and nurses and these crazy old people—they drivin' me crazier than I already am! I can't take it anymore, Cass! Now you got to come and get me. All I want is to go home. I don't belong in a place like this, and if you don't come and get me, I'll walk!"

"C'mon, Amos, man," Cass heard a voice say in the background.

"Man nothing!" Amos spat, his voice pulling away from the phone. "Give me back . . . Mothaf—"

"Hello?" a man's voice said over the phone.

"Hello?" Cass responded, suddenly worried that maybe Amos was being tortured and held against his will. "What's going on? Where's Amos?"

"This is Mark, one of the nurses," he explained.

She remembered him. "Mark. This is Cass, Amos's—What's going on? What's wrong with him? He sounds upset."

"He is."

"What's wrong?"

Lord, she didn't need this. Cass had to cater an event for a hundred people tomorrow night. Amos didn't fit into this equation.

"Well . . ." Mark sighed. "He needs an enema," he said matter-of-factly.

Cass's stomach gurgled. "What?"

"Shuddup, man!" Amos shouted from the background.

"Mr. Davis here is all backed up," Mark said, almost playfully.

"Go to hell!" Amos shouted again.

"We need to do an enema, and he's not happy about it."

Hell, she wouldn't have been happy about an enema, either. "Uh . . ." was the best she could muster.

Mark laughed. "All this could have been avoided if the old man had eaten his oatmeal."

"Fuck yo' oatmeal!" Amos grumbled.

"I think he hates oatmeal," she muttered absently.

"Apparently."

"Look, I can't deal with this right now," she said. "Isn't there anyone else he can call?"

"I don't think so," he said hesitantly. "Yours is the only number we have on file."

Cass needed to sit down. God help him if she *was* all he had. Cass leaned over her shopping cart to support herself. He had more than Cass. Amos had children who were biologically his. How come none of them had to suffer through his protests against enemas?

"Look," Mark finally said. "Normally, I wouldn't do this, but, uh . . . Amos keeps talking about how he'd like some home-cooked greens. Do you cook greens?"

Cass sighed. "Yes."

Mark was not shy about seizing an opportunity. "I think it'll help, and we can avoid the humiliation of having to hold him down to shoot anything medicinal up his behind. You can just drop them off at the nurses' station and say they're for me—Mark Sheridan."

Cass said, exasperated, "Mark, I really don't have time to make greens for Amos."

"C'mon," he pleaded. "If he's anything like my old man, they'll go right through him in no time, plus . . . you'd be doing me a huge favor because I don't want to have to do this to him any more than he wants it done."

Cass couldn't help but laugh at this wry admission. "Yeah, I don't think I'd want that job, either."

"The way I see it, if we work together on this, we can tag-team him. You make the greens, and I'll see to it that he eats plenty of them. It'll be worth the effort, I promise."

The man made a very convincing argument. She vaguely remembered meeting him that first day Amos had been taken to the nursing home. Cass had been so preoccupied with suddenly having to take on the responsibility of Amos that everything around her formed a big blur.

"Okay, you win," she finally said. "I'll bring them over tomorrow in time for lunch."

"No, we both win." He laughed. "Believe me."

"Will you be there tomorrow?" Cass felt silly as soon as she'd asked that question. He'd already told her just to drop them off for him.

"I can be," he said tentatively.

"No, I'm sorry. Um . . . don't make any special trips in for this."

"It's not a problem," he said. "I'll see you tomorrow at, say . . . eleven, eleven thirty?"

"Yeah, sure. That'll work."

After hanging up, Cass went back to her shopping, making a mental note to put mustard greens on the list. Yet thoughts of the phone call kept intruding. That nurse was about as manipulative as Amos. He didn't have to go the extra mile with Amos, making that request for greens. She could have told him to go to hell. People probably did that all the time. But he'd made her promise. He was even coming in on his day off to make sure Amos ate his greens. He was doing all of that for an old man who, as far as Cass could tell, was not a model patient.

Making a special trip to the nursing home wasn't something he had to do. So she could extend herself as well. Amos. Greens. And maybe a peach cobbler for Mark. Amos was obviously giving that man the blues, and making him a peach cobbler was the least she could do.

# Amos

He sat in the back of Sunnyview's main recreation room, staring around the place. Some of the residents sat around watching television; others had dozed off and were letting the television watch them. A small group of women sat together across the room, chatting while knitting hats or sweaters, talking over one another about their children and grandchildren. Two old men huddled over a chessboard near the window, looking as if they'd been sitting in those same positions since the beginning of time. He'd been watching them for an hour, and it seemed neither one of them had moved a muscle. Amos was beginning to think they were dead until one of them finally said something and the other one nodded.

Is this what his life had come to? Not that long ago Amos had been cock of the roost, singing, dancing, and gyrating onstage for audiences that could fill this room half a dozen times, hanging on every melodious word that fell from his lips. Women wanted him, and men wanted to be him. Tall, slender, Amos had been fine back then. A need to do a mental inventory clicked in his head. He looked down in disdain at the round belly on his lap. That didn't used to be there. Continuing his survey, Amos held up his hands and stretched out his fingers. Arthritis swelled his knuckles, but once upon a time, his fingers used to play some slick-ass notes on the piano. He closed his eyes and let his mind travel back to the vision of hundreds of bodies swaying in a smoke-filled room, dancing and spinning around on the floor out in front of him. Amos had been the captain of that carnival every time he set foot on that stage. And the women adored him! They threw themselves at him.

Amos could count on one finger how many women he'd chased in his life. One. A big, fine redbone in a yellow dress hugging on every curve like a jealous man. Melba Jean McCann. He had a woman sitting at home waiting for him, but Amos had forgotten Linda's name as soon as Melba Jean had told him hers.

*They were between sets, and he pushed his way through the crowd and shot over, like a bullet, to that woman sitting at the bar.*

*"Whatchu drinkin', sugah?" he asked, sidling up next to her.*

*She cut her pretty eyes at him and sized him up with a glance. "I've already got a drink," she told him dismissively.*

*If he didn't know better, he'd swear she'd just found his ass resistible. That was a first for Amos because, to every other woman in the room, he was the finest man around. Apparently, she hadn't gotten the memo.*

*"What's your name?" he asked, refusing to leave her side. The sharks were circling and waiting for him to leave her sitting there by herself.*

*The woman didn't say a word. I'll be damned, he thought. "I'm Amos Davis," he announced like she should already know his name. After all, it was on a big-ass poster taped to the front door, along with his picture. "I'm performing here tonight." Amos felt like an awkward schoolboy trying to get the pretty cheerleader even to notice he was breathing. But she wasn't giving him anything here. He had nothing to* work with. She didn't want a drink, wouldn't tell him her name . . . wouldn't even look at him. An unfamiliar desperation began to set in. Amos wanted this woman more than ever because she didn't want him.

"Damn, baby!" he exclaimed, picking up a napkin off the bar and wiping the sweat off his brow. "I'm just tryin' to be friendly."

She looked at him and shrugged. "I got plenty of friends."

He grinned. "You ain't got friends like me," he said. "I promise you that."

The woman blinked her big, beautiful brown eyes, looking through him as if he was invisible. She took another sip of her drink.

"C'mon, man," one of his bandmates said to him over his shoulder. "We back on."

An anxious knot burned in his stomach. Amos stared around the room at all them fools just biding their time, waiting for him to walk away and leave this gorgeous woman sitting by herself. He hadn't gotten a name, a number, nothing.

"Amos!" someone yelled to him from the stage over the noise of the crowd.

He turned abruptly and forced his way through the crowd again, back to the stage.

There are a thousand and one ways to make love to a woman, and Amos made love to that redbone from that stage with as much passion as he would've had he been spread out on top of her. He stroked every inch of her with song lyrics aimed directly at her, and before he knew it, she had broken free from all those dudes holding her prisoner at that bar and was making her way over to where he played. She stood there for the rest of the night, gazing up at him, held captive under his spell.

Melba Jean McCann. That was her name, and Amos loved her like a man possessed until dawn. Yeah, Linda was going to be pissed that he didn't come home all night. And yeah, he was going to have to come up with one hell of a lie to explain why he hadn't come home, knowing full well that she'd know he was lying. He loved Linda, but at the moment he was too busy loving Melba Jean to care.

Melba Jean rode him like he was a wild stallion, gazing down at him with those big eyes of hers, her lovely mouth calling out his name over and over again until the walls shook in that small apartment of hers.

"Keep it down!" someone banged on the wall and yelled.

Amos held on to her small waist and licked his lips at the unforgettable sight of her mouthwatering tits bouncing above his head. He was using her. She was using him. And as far as he was concerned, neither one of them needed to apologize for it.

"C'mon, baby," he said, willing back his orgasm. The least he could do was to give her some good loving. He would take care of her first before taking care of himself. Melba Jean was a dream walking. She was the kind of woman men fantasized about, but keeping a woman like this for his own was a whole other story. A woman like her could get a man killed. But for one night with her, he was willing to take his chances.

"Oh, Amos!" she said, breathless. "Amos!" Melba Jean tossed her head back. "Amos!"

"What kind of look is that you got on your face?" Jennie V. said, sitting down next to him. "If I didn't know better, I'd say you was up to no good."

Startled, he opened his eyes to the petite woman across from him. Jennie V.'s wavy gray hair lay slicked back on her head, and a crooked smile creased the corners of her mouth. She was a far cry from Melba Jean, but then again, he wasn't much more than a shadow of the man he used to be back then, either.

"Thinking about somebody I used to know," he finally said.

She eyed him suspiciously. "A woman?"

He smiled. "That obvious?"

"With a grin that dirty, yeah, it was pretty obvious. I suspect that good-looking soul singers like you must've had plenty of women dropping on the floor at your feet at one time or 'nother."

Amos shrugged. "I had my share," he said smugly.

"What was this one's name? . . . If you can remember, I mean."

"Oh, I remember her, all right." He recalled Melba Jean being the light he needed on dark nights. The sugar in his coffee. The cool glass of water he craved when his throat was dry. But just as quickly he remembered everything else. She was demanding. When she got mad, she was cruel. She'd ended up hating him more than any woman he'd ever known. His smile faded away as suddenly as it had appeared.

"You had feelings for the woman?" she asked, mildly surprised. "I can see it in your eyes. You cared about her."

Amos had never quite thought of it like that. Melba Jean had been a goddess who turned into a monster, and he'd had enough sense to run.

"What? You can't admit that you actually cared for the woman?" Jennie V. asked indignantly. She waited for him to respond, but Amos didn't. "Sitting there looking silly with that grin on your face thinking about her, but you can't sit here and say out loud that she meant something to you." She shook her head in disgust.

Amos clenched his jaws. He didn't have to explain himself to this woman. Jennie V. wasn't Jesus holding his salvation in her hands. She was a nosy old woman who had nothing better to do than to pry into his affairs.

"I'll bet you broke her heart," she said, continuing

relentlessly with her effort to get him to tell her something that wasn't any of her business. "A man like you never gives a damn about a woman's heart, though. A man like you will use a woman up and then toss her out like yesterday's garbage when he's finished with her," she continued gravely. "You think she's smiling when she thinks of you, Amos?"

"Shut the hell up, Jennie!" he growled under his breath. "I'm sitting here minding my own business, and I don't recall inviting you into it."

"I invited myself."

"Well, I'm uninviting you, so take your ass someplace else and leave me the hell alone!"

Offended, Jennie V. stood up to leave. She stood over him and stared down her nose at him. "You ain't no superstar soul singer no more, Amos. You just an old man losin' his mind and what's left of his life. Heaven or hell is closer to you now than it ever has been, so if I was you, I'd be thinkin' long and hard about making amends. You can't give back what you took from people, but maybe you can give somethin' back to the ones you leave behind. You say you got kids? Kids who came from these women you used up? Those kids don't think enough of you to come around and see about you."

Amos huffed bitterly, hit the forward switch on his chair, and started to roll away from the woman.

"Didn't none of them ask you to be their daddy," she called after him. "But you still accountable to them!"

Amos rolled back to his room and parked his chair in front of the window. His happy memories had turned into regrets. He knew why Melba Jean had turned on him.

*"I'm havin' your baby, Amos. Ain't you happy? We gonna have a family of our own now. Ain't you happy?"*

Toya. The little girl's name was Toya, and when she was born, she looked just like him. But back then Amos didn't have time. He'd walked away and kept on walking. For the first time since he'd met Melba Jean, Amos admitted to himself that he'd done wrong by that woman, by that little girl. He'd done wrong by all of them.

# *Toya*

Why couldn't she stay true to her word? Toya groaned, utterly disgusted with herself.

"Ummm, are you okay, baby?" Max asked as he rolled over and put an arm around her midsection.

Toya nodded. Half of her was upset that she had allowed Max into her bed—*again*. She really and truly had thought she had the strength to let him go. But loneliness had overtaken her. And Max was a warm body. And today she'd gotten something she'd been begging for for months: Max had spent the night. Toya didn't know what he'd told his wife. And just about now she didn't really care.

When he'd showed up at her place, she'd been surprised that he didn't immediately try to get her into bed. She'd told him about Amos, and he had actually encouraged her to talk about her feelings. It was a side of him she'd never seen. A side of him that made her love him even more.

"Like I told you last night," he said, propping himself up on his elbow, "anyone who doesn't recognize you for the prize that you are—and that includes your own flesh and blood—is a fool."

She couldn't help but note the irony of his words. He didn't know the number of times she'd called herself a fool with regard to him. She wanted to tell him that, but then again, she didn't want to ruin this moment.

"Thanks, babe, but it still hurts. All I wanted was for him to acknowledge me, acknowledge his mistake, say I'm sorry and try to do right. But now that I have a chance to face him, I'm scared. What if he doesn't say any of that? What if he wants to know why I'm even there?" She'd been thinking about that for the past three days. Cass wanted her to come. What if Amos didn't want to see her? That thought had kept her from calling Cass. But more and more, Toya found herself wanting at least to talk to her father.

Max shook his head. "I never understood how a man could turn his back on his own child."

His being a good father had actually been what initially attracted Toya to Max. He was in Macy's with his daughter to buy her some school clothes. He was lost when it came to figuring out what to buy, and Toya had stepped up to help. He informed Toya that although his daughter didn't live with him, she spent every other weekend at his home. He and his current wife had a son, but he made sure to include his daughter in everything they did. Through it all, as much of a jerk as Max could be sometimes, he loved and adored his daughter from his first wife. Toya loved that about him. His current wife, Jewel, couldn't stand the ex, or his daughter, and at one point she had asked him to choose. He told her in no uncertain terms that he was not turning his back on his child. And of course, the moment he said that, Toya's love for him was sealed. She wished that she had known a father's love like that.

"Babe, it'll be all right," Max said.

"Thank you so much for being here," she said, leaning in

and kissing him, pushing away any feelings of regret. "Thank you for making me feel better."

"My pleasure." He was struck by another thought, taking it another way, and smiled wickedly. "Let me make you feel better again." He moved in and began nuzzling her neck.

They were interrupted by a loud crash from the front door.

"What the—" both of them said, jumping up.

They heard someone scream, "Max, I know you're in there. I see your car!"

"Oh my God. That's Jewel."

Toya sat up in the bed in a panic. "Your wife? How does she know where I live?"

"Hell if I know," he said, scrambling out of the bed.

"Oh, God," Toya mumbled. This was the last thing that she needed.

"You slutty tramp. You want to sleep with other people's husbands! Come out and face me like a woman!" Jewel screamed like a madwoman.

Suddenly, images of her mother and Amos and the fight in the club popped into her head. It felt like déjà vu all over again. Only this time *Toya* was the other woman.

*Like mother, like daughter.*

Toya found herself wondering if Max's child was hovering outside, watching his mother crying and begging her husband to come home.

*Like mother, like daughter.*

"Max, get her away from here before my neighbors call the cops," Toya hissed.

"Dammit," he mumbled, stumbling as he tried to step into his pants.

He headed toward the door as she got out of bed and

slipped her robe on. Max stopped, and then nervously looked back at her.

"Max, I'm gonna kill you and that tramp!"

"What are you doing?" Toya asked when she noticed he wasn't moving.

Max shook his head. "Man, Jewel is crazy."

Toya was dumbfounded as Max made a left turn out of her bedroom and, instead of heading toward her front door and his crazy wife, eased open Toya's patio door and stepped outside.

"Sorry, baby," he muttered. "I'll call you later." Before Toya could say another word, Max disappeared.

Toya wanted to scream after him, but she was too appalled by his cowardice to move. She jumped when she heard another loud crash. She was about to call the police herself when she heard the woman yell, "Max, come back here!" Out the window Toya saw Max's Chrysler 300 speed out of the parking lot.

"Trick, this ain't over!" the woman screamed as she gave Toya's front door a final jarring kick.

Toya stood at her bedroom window, watching in disbelief as Jewel roared off after her husband. Had this really become her life? Was she really subjecting herself to this degree of humiliation? What the hell had she been thinking? And, most frightening of all, what was this psycho going to do now that she knew where Toya lived?

# Tomiko

*Dear Ms. Davis:*

*You don't know me, but my name is Mark Sheridan, and I work as a nurse at Sunnyview Assisted Living Center in Detroit. I don't know if you are the right Tomiko Davis, but you are certainly the most popular one on the Internet, and so I thought I would start with you. Like I mentioned, I work as a nurse at Sunnyview, and there is a man here named Amos Davis who claims to be your father. While he is in good spirits, he is very ill and his time may be limited.*

*He confided in me about you, and Ms. Davis, his eyes teared up when he talked about you. I don't know all of what happened between your mother and your father, but from what I can tell, he never stopped loving you. I hope you find it in your heart to come and see about Amos, and I hope to God that you are the right Tomiko Davis. Please respond so I know if my search is done or if it's just begun.*

*Best,*
*Mark Sheridan*

Tomiko must have read that e-mail fifty times before she realized she wasn't breathing. By the time she stopped to fill her lungs with air, her head was swimming and her heart was galloping so hard she thought it would burst from her chest. She wanted to look away from the e-mail, but she thought that if she did that, she would look back and it would be gone.

In a matter of minutes she experienced an entire cycle of emotions—surprise, panic, disbelief, and then anger. Was someone playing a horrible trick on her? She was well aware of scammers who wooed unsuspecting individuals like herself. When she responded—no, *if* she responded—what would this so-called Mark say? Oh, your daddy died, but he left you a million dollars. I just need your Social Security number and bank account information before I can get the money to you . . . from Nigeria.

Tomiko wasn't stupid. She watched *Dateline*! But suppose it wasn't a scam? Suppose it was real? Tomiko nervously chewed her bottom lip as she pondered what to do. Even if it was true and she called or even visited the nursing home, what would she say to him? So many years had gone by. She had been so young. But the memory of his leaving still hung fresh in her mind, and even now as she sat there staring at the e-mail, she began to relive those last moments before Amos left her forever.

*By the time Tomiko was six years old, things between Ruby and Amos had started to unravel.*

*Sometimes Amos came home from his gigs with all of his money, sometimes he came home with nothing, and sometimes he didn't come home at all. In the years the couple had been together, they had been put out of six different apartments within a ten-block radius. By the* time Tomiko was three, the sight of a man in uniform made her cry. *Why?* Because she thought anybody dressed in a uniform was the sheriff, coming to evict them again.

Every time the family moved, something got left behind—a favorite doll, a wool cap, a pair of shoes—but never the piano. Besides the fact it was too big to forget, Ruby couldn't leave it behind even if she wanted to. If she had, it would have been like ushering Amos out the door.

Amos said that the piano had once belonged to a former slave turned composer named Blind Tom Wiggins. Or at least that's what the white man who sold him the piano had told him. But there was no proof to back up the claim.

"The music I write on this here piano is proof enough!" Amos would bellow whenever the authenticity of the piano was challenged. "I don't care what you do, what they wanna take—you don't ever let them take this here piano."

Once Ruby suggested he pawn the piano so that she could get some food in the house and maybe buy herself and Tomiko new winter coats: "You got the gig in Chattanooga soon. It wouldn't even sit in the pawnshop for a week."

Amos looked at Ruby as if she'd asked him to put his mother out to pasture. Ruby hated and loved that piano. She eyed it the way she eyed the women she suspected Amos was sleeping with.

Once she got so mad at him, she doused it with kerosene and held a lit match over it. "You love this piano more than you love me!" she declared as the bright flame danced menacingly close to the lacquered wood.

That was the first time Tomiko saw Amos hit her mother. The sound Amos's open palm made on Ruby's tear-soaked cheek was as loud as the crack of a bat against a home run ball.

*The match flew to the floor, and the flame flitted out.*

*Ruby swung back and missed. Amos caught her by the waist, swung her up and over his shoulder, and carried her into the bedroom, away from Tomiko's wide, fear-filled eyes.*

*He slammed the door hard behind him. But that didn't block out Ruby's screams of anger. Tomiko heard a large thud, which was followed by Amos's warning: "Now listen here, Ruby, don't be pushin' me again!"*

*After a while, only soft sobs and whispers could be heard. Just before the sun slipped from the sky, the bedroom door opened and a red-eyed Ruby appeared.*

*"Hey, baby," she said, in a tired tone. "You want some White Castle for dinner?"*

*That's how they made up for things. White Castle burgers.*

*Tomiko's eyes swung to the bedroom. It was dark and quiet, and for a terrible instant she had the horrific feeling that her father was dead. And even more disturbing, the thought of him being dead brought her a sense of relief.*

*But that feeling was swept away when Amos appeared in the doorway, wearing his favorite hat cocked smartly to one side.*

*He winked at Tomiko before strolling into the kitchen to retrieve the dish towel that Ruby kept looped through the handle of the refrigerator door. Ruby and Tomiko watched as he walked over to the piano and carefully wiped away the glistening pool of kerosene. Afterward, he closely examined the wood and then raised the top and scrutinized the insides.*

*After a while he closed the top, balled up the towel, and shot it across the room, where it landed in the sink.*

*"So, Tomiko, what's it gonna be: single or double murder burgers?"*

Tomiko looked at her mother for guidance, but Ruby was staring at her bare feet.

Amos started toward the door. "You comin' or what?" he threw over his shoulder.

Tomiko threw her mother one last glance before racing to her father's side and slipping her little hand inside of his.

The last time Amos and Ruby came to blows was the last time Tomiko would see her father. She was seven years old and Amos was forty-six when he left them for good.

At forty-six he still had his looks, but the years of late nights, drinking, and smoking had started to leave their mark. Deep vertical lines lay across his forehead like train tracks. Dark, heavy half-moons hung under his eyes, and the pads of his fingers were callused and yellow.

The world was changing. Nightclubs that had turned into discos were now turning back into nightclubs and replacing live music with DJs spinning vinyl records. The gigs had begun to dry up, and Amos's income dwindled to almost nothing.

Amos kept a safe. It was small, square, heavy, and black. Sometimes Ruby would put on an Earth, Wind, and Fire album, sit on the floor with her back pressed up against the bed, and smoke one cigarette after another as she fiddled with the silver-and-black combination wheel.

Tomiko would peek into the bedroom and issue a warning cry: "Oooh, Daddy gonna get you."

"You hush your mouth 'fore I get the switch and tear your little behind to pieces."

Once, when Ruby had had one beer too many and Maurice White had sung a little too long, Ruby's frustration had bubbled over. She got up and walked right out of the house.

Tomiko scrambled behind her. "Where you going?"

Ruby, barefoot and dressed in only a half slip and bra, walked in the cold Michigan air down the street to a neighbor's house. When she returned, her cheeks were bright red, her teeth were bared, and she had a hammer in one hand and a hacksaw in the other.

"What you gonna do with those?" Tomiko asked as she followed Ruby back into the bedroom.

Ruby bent over and studied the safe's dial. She turned it left, then right and jiggled the handle as if she was giving the safe one more chance to cooperate.

"All right, then," she mumbled before leaning back on her haunches, raising the hammer into the air, and bringing the head down onto the dial.

Tomiko screamed as if she had been the one on the receiving end of the blow.

"Shut up, girl," Ruby warned before repeating the jarring crash.

Tomiko slapped her hands over her mouth, and her body flinched violently each time the head of the hammer struck the dial. Thwack, thwack, thwack!

Ruby pounded away until the dial popped out and hung from its springs like a dislodged eyeball.

She jiggled the handle again, but still the door did not open. Ruby then reached for the hacksaw and dragged the sharp blade over the coiled springs. The dial dropped to the floor with a plunk. Ruby swept it aside, leaned over, and pressed her naked eye to the opening. Sucking her teeth in disgust, she slung the hacksaw across the room in frustration. If Tomiko hadn't ducked, the blade would have ripped open her shoulder.

Incensed, Ruby picked up the hammer and began banging it against the walls of the safe. The sound was deafening. Tomiko placed her hands over her ears and begged for her mother to stop.

Flecks of black paint came away beneath the blows, but little else happened. Beside herself with rage, Ruby turned the hammer onto the living room walls.

By the time the downstairs neighbor came up to complain, she'd left five gaping holes in the wall.

"Ruby!" the neighbor bellowed from the other side of the closed apartment door. "Goddammit, Ruby, what you doin' in there?"

Ruby didn't answer. Instead, she went over to the record player and turned the volume up full blast. Maurice was wailing, "What used to be happy was sad . . ."

"Ruby, don't make me call the police!"

"Call 'em!" Ruby screamed. "And when they get here, I'll make sure to tell 'em about the weed you sellin' outta your apartment!"

The neighbor didn't say another word.

Tomiko heard the man stomp back down the stairs. Minutes later, he was sitting in his black Buick, revving the engine.

When he returned, he had Amos with him.

Amos was still cussing about being dragged off in the middle of a set when he walked in and saw Ruby sitting on the couch with the hammer resting on her lap. His mouth fell open when he saw the holes in the walls.

"Woman, have you lost your goddamn mind?"

Ruby just glanced at him. Tomiko was sitting beside her; she had the dial to the safe clutched in her hand.

"Is that . . . ?" Amos began.

Tomiko nodded her head and held the dial out to him. "I didn't break it. Mommy did."

Amos stepped forward and snatched it from Tomiko's hand. He brought the dial close to his face, and when he looked at Ruby again, the whites of his eyes had turned crimson.

Ruby gave him a sideways glance, chuckled.

Amos walked slowly through the living room and into the bedroom.

One moment he was in the bedroom, and the next moment he was looming over them.

"Why you fuckin' with my safe?"

Both Ruby and Tomiko jumped off the couch. Tomiko streaked across the room and tried to disappear behind the drapes. Ruby stood her ground, puffed out her chest, and raised her balled fists in the air like a prizefighter.

Blows were shared, hair was pulled, furniture was knocked over, and when Tomiko saw blood seeping from Ruby's nose, she screamed, "Please stop!"

But her plea fell on deaf ears.

Tomiko screamed and screamed until a window of opportunity presented itself. Some invisible force separated the warring couple. They stood barely a foot apart, lips skinned back, snorting air through their nostrils like rhinos. Tomiko stationed herself between them, planting her left hand on Amos's thigh and her right firmly on the soft center of Ruby's stomach. "Stop!"

Maybe it was the sound of her voice or the touch of her small hands; whatever it was, it snapped Ruby and Amos back to their senses.

Amos sighed and took a step back. He raised his hand to his face and began fingering the bloody trail Ruby's fingernails had carved into his cheek. His moment of distraction was brief enough for Ruby to stoop down and snatch up the hammer. She swung and landed a blow just above Amos's right temple. Amos howled and stumbled into the wall. Tomiko grabbed hold of her mother's hand and dragged her toward the apartment's open door.

Dressed in little to nothing, mother and daughter found themselves shivering on an unlit corner of their block.

*"Where we goin'?" Ruby asked through chattering teeth.*

*Tomiko had no idea. Out of the corner of her eye she saw Amos stumbling to his Cadillac. He climbed in, turned the ignition, and, without pulling the door shut, pulled it onto the sidewalk and pointed that four-wheeled beast down the street. After the car turned the corner, Tomiko never saw it again.*

That had been one of the worst nights of Tomiko's life. And now, sitting there in her office looking at the e-mail from Mark, she felt herself growing angry and disappointed all over again. Yes, the blow with the hammer had been one step too far, but Amos never gave her mother a chance to say she was sorry. He never responded to any of her calls. When she showed up at a nightclub while he was playing, his face filled with fear. He went straight backstage after the set and hurried out the door.

He never tried to contact Tomiko at all. She was left wondering throughout the rest of her childhood whether she had ever meant anything to him, her own father. He could have tried to claim partial custody. Hell, he could have taken her out to lunch one single time. But he simply vanished into the night. All the love between them had been left to curdle forever—until now.

Despite her long-simmering anger, the sense of curiosity she felt was strong. If this nurse was telling the truth and this man claiming to be her father was actually her father, this could be an opportunity of a lifetime. Yes, she thought as she poised her fingers over the keyboard in preparation to respond, I've got some things I'd like to say to Amos Davis!

# Cass

You're not on today, Mark," Cass heard the woman at the nurses' station say. As she approached, she saw a good-looking guy wearing loose-fitting jeans and a slate-gray mock turtleneck sweater.

He glanced over at Cass and smiled. "I had something to do."

Mark wasn't as tall as Darryl, or as lean, but it was easy to see that he was no stranger to the gym. The arms were fine, the shoulders were broad, the waist tapered nicely. But he wasn't her type, she told herself. He wasn't Darryl.

Cass held out a plastic container to him. "I'm sorry I'm late," she said, inhaling whatever cologne he had on but pretending not to, "but I lost track of time."

Mark took the container from her. "He'll appreciate them, for sure."

Did he look at everybody like this? Cass glanced at the space behind him and nervously rustled her fingers through her hair. "So how's he doing?"

"He's, um . . . on the mend, but I think he'd appreciate a visitor."

"Physically, he's okay?" she asked, ignoring his last statement.

"Therapy is slow," he explained. "Amos is stubborn."

She nodded. "He is. Always was."

"You know, he put on quite a show for everybody here the other day."

She understood right away what he meant. "He sang?"

"Sang the hell out of that song of his." He smiled. "One of the other patients recognized him and convinced him to do it, and then next thing we knew, he had people dancing in the hallways." Mark laughed.

A surprising wave of pride filled her, and Cass felt a smile creep across her face, too. "He had a voice that could shake the shingles off the roof."

"Yeah, well . . . he still does. He even signed a few autographs that day." He laughed.

Cass laughed, too.

"These smell good," he said, shifting suddenly, referring to the vegetables in the container.

"Thanks," she said. "My mom's recipe, actually. He always loved them."

"Maybe he'll be cool and save me some."

He was standing close, but not in a disrespectful, personal-space-invading way. Just close enough to feel nice, intimate but not creepy. And he had this way of looking deeply into her eyes when he spoke to her. That was a bit unnerving because he gave her the feeling that he was looking for something in particular.

"There's plenty there for both of you," she added, clearing her throat. "I made sure of it."

He cocked an eyebrow. "Cool."

Cass swallowed. He wasn't Darryl, but he was . . . hard to ignore. Of course, she wasn't interested in him like that, but if

Darryl wasn't in the picture, well . . . "I should get going." She motioned back down the hallway, taking a step in that direction.

He took a step forward. "You sure you don't want to say hello to the old man?"

She had nothing to say to Amos, not even hello. Cass had no interest in that man trying to pull her heartstrings. She had promised herself that she'd help find blood relatives for him. Whether any of them chose to come and see about him was their business.

"I've really got to go." Cass turned around and headed down the hall.

"Cass?" Mark called after her.

She turned around one last time. He held up the container. "Thank you."

Yes, he was a nice man. "You're welcome, Mark."

A part of her felt guilty about leaving without seeing Amos. Another part of her felt relieved.

It was after midnight when the sound of Cass's phone woke her up. By the time she picked it up, she got only a dial tone, so she turned over and went back to sleep. The next morning, Cass checked her voice mail.

The person leaving the message cleared her throat. "This is . . . umm, Toya." The woman cleared her throat again. "Amos's . . . You know what, it's late. It's . . . late." She hung up.

Cass started to press the Call button on her phone to redial Toya but then hesitated. There had been a lot of bad blood between Cass's mother and Toya's over Amos. Cass had seen her once. Linda had gone crazy one night and followed Amos's car to Melba Jean's house while Cass sat wide-eyed and afraid because she'd never seen her mother so angry, crying and cursing like she'd lost her mind.

"C'mon, Cass!" she'd yelled at the ten-year-old. "Get in the car!"

Linda came rushing from the bedroom, shoving what looked like Amos's gun into her purse.

"I'm sick of this shit!" she growled, gritting her teeth as she sped through the city streets. "I'm so sick of his ass!"

Before Cass realized it, Linda skidded to a stop in front of a small house on the other side of town. Amos's car was parked in the driveway. Her mother jumped out of the car and sprinted toward the front door. Amos must have heard her coming because he burst from inside the house and caught hold of her, stopping her from kicking the door in and rushing inside.

Cass's mouth hung open at the chaos going on in that woman's front yard. Her mother was kicking, screaming, crying, cursing. Amos had her wrapped in his arms. "Linda! Stop it, now! C'mon!"

The other woman, Melba Jean, stood in the doorway with wild hair, wearing an open robe and a slip underneath.

"Whatchu come here to do, Linda?" Melba Jean screamed, her arms flailing in the air. "Yeah, he with me! He always with me! And he gon' keep on bein' with me 'cause you ain't woman enough to keep him!"

Amos held Linda's arms pinned to her sides, but she reached desperately for her purse with her free hand. If he hadn't held on to her like he did . . .

A skinny little girl rushed past her mother in the doorway and ran out into the yard, screaming, "Leave us alone! Leave us alone!"

"Get back in this house, Toya!" the woman yelled.

"I hate you!" Linda screamed. "I hate you, Amos!"

"Yeah, I know," he said. Amos held her close and whispered something into her ear. Linda gradually stopped fighting, and the tears started to flow like a river down her cheeks.

"*Amos!*" *Melba Jean called out.* "*Amos, whatchu doin'?*"

*The little girl, Toya, stood at the top of the steps with her mother, wrapping her arms around the woman's hips. She looked across the yard over to the car where Cass sat staring, and for a moment the two of them locked gazes. Cass didn't realize it at the time, but she was crying, too.*

*Linda jerked free from Amos's grasp, glared one last time at the woman, then back at him.*

"*Go on home, now,*" *he said calmly.* "*I'll be there shortly.*"

*Linda spit on the ground in front of him.* "*Don't bother,*" *she said.*

"*Don't bring your ass back to my house!*" *the other woman shouted.*

"*Shuddup, Melba Jean!*" *Amos said angrily.*

"*You can't have everythin', Amos!*" *Melba Jean continued. Amos slowly made his way to her front door.* "*I want you to choose! You choose today! I ain't gonna keep . . .*" *Her voice disappeared behind the closed door.*

*Cass stared at that house that Amos had disappeared into, and something told her that he wasn't ever coming out again. The curtain in the front window moved, and Cass saw small brown eyes seeking hers, looking as helpless as Cass felt.*

*Linda drove home without saying another word. But the first thing she did when they got back to the house was to gather all of Amos's clothes together and toss them out into the grass in one big, messy pile.*

Cass pressed the Call button on her phone and waited anxiously as it rang.

"Hello?" a woman answered groggily.

Cass opened her mouth to speak, but the words caught in her throat. "Toya?" she said finally.

"Yes?"

"It's Cass . . . Cassandra Edwards. I, um . . . I got your message."

The woman hesitated a long while before responding. "How is he?" She seemed to force herself to ask.

"He's all right, I guess. Grumpy, but . . . you know how he is."

Again, Toya took her time answering. "No, I'm afraid I don't, Cassandra."

Toya's tone left little open to interpretation. She obviously wasn't a member of the Amos Davis fan club.

"Well, I want to give you the number for where he's staying. You can call him there. I'm sure he'd be happy to hear from you."

The riveting silence on the other end of the phone sent regrets running up and down Cass's spine. The soft click of the phone being hung up in her ear pretty much filled in the rest of the blanks.

# Amos

"Pappa. Pappa, it's me. Pappa, it's Mary."

The white-haired man looked at that woman like he had seen a ghost. She leaned across the table toward him and took hold of his hand. Even from where he sat, Amos could see that she had tears in her eyes. "I'm your daughter. I'm Mary."

How could a man forget his own flesh and blood? Amos shook his head, disturbed by the thought. Was he going to end up like that dude? He wondered if Cass had been here to visit him more times than he remembered. Maybe he'd just forgotten that she was here. Maybe his mind was as bad as the mind of that woman's father. Lord have mercy! What would be left when his mind was gone?

The white-haired man's eyes grew wide, and he peeled the woman's hand off his. "You're not my Mary," he said, his voice shaking. "I don't know who you are, but my Mary's just a little girl. She's six years old and in the first grade."

"Damn shame, ain't it?" Jennie V. said, sitting across from Amos; she was knitting and shaking her head. "It breaks that girl's heart when she comes here and he don't remember who she is. She's the only one who does come to see him."

Amos didn't know what to say to that. At least that man's daughter *was* coming to visit him.

"The sad thing is," the old woman continued, "she's all he talks about. He goes on and on about his Mary, missing her and bragging about her visits and the care packages that she sends, but when she gets here, half the time he don't even claim her."

Amos cleared his throat. He could be just like that old man. Cass probably had come by more than he remembered. The thought scared him. Was he capable of forgetting who she was, who Miko was, when either one of them could've been sitting up in his face, trying to get him to realize his daughters were visiting?

"How many kids you got?" the woman probed.

"Three," he said, without hesitating. "Cassandra and Tomiko," he sighed. "Toya."

Jennie V. frowned. "Why'd you say it like that?"

"Say what like what?" he asked, annoyed.

"Toya," she asked. "You got something against that last one?"

Amos huffed. "There you go again, trying to read something into nothing. I got three kids, Jennie. Leave it at that."

He had loved that little girl like he had loved the others. It wasn't right that he had left her out in the cold because him and Melba Jean didn't know how to act.

"You all right?" Jennie V. asked, studying him like she was reading a map. "I just asked a simple question. That's all."

"I'm fine," he said, recovering.

"I've got to go!" The old man sitting with Mary lurched to his feet and started to walk away. "I can't. I've got to go!"

Mary followed after him. "Don't do this, Pappa! Just talk to me! Sit down and let's talk!"

She was too desperate, and she needed more than he had to give.

"Why don't she just leave him alone?" Jennie V. said kindly. "He can't remember what he can't remember, and it ain't his fault."

One of the orderlies rushed over to the old man and helped him out of the room before he fell and hurt himself. Another one went over to Mary, sat her down, and tried to console her. The woman broke down in the recreation room, in front of everybody, crying like a little girl whose heart is broken.

*"Why you doin' this to me, Amos?" Melba Jean begged and pleaded, and when that didn't work, she cussed and fussed, threw things and threatened. "She ain't better than me! You come here and you know what you mean to me, and then go home to her like she's better than me! I love you, too, Amos!"*

He never said Linda was better. But she wasn't worse.

*"I'm the one who had your baby, Amos! That's your flesh and blood layin' in that crib in the bedroom! You need to be here for her! For us!"*

Thick and fine, Melba Jean. She was every man's dream, and the first time he laid eyes on her, he knew he had to have her. At one time he even convinced himself that he loved her, but then he realized that she was the type who was always going to be hungry and never get full. No man could ever be enough for Melba Jean.

"Come back next week, Mary," the orderly told the woman as she walked her toward the door. "It'll be better next week."

Women were greedy. At least, the ones he'd come across were greedy. They wanted to own him like property. That's how it felt whenever he was with one for too long a time.

They would do whatever it took to lure a man in and hook him like a fish. Sex, a nice home-cooked meal, sweet smiles, and agreeable dispositions to start, and sometimes babies he didn't plan for.

*"You said you were on the Pill!"*

*"What difference does it make? She's here now!"*

Amos had just signed a contract with a new independent label in Detroit, D-City Records. He'd been working on recording his second album and was getting ready for his first cross-country tour. He and Linda had been together for years, but finally, he'd gotten the break he'd been waiting his whole life for. Linda was tripping at home about his going on the road, and Melba Jean was tripping on the other side of town because he wasn't coming to her.

*"Her name's Toya."* She held that baby like she was a sack of gold. Melba Jean looked at him as if she expected him to drop to his knees, beg for her forgiveness, and reach out to take that child in his arms.

*"That's a pretty name, Melba."* He didn't reach out to Melba Jean or that child.

Melba Jean tried to smile. *"She look just like you. Come see. Come look at her, Amos."*

He needed a child like he needed a hole in his head, and he needed her momma even less.

*"Come look at her."* The look in that woman's eyes changed and filled with heartache when he didn't move.

Amos had what he wanted more than anything in the world. He had his contract, his record deal.

*"Are you sure she's mine, Melba Jean?"*

*"You sonofabitch!"* Her lips quivered and tears flowed down her cheek.

"Looks like you just went off to someplace else," Jennie V. said, mercifully disrupting his memory. "Where you been this time? Back with that woman that had you grinnin' the last time we spoke?"

Amos straightened up in his seat. "She didn't deserve how I treated her," he confessed uneasily. Why he felt Jennie V. needed to know this was a mystery to him, especially when all she was going to do was throw it back in his face.

"Most women don't," she said curtly.

He scowled at her.

"You had children with her?"

He nodded reluctantly. "One."

"One's plenty. That the one named Toya?"

"I wasn't there like I should've been," he admitted.

Jennie V. folded her arms across her chest and convicted him with that smug expression on her face. He should have kept his mouth shut.

"How come I'm not surprised?"

He glared angrily at her. "I don't give a damn what you think, woman!"

"Then why you sittin' here tellin' me all this?"

He opened his mouth to say something smart to her, but realized he had nothing to say.

"I already know," she said. She leaned close to him. "Because I'm all you got, old man. Guilt done built up inside you like poison, and you got to get it out. I'm here, and I'm listenin', but I'm not the one you need to be talkin' to, and you know that."

He did know that.

Jennie V. turned around in time to see poor Mary being ushered to the door, sobbing. "She loves her father, which is why him not rememberin' her breaks her heart." She turned back to Amos. "Can any of your children say the same about you, Amos?"

Jennie V. left him sitting there alone with his thoughts. Every man left behind a legacy when he died. Amos had a gold record, and for a time that's all he ever thought he needed to leave behind. He'd been wrong about that, though. He had his girls, and he was finding out he had another kind of legacy: none of his daughters cared whether he lived or died.

# Toya

That bastard hadn't even bothered to call.

Toya didn't know if Max's wife had cut him into a million pieces, if she was going to come back for Toya, or what that scorned woman had up her sleeve. But one thing Toya did know: she was done with Max. For real. The part of her life that included Max was over.

Now she had to deal with another part: what to do about her father. She'd spoken to Cass this morning. Toya had felt strange talking to the woman. And honestly, a part of her felt bitter as well. That's what made her hang up the phone on her. Cass might as well have had Amos's blood flowing through her veins because she'd gotten more from him than Toya ever had. More love. More money. More everything.

Toya had wanted to tell Cass she'd think about coming to Detroit. She was torn over what to do. She desperately needed to talk to someone, which was why she was on her way to talk to the one person she should've turned to in the first place—her best friend, Misty.

The two of them had been best friends ever since Toya and her mom moved to Flint. But even though they shared everything, Toya had never opened up about her father because Misty was a no-nonsense type of person. Misty did not hesitate to make her face some hard truths about the woman she'd become. But maybe that's what Toya needed right now. Thinking straight about her father was hard, for sure.

"So did you get your door fixed?" Misty asked after Toya had filled her in on everything.

Toya nodded. "Yeah, they fixed it this morning. The apartment manager made me pay two hundred dollars. You'd better believe Max is going to give me my money back."

"And that buster still hasn't called?"

Toya shook her head. "Nope. But he wasn't kidding when he said his wife was crazy. I swear, if that woman had had a match and some lighter fluid, she would've burned down the whole apartment building."

Misty looked scared for her friend. "Well, I hope you stick to your guns and don't go back to Max. You don't need that type of drama."

Misty couldn't be more right. Toya had bigger things to focus on, and she pushed thoughts of Max aside once and for all.

"So what are you gonna do?" Misty asked.

Toya took another sip of her Patrón. She wasn't a heavy drinker, but she needed something to calm her nerves and a glass of wine definitely wouldn't do it.

"I told you, I'm done with Max."

"Not about Max," she said, waving that subject off. "I'm talking about with your dad."

Toya was glad Misty had brought up the subject. She hadn't known how to work around to it. "I don't know." She sighed. "There's a part of me that wants to see him."

"Then go."

"But then there's a part that's, like, for what? I mean, what valid reason can he give as to why he wasn't in my life?"

Misty straightened up some in her chair. "Why don't you ever talk about him?"

Toya shrugged. "What is there to tell? He ain't never been around. He stayed with us off and on for a few years, and I haven't seen him since the last time he went out for milk and didn't come home. I don't know anything about him. Truth be told, he could walk up and slap me in the face right now and I wouldn't know it was him."

She could tell Misty didn't like that kind of talk. "Well, if he's dying—"

"Nobody said anything about dying."

"Well, Alzheimer's, dementia, whatever, it's all like the step before death," Misty pointed out.

"Where'd you get that from?"

"I don't know. I guess I saw it on *Dr. Phil* or something." Misty was always watching some talk show and felt that made her an expert on everything from dysfunctional families to baby daddies.

Toya sipped her drink, considering. Her thoughts kept coming back to one thing. When Cass had filled her in on Amos's condition, Toya was surprised at the utter indifference she felt inside. "All I know is my father didn't want to know me when his brain was functioning right. Why should I believe he wants to get to know me now? Maybe this is Cass pushing this. I mean, what if I get there and he's like, 'I didn't want to see you.'"

"Well, if you won't do it for him, do it for yourself. You need some closure."

"Oh, so now you're starting to sound like Dr. Phil."

Misty leaned forward in protest. "No, just hear me out. You

should talk to your father for no other reason than to help yourself heal—because, trust me, girl, you got issues."

"What?"

Misty sighed with apparent frustration. "Look, I'm your girl, so I'm gonna keep it real. Your unhealthy relationships, all these married men you date, I think it has to do with your dad."

"So you take one psychology course at the community college and now you're an expert?"

Misty threw up her hands. "Fine. Get smart all you want."

"Look, Misty, I appreciate your trying to give me your little input. But just because you took one class, watch a lot of TV, and you've been with the same man for the last nine years doesn't make you an expert."

"Then answer me this: Why do you keep dating men who aren't available? Even in high school, you only messed with boys with girlfriends. There's a systematic problem." Misty folded her arms across her chest and glared at her friend.

Toya couldn't deny the truth of what she'd said. "I can't help it that's who I attract."

"Really? Every single married man you've been with has broken your heart, yet that's all you keep getting and it's all because that's the only kind of men you attract? No single man wants you, right?"

Toya didn't reply as she toyed with the ice in her glass.

"Are you even listening to me?" Misty said.

Toya finally looked up at her friend. "Yeah, I hear you. You think because I didn't go to father-daughter dances, I'm all jacked up."

"No." Misty sighed heavily. "I'm just saying if you've never been shown the power of love by a real man, how would you know what it looked like?"

That agitated Toya so much, she stood up abruptly. "Misty, go somewhere with that shade-tree psychology," Toya snapped.

"Okay, fine. But I'm telling you, I'm right about this."

"Even if what you were saying is true," Toya continued, "I don't see how me going to talk to my father is going to change anything. He's a liar and a cheat."

"Just like every man you date." Misty sat back and leveled a stare at her.

"That's because men are low-down dirty dogs," Toya said. Misty continued staring at her, and Toya flinched in dismay. "Why are you looking at me like that?"

"Because you sound just like your mother."

Those words stopped Toya in her tracks. *Like mother, like daughter.*

Misty came over and grabbed her friend's hand, then led her back to the sofa. "Toya, the last thing you want to do is have your father die with all your questions unanswered," she said, sitting her down.

"I don't have any questions," Toya said defiantly.

"Yes, you do. There's something you want to know, if nothing other than why? Why did he leave you?"

Toya let Misty's words sink in. "Okay, so I go see him. Then what?"

Misty shrugged. "You ask questions. Maybe you'll get answers, maybe you won't. Maybe you'll forgive him. Maybe you'll make peace with him. Maybe you'll better understand why he abandoned you. Or maybe you'll decide you were better off not knowing him. But at least you'll know. I know you want a healthy relationship. I know you want to love and be loved. But you got to deal with those demons from your past first."

Toya finally managed a smile. She didn't know if Misty had ever talked that long in one stretch. "Forget Dr. Phil, I guess you're going for Oprah's job."

"Ha-ha-ha. Crack jokes all you want," Misty said. "But maybe if you heal your relationship with your dad, you can find the Prince Charming who was meant for you."

Toya swallowed her drink, and as the liquid burned her insides, she couldn't help but wonder if what her friend was saying was true. She finally deduced that the only way she'd ever find out for sure was to pay a visit to Amos Davis.

# Amos

The delicious, savory flavor of Linda's turnip greens exploded in Amos's mouth, and he chewed slowly, appreciating every heavenly, delectable bite. Mark sat across from him, enjoying a bowl, too.

"The only thing missing," Amos said, smacking his lips, "is the corn bread. Next time you hear from Linda, ask her to make some corn bread to go along with the greens."

"I don't know who Linda is, but your daughter Cass made the greens," Mark told him.

Amos looked surprised. Linda had passed away. He'd forgotten that. How could he forget something like that?

"You should call her to thank her for saving your ass," Mark said with a smirk, referring to the threatened enema that both men had been trying to avoid. "Literally."

Of course, the thought crossed his mind from time to time to call her, but Amos always stopped short of doing it because he had no idea what to say to her. Cass didn't seem all that interested in hearing from Amos anyway. She knew where he was, and if she'd wanted to see him . . . Unless she'd mailed these greens, she'd swung by and left without saying a word to Amos. He'd have been lying to himself if he didn't accept the sting of knowing that.

"So," Mark continued, "she's single?"

Amos was startled out of his reflection. "Who?"

"Your daughter, man," he asked.

"How the hell should I know?" he snapped.

"She's your daughter."

She was, maybe not by blood, but Cass was his. He looked away, embarrassed that he didn't know if she had a man or not, or kids.

"She's a good cook," Mark supplied.

Amos nodded. "Like her momma."

"Pretty woman," Mark added.

Amos looked at him. All of a sudden, it dawned on him that this fool had a thing for the girl. "Like her momma." He smiled mischievously. He relished watching the young brotha squirm a little.

"It's just—I'm just making an observation," Mark finally said.

"Course you are."

"She's got to have somebody," Mark continued. He couldn't help fishing. "A woman like that, of course she's got somebody." He shrugged.

"You'd think so," Amos muttered.

"But you don't know?"

Amos reluctantly shook his head. "No, son. I don't know."

"I was thinking about . . . you know." He shrugged.

"Nah," Amos said, even though he did know.

"The jazz festival's next weekend. I was thinking about asking her if she wanted to go."

"Why you tellin' me this? You want my permission to ask out my daughter?" Amos teased.

Mark frowned. "No, man. I'm just letting you know."

Amos didn't bother with a response. He decided to let him sweat a little.

"She should like that, right? Jazz? I mean, she grew up around music, with you, right? Of course she'll like it—if she decides to go."

He dug this kid. Mark had taken good care of Amos since he'd been here. If Cass didn't have a man already, she could do a lot worse than him.

Mark pulled his cell phone out of his pocket and looked at the screen even though the thing hadn't even rung. Mark was always fumbling with that damn device. Amos had never understood the fascination with portable phones. He used to have one, but after he lost it, he never bothered to try to get another one.

Mark started grinning all of a sudden. "Guess who I just got an e-mail from?"

Amos stared at him like he was crazy. "How the hell should I know?"

Mark looked at him. "Your other daughter, man." He laughed. "Tomiko."

All of a sudden those greens weighed like a stone in his stomach. Without realizing it, Amos held his breath. "Miko?" he whispered.

The smile faded from Mark's face. "Told you I'd try and find her for you, man," he explained. "She's got a Web site, got the covers of all her books on it. She's famous."

Miko loved stories from the time she was born, so Amos wasn't surprised she had become a writer.

"I told her where you were. I asked her if she'd be open to seeing you."

The question closed the back of his throat. Amos swallowed and finally managed to squeak, "What she say?"

Mark started to read the e-mail: "'I haven't seen my dad or heard from him in years. It's been hard not knowing where he was or if he was okay, but at least now I know. They say that the apple doesn't fall far from the tree, and my dad and I have always had being creative in common. Tell him that I've never stopped loving him and I've never stopped loving the music.'"

Amos waited with anticipation for Mark to say more, but Mark had come to the end.

"That's it?" Amos asked anxiously.

Mark nodded. "It's a start, man. It's more than you had when you woke up this morning."

But had she forgiven him for leaving her behind the way he did? Would she come to see him and give him a chance to explain why he'd stayed gone so long?

Mark's pager suddenly went off. "I've got to go, Amos," he said, hurrying out of the room.

*It's more than you had when you woke up this morning.*

Amos let out a long sigh. Mark was right about that. A connection had been made, even if it was through some other cat's e-mail. But Miko was close, so much closer than she had been to him in years.

# Cass

"Don't you ever get a day off?" Cass asked when she looked up and saw Mark walking toward the nurses' station.

He gave a nonchalant wave with his hand. "Plenty, but can I help it if you just happen to stop by when I'm on duty?"

He came up to her, closed his eyes, and took a deep breath. "Smells delicious."

Cass had brought enough food to feed a small army, so she figured it ought to be plenty to tide Amos over for a few days. "Leftovers," she said simply. So Nurse Mark made her jittery all of a sudden. Cass willed her shaking nerves to calm down and get right again. She felt ridiculous. She noticed the faded spot on his finger where a ring had been. "You lose something?" she asked, staring at it. Cass could've kicked herself for even noticing and she really could've kicked herself for even mentioning it.

He stared down at it, looking uneasy. "Yeah. My wife," he admitted.

"Got kids?" she asked, surprising herself.

He looked a bit caught off guard by the question, and then nodded. "Two. Boy and a girl."

"They live with their mother?" Cass wasn't asking to be nosy. She was asking because Mark seemed like a decent guy, and for some reason he'd taken to Amos.

"We share custody," he volunteered.

She studied him, trying to figure out how this fit with what else she knew about him. Mark was one of the good guys, plain and simple. He wasn't drop-dead gorgeous like Darryl, but he had a warmth and kindness in his eyes that pulled you in if you stopped long enough to notice.

"Why don't you go back and at least say hello to the old man?" He tilted his head toward the recreation room. "I know he'd like to thank you personally for the food, seeing as how he hates the cooking around here so much."

Cass had been working real hard to avoid Amos. She figured that by bringing him food from time to time, she would be off the hook for visiting, but she hadn't seen him in over a month, so reluctantly she agreed.

She walked with Mark down a wide hallway until they reached a room filled with residents sitting in small groups with one another, talking and laughing. Cass was surprised by one couple walking into the room and gasped quietly when the man slipped his arm from around the woman's waist to her behind.

Mark laughed. "They're not dead, Cass."

Eventually, she spotted Amos sitting alone across the room, his gaze fixed on the television he wasn't really watching. He looked old and small, inconceivably sad and alone. The Amos she'd known as a kid had had an endless stream of people in his life. Never in a million years would she have imagined that she'd see him like this. Mark gently put his hand on her back and guided her forward.

"You got a visitor, Amos," he announced.

It could've been her imagination, but Amos's eyes seemed to light up like beacons when he saw her.

"Li'l Mama Cass!" he exclaimed, and patted the seat next to him. "'Bout time you stopped by to see an old man. Been feedin' me good enough. Kinda rude of you not to at least say hey to me every now and then."

"I'll see you later, Cass." Mark smiled as he left.

Cass was surprised by the look of appreciation and even admiration in his eyes as he said good-bye. He stared at her like she was Tyra Banks or somebody.

"You bring me somethin' to eat?" Amos asked.

Cass forced a smile. "They're warming it up for you, Amos."

He nodded. "Where'd you learn to cook like that? Linda cooked all right, but she wasn't anywhere near as good as you."

Cass couldn't help but laugh. "I like to eat, so . . ."

"The mess they serve here tastes like paper. They don't know how to season anythin', and all they got on the table is salt and pepper." He frowned. "A man needs some seasonin', baby girl. Know what I mean?"

And it dawned on her right then what was missing in Amos now: seasoning. He'd lived too fast and too hard and had used it all up, years ago. She felt sorry for him. Amos had been the Pied Piper to so many people when he was younger. He'd been almost worshipped, and it seemed like the magic of him would never end.

"Where is everybody, Amos?" She surprised herself with that question. It came up out of the fear that anybody could end up like him.

He looked in confusion around the room and then turned his attention back to her. "You can't see?" He laughed uncomfortably.

"You know what I mean," she continued. "Your friends? Wife or girlfriend? Your children?"

All the joy vanished from his eyes. "What's it to you?" he asked, hurt. "You askin' because you care or are you just being nosy?"

She felt sorry for him, but she felt sorrier for herself and others like her, the ones he'd wiped his shoes on as he walked over them. She felt sorry for women like her mother, Linda, who never could shake him from her system, even years later, after he'd left her and moved on to somebody else, whom he'd obviously left behind, too, because if he hadn't, she'd have been here.

"Somebody else should be coming here besides me," she said, caught off guard by the tears filling her eyes. "Where is Toya, Amos?" she blurted out. "Melba Jean? Where is Fat Don? B. B. Bruce? Tiny?"

He searched his memory for the people Cass had named. Some of them had performed with Amos, and rushed to his side every time he even mentioned the word *band*.

"You know we down, Amos, man," Fat Don, a bass player, used to say. He was always ready to play and worshipped Amos like he was James Brown.

"Count us in, too," Tiny would volunteer for him and B. B.

Amos had been king of the mountain, but now he was just an old man.

He cleared his throat. "People move on," he said. "They grow apart is all."

"But . . . isn't there anybody, Amos?" she asked earnestly. "Am I really all you have?"

Amos swallowed and looked nervously at the television. Yet after a short pause he seemed to recover. With some of the old boom back in his voice he asked, "You married, Cass?"

The abruptness of his question threw her. The old man was

trying to change the subject, but she wasn't too keen on what he was trying to change it to because her life was none of his business.

"So you don't have anybody else," she said softly. She remembered him always being surrounded by people, having more friends than he knew what to do with, with total strangers dropping to their knees on the street when they saw him, practically kissing his feet.

He pressed her. "You got a man? You got kids?" Something sad and dark filled his eyes. Loneliness. Loss?

"Why do you want to know?"

He shifted uneasily and turned away from her. "You don't wanna tell me," he said, sounding disappointed.

"You haven't been interested in anything to do with me in years, Amos," she said, surprising herself by being so blunt. "All of a sudden you care now?"

He sat there, quiet and thoughtful. Cass couldn't remember a time when she'd ever known Amos to think before he spoke. Usually, he'd blurt out something he'd have to apologize for later.

"I should know if my daughter has a man," he said, swallowing. "I should know if she has children."

"Your daughter? Amos, I haven't been your daughter since I was in the fourth grade," Cass blurted out.

Amos always did have a way of looking at her that made her want to crawl up in his lap and stay there. But Cass was a grown woman now, and that didn't work anymore. That look from him, though, still had a way of peeling back layers, and Cass couldn't help but concede, even if she was too big now to crawl into his lap.

She sighed. "No. I'm a widow, but yes, Amos . . . I have a son. He's twenty-four, and his name is RJ."

Amos nodded, gratified that she'd answered his questions.

"Too pretty a woman not to have a man," he muttered, more to himself than to her.

Shit, it wasn't like she wasn't working on that dilemma. Cass had a man in her sights—Darryl—but Amos didn't need to know all that.

"You met that man nurse who work here?" he suddenly asked. "Mark?"

Cass kept her face neutral. "Yeah, I've met him."

A sly smile crept across his mouth. She wasn't always the brightest bulb in the pack, but Cass eventually caught on.

"You trying to fix me up with your nurse," she said.

"What's wrong with him?" Amos shrugged.

Cass shook her head and picked up her purse. "I've got to go."

"Cass, c'mon. He ain't bad-lookin'. Nice guy, too."

"All of a sudden now you're a matchmaker, Amos?" she said indignantly. "Really?"

"I'm just sayin' . . . he ain't a bad dude."

"Then you date him."

"I ain't the one he's diggin', Cassandra," Amos said meaningfully.

Digging? Another surprise. "What makes you think he's digging me?" Cass asked reluctantly.

"He asks me about you."

She was trying to process all of this information. Yes, Mark was friendly, but that was part of his job. He was supposed to be friendly. Mark was nice-looking. That wasn't part of his job, but it didn't hurt that he was. But Mark wasn't Darryl.

"I, uh . . . Well, that's nice, but I'm not interested."

Amos cocked his head to one side. "You like girls?"

She was shocked. "No! Just because I'm not interested in him doesn't mean I don't like men. He's just not my type."

He nodded. "Well, if he ain't your type, he ain't your type, baby girl."

The two of them stared at each other in awkward silence before she finally decided to leave. "It's been good seeing you, Amos," she said, standing up.

"I always enjoy seein' you, too, Li'l Mama Cass."

That name brought an unexpected smile to her lips that she shared with him before she left. Amos's charm had never failed to work its magic on her, even after all this time.

She started to walk away. "So, can I tell him it's all right to call you?" He almost shouted. "They've got your number on file. Right?"

# Toya

Toya dove to the ground at the sound of gunfire. When she got her bearings, she realized that it was a car backfiring.

"Relax," she mumbled as she pulled herself up off the ground. She'd been waiting for Jewel to pop up and attack her, so every time she heard a strange noise or saw something suspicious, her mind started racing. But Toya knew she needed to let it go. Jewel—and Max, for that matter, since she hadn't heard from him—had obviously moved on. She needed to do the same. Besides, she had bigger problems to deal with, like how in the world she was going to tell Melba Jean that she was going to Detroit.

"Might as well get it over with." Toya took a deep breath and eased through the back door into her mother's kitchen. Melba was standing over the sink, washing dishes. "Hey, Ma."

"Hey, sweet pea. Hope you brought me some money. These folks talkin' 'bout my check must be 'lost in the mail.'"

Toya assured her mother that she'd float her a couple of dollars. They made some small talk so Toya could work around to the subject she'd come to discuss. She finally cleared her throat and said, "Momma, I, ah, can, umm, can we have a real conversation?"

"Ain't that the kind of conversation we have all the time?"

"I need you to shoot straight with me."

"That's the only way I know how to shoot."

Toya took a deep breath before continuing. "I would say that's true for just about everything, except my father."

That stopped Melba cold. She held the dishtowel in midair, and when she turned to face her daughter, her eyes were blazing. "Is there a reason you're comin' in my house talkin' 'bout that man?"

"That man is my father."

"That man was your sperm donor. I'm the one that took care of you."

"I know that, Momma. And my wanting to know more about him doesn't take away anything that I feel about you."

"Humph," she said, turning back around.

"Momma, please? Can we just talk about this? I don't understand why you've kept him from me all these years."

Without warning, Melba slammed a pot down in the sink so hard, it made Toya jump. Her mother spun around, and the fire in her eyes was replaced with hot tears.

"Kept him from you? Kept him from you?" she spat. "I begged that man to come back to you, to us."

"I-I didn't mean it like that, Ma," Toya stammered. "I just need you to talk to me about him."

Her mother stepped toward her, and for a minute, Toya thought Melba Jean was going to hit her. Instead, she stood face-to-face, glaring. "What you want me to say, Toya? Do you want to hear how I loved that man to the core of my soul? Do you want me to tell you how I gave that man everything I had to give? How I took his mess—his women—for years? How I listened to his promises, his lies? How I wanted to kill myself when he left me for someone else? How I waited and waited for him to leave her, and when he finally did, he found someone else and started a whole new family? How on the most horrible day of my life, he wasn't even there? Is that what you want to hear? Or maybe you'd rather hear how he came back into my life, fed me more pipe dreams, then just up and left again when he got tired of me? Do you want to hear about the loaded pistol I put to my head trying to end my pain and how you came and tugged at my skirt and asked what I was doin'? Do you want to hear how you saved my life that day because I was so heart-broken I didn't want to live?" She paused, her breath coming in ragged gasps. "Is that enough for you or should I go on?"

Tears were raining down her mother's face. Toya was frozen in place. Melba was so angry she was shaking.

"I even humbled myself and went to one of his band mates, Big somebody or other, and begged him to talk to Amos about doing right by his child, even if he didn't do right by me. And that big bastard told me I wasn't nothin' but a blade of grass in Amos's world. That there were too many other women standin' in line trying to get to him and that I wasn't anything special even if I did have that man's child. They knew how bad things were for us, and nobody would help us."

"I . . . I had no idea," Toya managed.

Melba inhaled like she was trying to calm herself down. "Well, now you do. So you gon' have to excuse me if Amos Davis ain't somebody I feel like talkin' about." She went back to washing dishes, only this time she was slamming pots and pans in the dishwater.

"I'm sorry, Momma. I just . . . I just need some answers."

"Whatever, Toya."

Toya weighed her next words carefully. "I wanted you to know, that, umm, I am gonna go to Detroit tomorrow."

Melba paused. Her breathing was labored as she finally said, "If you're lookin' for my blessin', you can keep lookin' because you ain't gon' get it."

"Momma." Toya took a step toward her mother.

"Don't 'momma' me. Just go and leave me alone," Melba said, her voice cracking.

Toya backed up slowly toward the door.

"Just know one thing," her mother said, turning to face Toya. "If you go see that man, don't expect any miracles from him, Toya. Amos might be good at makin' babies, but he don't care one way or another about takin' care of 'em."

Toya considered her mother's words. "Miracles?" she asked, meekly.

Melba Jean shrugged. "Just don't get your hopes up, baby. He can make you believe in 'em, but Amos ain't never been good at deliverin' on 'em."

# *Tomiko*

Still wearing her favorite flannel gown, the white one speckled with multicolored unicorns, Tomiko made her way from the kitchen down the hallway and into her office. She carried a cup of fresh-brewed coffee in her hand, sure that the strong, dark concoction would assist her in jump-starting her day. It was still dark outside, and not even the birds had begun to stir.

She sat down at her desk, switched on the lamp and then the computer. The dark room seemed to spring to life beneath the glow of light, and after Tomiko had a long sip of her coffee, she felt herself begin to come alive also.

As always, she began her day by checking the variety of social networking sites she subscribed to. She responded, liked, and retweeted for thirty minutes. By the time the sun slipped over the horizon, she was reading through the e-mail that came into her public e-mail address and then, finally, she turned to her personal e-mail address.

She had notes from her publisher, her assistant, and her publicist. A long, tiring letter from a girl named Claudia whom she'd gone to high school with. Tomiko didn't know how Claudia had gotten her private e-mail address. She sighed as she deleted Claudia's e-mail, along with announcements from a variety of online retailers.

Her coffee had grown miserably cold by the time she read the e-mail from Marjorie's Mr. Wonderful: Greg Miller.

> *Tomiko,*
>
> *I have two nephews and a niece who love your books. I have to admit that I am also a fan.  : )*
>
> *Please let me know when your calendar opens up. I would love to get to know the woman behind the words.*
>
> > *Best,*
> > *Greg*

He had sent an e-mail. Even though Marjorie had given Mr. Wonderful her number.

Tomiko smiled, read the e-mail again, and then moved it into her to-do folder.

The next e-mail she came upon was from Mark Sheridan. His name seemed to glow on the computer screen. Tomiko felt her heartbeat quicken. What did he have to say? Was Amos dead? Tomiko pushed away from the desk. She didn't want to know. Her hands began to tremble.

It was ten minutes before she finally found the nerve to open the e-mail.

> *Hello Tomiko,*
>
> *So glad that you responded and even more excited that you are indeed the right Tomiko Davis!*
>
> *When I read your email to Amos he was happier than*

*any of us have ever seen him since he was brought here.
Just like I suspected, he has a million questions that I am
not equipped to answer. I think it would be great if you can
speak to him yourself. So I was wondering, would you be
open to doing a video conference call? I think he would be
thrilled to see you.*

*Please let me know your thoughts.*

*Have a great day!*
*Mark*

Tomiko's heartbeat slowed. "He's still alive," she whispered.
She hurriedly responded:

*My schedule is open. Whatever day or time works for you
works for me.*

T

Tomiko stared at her response and then added:
*Thank you so much for doing this. Have a great day!*
Just as she pressed Send, her telephone began to ring.
Tomiko looked at the caller ID and saw that it was Marjorie.
She picked up and sang, "Hey, guuuurrrlll!"
"It's time!" *Pant, pant, pant.*
In the background Tomiko could hear Dwight demanding
that she give him the phone.
*Pant, pant, pant . . . ooooooo-weeeeeeee . . .*
Tomiko's uterus contracted.
"I need you here. You said you would be here!"
"I'm coming, Marj. Just hold on," Tomiko squealed as she
jumped up from her desk. "How many minutes apart are the
contractions?"

"Ow . . . ow . . . ow . . . zero . . . zero . . . Oh, God . . . Oh, God . . ."

Tomiko heard the sound of a car door slamming shut, some shrieking, and then the phone went dead.


Tomiko drove like a bat out of hell. Thank God rush hour was over and the roads were clear. She reached the Holland Tunnel in record time and tore through the underground viaduct at breakneck speed. By the time she parked the car and took the elevator up to the maternity ward of New York Hospital, she was perspiring so heavily that her T-shirt was plastered to her body.

Tomiko burst into the hallway, wildly swinging her head to the left and then right, and spotted Dwight standing alongside the bank of elevators with his cell phone pressed to his ear.

"Dwight?"

He looked up, and his face lit with a smile. "I'll call you back," he said to the person on the other end.

"Damn, girl, did you fly?"

Tomiko rolled her eyes. "Where is she? Is the baby here?"

Dwight raised his hands. "Whoa there, Nellie!" He laughed. "They gave her a epidural so she's resting comfortably."

"An epidural?" Tomiko coughed. "She specifically said she wanted to have a natural childbirth."

Dwight made a wry face. "Yeah, that was until those pains started ripping through her. After that she was screaming for drugs." He threw an arm around her shoulder and pulled her into him. "I'm glad you're here, sis."

They had that type of relationship. Like siblings—she, Dwight, and Marjorie. And even though she had never had any romantic thoughts about Dwight, he was, in her mind, the model of the man she hoped to end up with.

They strolled down the corridor toward the delivery suite. When Dwight pushed the door open, Marjorie turned glazed eyes in Tomiko's direction and asked, "What took you so long?"

Hours later, little Emily arrived. Wrinkled, tiny, and wailing like a banshee, but unmistakably adorable. Tomiko's eyes brimmed with tears of joy.

New father stood alongside new godmother and gazed lovingly down at the miracle squirming in Marjorie's arms.

They were so enraptured that they didn't notice the tall gentleman who'd crept silently into the suite. He stood watching the age-old tableau before clearing his throat and saying, "Already smitten, huh?"

Three pairs of eyes swung his way.

Tomiko didn't know Dwight could look any happier. But the arrival of the stranger seemed to add another layer of light to his face.

"Hey, man!"

The two men shook hands and then embraced.

"You know I had to come. Congratulations!"

"H-hi, Greg," Marjorie stammered as she used her free hand to smooth down her bird's nest of a mane. "I-I didn't know you were coming." She shot Dwight an annoyed glance and then forced a smile.

Was this Greg? *The* Greg?

"Greg Miller, this is Tomiko Davis."

Greg dramatically pressed his hand to his chest. "*The* Tomiko Davis, who never responds to my e-mails?"

Tomiko blushed. "Guilty," she admitted.

They shook hands over Marjorie's swollen stomach.

"Nice to finally meet you."

"Same here."

An awkward silence fell over the room.

"So," Dwight said as he clapped his hands together, "I think maybe we need to let mom and daughter get some rest and—"

"Of course, of course," Tomiko said as she gathered her purse and shawl from a nearby chair. "I'll come back and see you later, okay?"

She leaned in and planted a kiss on Marjorie's cheek and then turned to Dwight and embraced him. "I'll see you both . . . I mean you three, later on!"

Why she felt like running, she didn't know, but she couldn't get to the door fast enough. She curled her fingers around the knob and pushed. The door seemed stuck. She pushed again, feeling annoyance with the hospital for not fixing the doors. Tomiko could feel the others' eyes boring into her back. Her cheeks grew hot with embarrassment. Suddenly, Greg appeared beside her. He closed his hand over hers, turned the knob in the opposite direction, and pulled.

"You were pushing."

"Uhm, yeah."

"And leaving without even saying good-bye."

Tomiko kept her eyes lowered. His hand was still resting atop hers.

"I don't know what's wrong with me. I guess the new baby . . . I don't know . . ."

Finally, Greg removed his hand. "I understand."

Tomiko raised her eyes to meet his. They were a deep brown, and warm like his hand. *Grow some balls, girl!* She screamed in her head. It wasn't like he was going to take a bite out of her. "Well," she heard herself say, "if you have time, maybe we can grab a bite to eat or a cup of coffee."

His brown eyes sparkled. "I'd like that very much."

# Cass

Alma had big ideas, and she had a way of dragging Cass right along with her. Her latest brainstorm was almost too big for Cass to comprehend. She wanted to, in her words, "take their catering business to a whole other level," which sounded absolutely frightening to Cass.

"Weddings and funerals will always be in style," Alma said with a determined look in her eyes. "Why just cater the food when we can plan the whole event?"

Cass looked confused. "Weddings or funerals?"

Alma shrugged. "Both."

She had drafted a thirty-page business plan with some pretty convincing financials. "This could be huge, Cass," she explained, laying all of the documents on Cass's coffee table in her living room. "We can cater an event, provide the location, manage guest lists, and even organize music."

Cass frowned. "Alma, I don't know. I'm not a mortician or funeral director. And besides, who's got time to do all of that?"

"We hire people, Cass."

"With what money?"

"With money we've made from what we do now."

Cass looked surprised. "We have money?"

Alma rolled her eyes. "Cass, I show you the books every

month, and every month you sign off on them. Of course we have money."

"I've never really paid attention to all that, Alma," Cass said, dismissively.

Alma looked stunned. "Then you are one clueless broad," she shot back, "and a horrible businesswoman."

Cass sat up, taking offense. "Of course I'm a horrible businesswoman. I told you that a long time ago."

"Cass, I know you can't be dumb enough to trust me like that."

"You're my friend!"

"I'm your business partner first." Alma pointed at her. "Don't you forget that. We have put twenty-five thousand dollars back into this business."

Cass looked shocked. "Twenty-five thousand?"

"Girl! What?"

"Why didn't you say something?"

Again, with the eye rolling. "You are amazing. Absolutely amazing."

"I'm not dumb, Alma," Cass fired back. "I'm just—"

"What?"

Cass was hurt. "I cook. I love to cook. I don't love to run a business."

"I swear, girl, you wander through this world like you're six inches off the ground. I don't get that."

"That's not true," Cass protested. But deep down, she knew that Alma was right.

Alma seemed to sense that she had been a little harsh with Cass. She got up off the floor and sat down next to her on the sofa. "You need to wake up, Cassandra," she said tenderly. "You can't disappear into a kitchen or lurk around in the corner of a room for the rest of your life. There's just too much going on."

Cass knew where this was going, and she didn't want to hear it. "I know, Alma," she said sternly, hoping the woman would just drop it. "I already know."

"You can't be careful enough sometimes," Alma continued. "Sometimes, things just happen and there's nothing you can do to—"

"Enough!" Cass said angrily.

"Cass, we can talk about this! I know how you feel. I understand what you've been through!"

Hot tears filled Cass's eyes. "Will you stop it?"

"You've never opened up! You've never—"

"And I won't!" she said hoarsely. Cass got up and walked away from Alma, who sat there looking dumbfounded. Cass paced back and forth and ran her fingers through her hair. "We can talk about this later."

Alma quietly gathered her presentation materials and stuffed them all back into her briefcase. She quietly walked past Cass to the front door. "I'll see you tomorrow."

"I'll be there," Cass muttered.

Alma had been e-mailing and texting her nonstop about that new business plan she'd been working on, pummeling her with plans and scopes of work and—Cass was ten minutes late to the restaurant the next day and stopped dead in her tracks behind the waiter escorting her to the table. Of course, Alma noticed her entrance.

"Cass!" She stood up and yelled across the room.

Cass turned as red as she possibly could.

Darryl stood up beside Alma.

It took every ounce of willpower she had to make her feet move, first one and then the other. Cass's stomach started doing somersaults, and she realized that she wasn't breathing.

Panic started to overwhelm her. Cass had to think of too many things at one time, walking, breathing, not throwing up, smiling, holding out her hand for Darryl to shake, and not kicking Alma in the shin.

"Can I get you something to drink?" the waiter asked. He'd appeared out of nowhere like magic, but Cass was grateful.

"Grey Goose with lime, please," she ordered.

Alma and Darryl both stared at her.

The waiter cleared his throat. "We don't start serving cocktails here until after lunch," he explained.

"How about some coffee?" Alma volunteered on her behalf.

Cass chuckled nervously, realizing her faux pas. "Coffee. Perfect." She shot Alma a glance, but Alma had turned her attention back to Darryl.

"Darryl, I believe you know Cass Edwards, the best caterer this side of the Mississippi," she said proudly.

"So I've heard." He smiled, revealing rows of teeth too perfect and too white to possibly be real. "So I've heard."

Cass swiped her sweaty palms across her lap underneath the table.

"I've seen you," he said, looking as if it had suddenly dawned on him that the two of them had actually breathed the same air before now. "I've seen you around at some of the receptions the band and I have played around town."

Cass tried her best to look surprised. "Oh, really? Wow." At least he had noticed she was alive. "Awesome."

What? Who the hell still says "awesome"?

"I was telling Darryl about our plans to expand our business," Alma explained.

Damn! She was beautiful. Cass realized all over again just how beautiful Alma really was. Out of the corner of her eye, she saw Darryl was mesmerized by Alma's beauty, unable to take his eyes off of her. All of a sudden, Cass didn't want to stay here any longer or she would just stab Alma in the throat with a butter knife.

Alma continued talking: ". . . bundling our businesses together in collaboration to create one-stop shopping for people planning weddings."

"Or funerals," Cass added dismally.

Alma had a strange look on her face. "Or funerals . . ."

"Bar mitzvahs," Cass blurted out.

Darryl smiled. "As a matter of fact, I've actually done a few of those."

He wanted Alma. Cass could see it in his eyes. Of course he did. What man didn't want her? Cass's loathing of that woman swelled with each passing moment.

"I can do the bulk of the planning," Alma talked on and on. "And I can work with clients to find the venue, help with decorating and guest lists. You, Cass, can work with them on deciding on menus and, of course, in choosing a wedding cake."

"That leaves me with the entertainment side of things," Darryl chimed in.

"Exactly." Alma smiled at him.

Why did she do that? Cass stared at her with dismay. She did that shit on purpose. Darryl might as well have been ice melting into a giant puddle at that woman's feet.

They ordered breakfast. Alma and Darryl talked throughout

the meal. Cass brooded mostly in silence as she ate. She used to be fine. She used to be a normal woman who knew how to sit across the table from a man and have a normal conversation without breaking out into a sweat. She used to know how to do exactly what Alma was doing, batting her eyes, touching his arm, and laughing at every dumb thing that came out of his mouth.

Her food tasted like cardboard, but Cass continued wolfing it down like she hadn't eaten in months. Alma's long, tall, skinny ass barely touched more than a few forkfuls of eggs. The two of them kept on talking to each other like she had left the room. Hell, she *could* leave, and they wouldn't notice. He couldn't see anything beyond Alma's almond-shaped eyes. He couldn't hear anything above the sound of her cackling laughter.

"I have a lawyer friend who can draw up a contract," Alma said.

"That's fine," he said, wiping his mouth with his napkin. "I have a lawyer friend who can look it over for me."

"Of course." Alma held out her hand to him. "I think this is going to work out great."

He nodded, shaking her hand. "I think you're right."

Both of them turned to Cass, who had just finished stuffing a buttermilk biscuit into her mouth. Feeling trapped, she could only nod.

# *Toya*

Toya glanced down at her ringing cell phone and immediately pressed Ignore. Max had finally called her. No, he
had been blowing up her phone. And she'd been ignoring him.
But this time when she pushed Ignore, he called right back.
Toya couldn't believe the nerve of him. She pressed Ignore
one more time, and a few seconds later the phone rang again.
He had to have known that she was ignoring him because she
was sending the calls straight to voice mail. Her cell vibrated,
letting her know he'd left a message, which was followed by a
text that said, "Call me!!!"

"Would you leave me alone!" she yelled. "You know what?"
she muttered. "I know how to deal with you." She handled the
steering wheel with her left hand as she deleted Max's number
from her phone with the other.

"Yeah. Take that, Max. You probably just want to give me
some cockamamy story about why you left me with your
crazy wife. Thanks but no thanks."

Toya arrived at her job with exactly three minutes to spare.

"Hey, Julie," she said to her friend who worked in the
Misses Department.

Julie eyed her strangely and gave her a half wave.

"What's up?" Toya asked.

Julie looked around and in a conspiratorial whisper said, "Girl, you're in the middle of some major drama."

Julie stopped talking when their supervisor, Carol, walked toward them. Looking around, Toya noticed several other employees staring at her as well.

"Toya, may I speak with you in my office, please?" Carol said, more as a demand than a question.

Toya glanced down at her watch to make sure she wasn't late. It was straight up two o'clock, so that couldn't be what had Carol so upset.

"Yes?" Toya said, once they were in Carol's office.

"Look," her boss began, "what people do on their personal time is their business. Even though I have no respect for a woman who sleeps with a married man, I don't get in my employee's affairs, and I mean that literally."

Toya's eyes grew wide. It was no secret that Carol's husband had left her for another woman. So maybe that's what this was about.

"Even though I think that men who cheat on their wives are the scum of the earth, and that the women they cheat with are just as low-down and dirty," Carol continued.

"O-kay," Toya said. "What does that have to do with me?"

"Because your lover's wife isn't willing to turn the other cheek and let bygones be," she said, unemotionally.

"Excuse me?"

"I just spent the last hour pulling these down from all over the damn place," Carol said, slamming the photocopied pictures down on the table. They were butt-naked photos of Toya in several sexual positions. Her mouth dropped open, and she gasped. She'd sent those pictures to Max a few months ago.

"Where did those come from?" Toya asked, horrified.

"From the woman who security had to stop from plastering them all over the place—in the dressing rooms, at the registers, on the mannequins. In the Children's Department."

She pushed a photocopy toward Toya. "This is the one she put in the boys' dressing room."

Toya wanted to cry when she saw the picture of herself with her legs wide open, a vibrator poised at her crotch. A seductive smile on her face. Across the top in a black Magic Marker were the words "Hey, kids, you're not the only one who likes to play with toys. This Macy's employee does, too."

Toya wanted to die.

"The woman started screaming, saying she was going to kill you and us, too, for hiding you because she was sick and tired of your having an affair with her husband." Carol managed to keep her voice controlled, but her eyes were like liquid fire. "We managed to calm the psycho down and convince her that you weren't here. But I actually feel sorry for the woman."

Toya didn't know what to say. All she could do was stare at the photocopies.

"Who saw these?" Toya said, scooping them up.

"Every-damn-body," Carol barked. "Now some woman is threatening to sue us because her seven-year-old son saw this while he was trying on some clothes."

"I'm sorry," Toya said, stunned.

Carol took a deep breath. "Toya, you know I like you. Despite your habitual lateness, I liked you as an employee and as a person. And you have an impeccable sense of style that the customers loved."

Toya couldn't help but notice how Carol was using the past tense.

"But this behavior is unacceptable. You have subjected your

coworkers and our customers to embarrassment and humiliation. So I'm going to need you to clean out your employee locker."

"You're firing me?" Toya asked in disbelief.

"I'm afraid so."

"You can't fire me."

"I can do anything I want, especially since you have left the company liable to a lawsuit because of your indiscretions," Carol said with a smirk.

Toya wanted to scream, curse the woman out. But she didn't have the energy. She snatched her purse up and stomped away.

"We'll mail you your last check," Carol called out after her. "And maybe next time you'll think twice about messing with another woman's husband," she added, her voice laced with venom.

Toya was too upset to respond. She slammed the door as hard as she could.

Jewel had told her this wasn't over. Toya had just had no idea this would be the price she'd pay.

# Tomiko

She had prepared for the call as if she were meeting the president of the United States of America. She got her hair done and her eyebrows tweezed. She had a habit of talking with her hands, so a manicure was a must, and even though he wouldn't see her feet, she treated herself to a pedicure, just in case. She spent an hour trying to decide just where she should sit in her house. The bedroom seemed inappropriate, the kitchen a little too informal. When Tomiko video-conferenced with book clubs, she often used her bookshelves as a backdrop, but now that seemed like bragging. She didn't want Amos to think she was taunting him with her success. *Look what I've accomplished after you left!*

In the end, she chose to sit on the cream-colored couch in the family room, which was sparsely furnished but tasteful. All Amos would see was the couch, the brick wall behind the couch, a pair of glass hurricane lamps, and her.

Tomiko sat cross-legged on the couch with her laptop balanced on her thighs. She watched the time—hadn't Mark said noon?—and resisted the urge to gnaw on her freshly painted fingernails. When the chime on the computer sounded, she almost jumped out of her skin.

She held her breath and hit the Answer button.

There he was. There was her father. He seemed so old, so frail. The last time she'd laid eyes on him, he had been a giant and she had been the small one. His eyes sat deep inside of his skull, but they were still bright. What little hair he had left on his scalp was silver.

"Miko, is that you, baby?" he asked hesitantly. "Can you hear me on this? Can you see me, Miko? Can she hear me?" he asked someone else in the room out of the frame.

"She can hear you. Say something." A man's voice responded.

Tomiko stared in awe of this stranger, waiting to feel something. "I hear you," she eventually said. The word *Daddy* stuck in the back of her throat.

She'd expected to feel happy or sad or even angry at seeing Amos again after so many years, but instead, she felt absolutely nothing.

"H-how are you?" she asked, politely, as if they were meeting for the very first time.

Amos grinned and then waved like a child. "Hi!" he said excitedly. "Fine! I'm fine!"

He was lying. She could tell by looking at him that he was anything but fine.

Amos's smile slowly faded. "I can't believe I'm talking to you, darlin'. I can't believe it."

Tomiko couldn't believe it, either, but where was the love? She'd loved Amos with all her heart and soul for as long as she could remember, but right now, in this moment, that love was nowhere to be found. And that's what broke her heart.

"Yeah," she said, starting to tear up. "I can't believe it, either." Daddy. Say the word, she commanded herself. But she couldn't.

A shadow of confusion gradually washed over Amos's expression as he stared, puzzled, at the screen. Then he scratched his head and took a deep breath.

"Put your momma on the phone, honey," he suddenly said, looking worried.

"I don't live with Mom," she responded carefully.

He nodded. "Tell her . . . tell her I'm playing tonight at Barstow's and that I won't be home until . . . until . . . I won't be home," he finished, absently.

"Amos," she heard the man saying again in the background. "How you doing, man? You all right?"

Amos nodded, his gaze averted to the other person in the room with him. "Miko is my baby doll." He smiled, turning his attention back to the screen. "Ain't that right, Miko?" He smiled. "Tell your momma I'll be home soon as I can."

Tomiko hadn't realized she was crying. "I'll tell her, Daddy." The word tasted so bitter in her mouth.

"Wait up for me if you can," he whispered.

She nodded. He used to tell her that all the time, and of course, she never could. "I'll try."

Amos laughed. "You know I'ma wake you up if you can't." He pressed his finger to his lips. "Don't tell your momma."

She laughed too. "I won't."

Amos smiled warmly at her, and then started humming a soulful melody that took her back in time. And then he started to sing. "And if that mockingbird don't sing, Papa's gonna buy you a diamond ring . . ."

Tomiko cried, hanging on every word until he finished.

"Daddy's got to go and make some skirts swing," he said at the end.

Tomiko dried her eyes. "Make 'em swing until they fly away, Daddy."

He laughed. "G'night, my love."

She waited for the image of him to fade from the screen before finally turning off her laptop. He'd done it again. After all these years, Amos had crawled inside the space in her heart and filled it up as if he'd never left. He'd made Tomiko feel as if she was the most special girl in the world and made her forgive him for ever breaking her heart in the first place.

# Cass

Alma had called and told Cass to meet her at three o'clock at an abandoned building on the outskirts of downtown Detroit. Yet by three thirty the woman still hadn't showed, and the last three times Cass called her, Alma's answer had been a frantic "Girl! I'm on my way!"

The sight wasn't pretty, Cass thought, sitting inside her car with all the windows rolled up and her finger poised to speed-dial 911. Every building on the block was boarded up and empty. The neighborhood looked like the set for some science fiction movie in which all the residents had been taken away by aliens. Thanks to the recession and the crippled auto industry, that wasn't too far from the truth.

"Real estate is dirt cheap," Alma had explained. "Don't you want to move your office out of your kitchen and into some-place nice?"

Sure, she did. But this place wasn't nice. It was a disintegrating five-story disaster. If the wind blew too hard, the place would fall apart. Maybe the building was cheap, but the cost to repair it and bring it up to code would cancel out what they saved in buying the place.

Where the hell was that woman? Cass dialed her number again and got Alma's voice mail. "Alma! I been here going on forty-five minutes," she said, annoyed. "If you're coming, then come on." She checked her watch. "I'm going to sit here for ten more minutes. If you're not here, I'm leaving."

As soon as she hung up, a tap on her window scared the mess out of her.

Darryl. Precious God, he was beautiful.

Cass came to her senses enough to remember how to roll down the window.

"Hey there," he said, hovering above her with his hands in the pockets of jeans that looked as if they had been made for him. He was also wearing a fitted white V-neck T-shirt and a black sports coat. Every tooth in that man had been strategically whitened and placed in his mouth by angels. Dark, hooded eyes twinkled like they had stars in them. Could she be any more in love with him than she had thought she already was? Yes. Absolutely yes! "Thought that was you sitting here." He leaned down and looked in her car. "Alma's not with you?"

Cass's heart had leaped into her throat and was pumping so fast that it closed off her windpipe. She felt her mouth moving, but not until he gave her a look like she was crazy did she realize she hadn't uttered a word.

"No," she said, quickly. "No, she's, uh . . . I called her, and she said she was on her way."

Alma hadn't told her that Darryl would be coming. And now the plan was all starting to make sense. She'd invited Cass. She'd invited him here, too. But now, all of a sudden, Alma, the person who'd set this whole thing up, was a ghost. Depending on how the next ten minutes unfolded, when she *did* see Alma again, she was either going to punch her hard in her stomach or kiss her.

"Wow," he said, staring over the top of Cass's car at the building. "So this is it."

Her palms were sweating. How come she had to have such sweaty hands? "I guess so," she said, trying not to sound as nervous as she was.

She took slow, deep, silent breaths to help calm her nerves. Alma had set her up, and she could've choked that woman for putting her in this position, but wasn't this the opportunity she had been looking for? She was out here alone with the man of her dreams. She didn't want to end up growing old by herself like Amos. She had promised herself that if she ever got this opportunity, she'd step up her game.

Cass cleared her throat. "Maybe we should check to see if the door's unlocked." As she opened her car door, he stepped aside and then held out his beautiful, strong hand to take hold of her hot, sweaty one and help her out of the car.

"I'm sure it is," he said, oozing charm. "I wouldn't waste a good lock on a place like this."

"Alma's got a vision, I suppose." Cass chuckled nervously as the two of them made their way up the sidewalk.

"Is that what you call it?"

The place had been condemned for all the right reasons. The door was unlocked, and inside it was even worse than the two of them put together could've imagined. They both stood there, dumbfounded. Holes yawned wide in the ceilings and the floors. Stair railings had been torn from staircases and left scattered on the ground. Electrical wires hung exposed from where light fixtures should've been. Something—Cass wasn't sure what it was, but it was brown and furry and had reddish-gold eyes—raced through one of the doorways, making a noise that made the hair on her arms stand straight up.

Cass jumped toward Darryl, and he caught her in his arms and laughed.

"Let's hope it's more scared of us," he joked.

"I'm sorry," she said, embarrassed, pulling away from him. Oh, Lord! She felt like a fool.

"Don't be." He smiled down at her, nearly blinding her with the glare from those perfect teeth.

Cass wasn't sure, but she thought she might be blushing. Since she hadn't blushed in twenty years, though, she wasn't sure.

"So," he said, strolling out into the center of the room, "what exactly do you think she had in mind for this place?"

Cass did her best to compose herself, but she kept one eye on the corner into which that creature had disappeared. "I think she wants to open it up, at least this part of it, and turn it into an event center or something. And then we'd put a kitchen in back, probably." Cass slowly walked around the room.

"What about upstairs?" he said, looking up through one of the holes in the ceiling.

"Not sure." She shrugged. "Maybe we could make smaller rooms for smaller parties?"

"Or a studio?" He gave Cass an inquiring look.

"You make records?" She thought he just sang at weddings.

He looked away, sheepish. "I try. Been trying for too long, maybe. I could record other artists, though." Now he was the one blushing. "At least I'd like to."

Seeing him vulnerable did wonders for her own courage. "That could be nice." Nice? From the look on his face, "nice" wasn't the response he was looking for. "I mean, that sounds exciting, Darryl," she quickly added. "Really."

Disappointment washed over his face, but he did his best to cover it up.

"It's funny," he observed. "All these years we've been working around each other, at all the same parties, and this is the first time we've ever had a conversation."

It was the first time *he'd* had a conversation with *her*. Cass had had a hundred conversations with him in her head, and in all of them he always told her that he was madly in love with her. But if she ever told him that, he would think she was some kind of stalker.

"Well, if Alma has her way, we'll all be in business together."

"I think she'll get her way." He winked.

Darryl slowly circled the room, nodding his head and humming Nat King Cole's "Unforgettable." Without warning, he glided over to her, wrapped one arm around her waist, and took hold of her hand.

"That's what you are," he crooned, slowly leading her around in wide circles. "Unforgettable, though near or far."

Cass offered up herself into the real-life fantasy he had swept her into. Darryl smelled so good. A muscled arm pressed against her side, and he guided her around that space like they were floating in the air.

"I think I'm starting to get a feel for Alma's vision," he said, gazing into Cass's eyes.

She nodded. "Yeah. I think I'm feeling it, too."

Alma was always preaching about the power of positive

thinking. Well, right now Cass was thinking pretty damn positively, and it was actually paying off. She was tired of sitting back, daydreaming about the kind of life she wanted. Cass could have it. She could have him, and she decided that all her dreams could come true if she put her mind to it.

# Amos

"I hear you're about ready to run a hundred-yard dash," Mark joked, following Amos into his room after he'd finished therapy.

"No, I'm ready to run my ass up out of this joint," Amos snapped irritably. His hip ached, his arms ached, and as far as he could tell, there was no reason for him to stay here. He wanted to go back home, to his own house, where he could do his own thing, which didn't include physical activities designed for men forty years younger than he was.

Mark helped him out of his wheelchair and into bed. "Eventually, that could happen. But for now . . ."

"For now," Amos grunted, positioning himself in a bed he'd come to hate, "you call Cass." He glared at Mark. "And you tell her to come get me out of here and take me home."

Mark stood there like he was deaf. He did that sometimes, just stood there and let Amos pitch a fit like some emotional schoolgirl.

"Y'all think I'm crazy, but I ain't crazy. I'm old. I forget things sometimes, but forgettin' don't make me crazy. I want to be back in my own house, eatin' my own food, watchin' my own TV without people starin' at me all the time like my head's gonna blow up!" He waited for Mark to say something, but the man was going to let it all ride. "I don't belong here, man! I ain't crazy, and I don't belong in this place!"

"You forget more than you remember, Amos," Mark eventually told him. "You've lost more than you know."

Amos stared at him, his eyes wide. The fool sounded like a broken record.

"I was here yesterday," Mark continued. "We talked, Amos. We talked for a while. Do you remember that?"

Amos tried to remember the last time he'd seen this man before today.

"You said you and me played together at some run-down club in Colorado called the Roxy. You sang and played piano, and I played drums. Some girl in a blue dress danced at the foot of the stage and stared up at you like you were Jesus. And then you got pissed at me for messing up the rhythm. You remember that conversation?"

No. Helplessly, Amos realized that he didn't remember telling Mark about that night at the Roxy. Unexpected tears filled his eyes.

"It was like it was happening all over again for you, man. You were there. You were living that moment again, and it was as real to you as this conversation is to me now," Mark said sadly. "It was a good memory, brotha. At least for a while it was good. And then it turned into something else, something . . . that left both of us confused and angry."

Mark waited for Amos to respond, but Amos just sat there.

"Every good thing that ever happened to me is behind me," Amos eventually said. He looked at Mark and forced a smile. "You got no idea who I used to be, son, of the life I used to live." Amos's eyes clouded over with tears. "I used to be something," he said, proudly sticking out his chest.

"I'm sure you were, Amos," Mark said, quietly.

But Amos hadn't been that man in many, many years. "Know what did me in?" he finally asked.

Mark shook his head.

"Rap music," he said, with disdain. "I thought disco was gonna do it, but I made it through disco all right. But when that Rum DMS and Kool Modee came out," he shook his head, unaware that he'd butchered both names. "Music like mine fell by the wayside. Nobody had any interest in soul music anymore. They was too busy listening to that hip-hop gang music about killings and the hood." Amos shrugged. "My old ass looked foolish trying to sing that mess."

"Good music never goes away, Amos. People love the kind of music you sang. It's timeless."

"Yeah, but I ain't timeless," he admitted. "I sold my soul to make music. I made all kinds of sacrifices for it, walked away from folks for music. I'd turn my back on the whole damn world if that's what it wanted me to do. As long as I had it, could play and sing it, nothing or nobody else mattered. Now," he said, shrugging. "Now I got nobody. I got nothing, not even my music."

Music had taken control of Amos a long time ago, and he'd spent his life chasing after it, after the promise that it offered, only Amos could never quite catch up to it. He never quite caught it.

"It was a love affair that I craved more than I wanted to take my next breath, but it was never quite as sweet as I thought it would be," he admitted, painfully. Amos turned his gaze to the window and looked out into the darkness. "I got shit to show for it, Mark. I got nothing."

"You've got your family, Amos," Mark offered.

Amos laughed. "What family? Son, I got no woman, no friends."

"Cass? Tomiko?"

"I forfeited those girls a long time ago," Amos confessed. "Ain't you been paying attention? Music was my everything. Not my girls. And I made sure they knew it, and now I'm paying for it. I can't blame them for how they feel. Nah, man. I can't blame any one of them."

# Toya

Cassandra Edwards had some hella nerve. Toya held the phone away from her ear, trying to make sure she wasn't being punked or something.

"Toya, are you there?" Cassandra said.

Toya put the phone back to her ear. "Yeah, I'm here, but you 'bout to be talkin' to the dial tone. I know you don't know me, but I'm not the one."

Cass took a deep breath. "I'm sorry. It's just that I've left you a lot of messages, and you're ignoring them."

"I told you I didn't get no message," Toya lied. "My voice-mail is broken." Toya had gotten Cass's messages, all thirteen of them. She should have just told the girl she was coming to Detroit tomorrow, but the words wouldn't form. She wanted to go see about Amos on her own, because if it didn't work out, she didn't want any pressure when she turned around and hightailed it back home.

*It's going to work out.* Toya had been telling herself that all day. Her raggedy car barely could make it down the street, and she'd almost used that as an excuse to back out. But then, she'd decided to take the bus. Still, Toya thought she wouldn't tell Cass she was going—just in case it didn't.

"Well, can you call him, please?" Cass asked.

"Look, I'm kinda busy," Toya replied. "I've picked up a lot of hours at work and—"

"Toya, he's not my responsibility," Cass said firmly. "He's not my father."

Now Toya was getting pissed. "Girl, miss me with that bull." How was Cass going to try to make her, of all people, feel guilty? "That man was more of a father to you than he ever was to me. So go somewhere else with that guilt trip. You and whatever other kids he has can work that out. I'm not in the equation."

"Don't you want to try to make peace with him?"

*Yes.* "No," she replied.

"Toya, can you live with yourself if something happens to your father and you haven't made peace?"

Toya was tired of playing games. She didn't have to lie. She didn't even owe Amos a lie. "Cassandra, let me be very clear. Years ago, Amos Davis made a choice that he would not be in my life. It was a decision that *I* had no choice but to live with. And as difficult as it was, I lived with it. I may have been jacked up because of it, but the fact remains that I lived with it. So don't come here laying some guilt trip at my feet."

"He's not healthy, Toya."

"Yeah, so I've been told," Toya said, even though hearing those words made her feel a pang inside.

Cass actually sounded like she was crying now. "I can't do this . . . I can't do this by myself."

Now, why did she have to go and break out the tears? "Fine," Toya huffed.

"So you'll call him?" Cass said hopefully.

Toya paused. She might as well go ahead and tell Cass she was coming. The girl seemed like she was stressed out to her limit.

"Fine, I'll come see him."

It was Cass's turn to be quiet. "Thank you," she finally said. "I think that'll mean a lot to him."

"Well, I'm not making any promises. But I'll come. Day after tomorrow."

"Okay," Cass said. "I guess, um, I look forward to meeting you."

"Yeah, whatever," Toya muttered.

Toya leaned back and began flipping the TV channels. She needed to be online, looking for a job, but not a lot of places needed personal stylists, and she wasn't looking forward to rejections.

She stopped at the sight of Bill Cosby dancing on her TV screen. He was in one of those colorful sweaters, doing a dance to entertain his family on *The Cosby Show*. The sight made her smile—even though she'd probably seen this episode fifty times. Like always, though, Toya imagined herself in the Huxtable family. She'd spent years as a teenager wishing she could take Vanessa or Rudy's place. Hell, she would've even taken Theo's place—anything to know a life like that.

*This the life God gave you so you need to learn to love it.*

Her mother's words resonated in her head.

Her mother.

Toya had tried to call her mother all last night and all day today. But Melba Jean was being her usual stubborn self.

Toya just hoped that her mother would forgive her for what she was about to do.

Toya sighed as the doorbell rang. If only her mother knew the lengths to which Toya was going in order to see her father. It had to be something she desperately needed if she'd called *him*.

"Hey, Max," Toya said, swinging the door open.

He stood there with a cocky grin on his face.

"Hey, sweet thang," he said, strutting in with the swagger of Denzel Washington. "I'm so glad you called me." He walked over and plopped down on the sofa.

"I didn't have any other choice," she said. And she didn't. As bad as Toya wanted to go see her father, the bottom line was she had five dollars in her savings account, and her checking account was overdrawn. She didn't have the one-hundred-thirty-dollar bus fare to get to Detroit. She'd asked Misty, but her friend was just as broke as she. So that had left only Max.

It had pained her to call him, but in the end, she told herself he owed her that much since his psycho wife was the reason she'd lost her job in the first place. Besides, he needed to reimburse her for that door his wife broke.

"So what's going on in your world?" He looked around like he was expecting a whole lot to have changed. "You wanna fix me a drink?"

"Nothing is going on in my world, and I don't want to fix you a drink," she said flatly. "It's like I told you over the phone, I had to use my money to pay for the stupid door your crazy wife broke!" She took a deep breath, trying to keep herself from getting worked up. "I'm not trying to play any games. I'm just in a serious bind."

"Yeah, your father is sick." He leaned back and put his feet on the table, eyeing her skeptically. "Are you sure you're not trying to get this money to go see another man?"

Toya huffed. "Max, I'm not running game on you for a measly one hundred and fifty dollars. You know I'm broke, and I'm trying to buy a bus ticket to Detroit. Hell, you can even buy the ticket yourself."

He continued to assess her like he was trying to figure out if she was telling the truth.

"Are you gonna give me the money or what?" she asked.

He flashed a toothy grin. "Whatchu gonna give me?"

Toya stomped back toward the door. "You know what, forget it!" she said.

Max jumped up and grabbed her. "Hey, babe, chill. Why you trippin'?"

"'Cause I'm not prostituting myself for a hundred and fifty dollars."

He tried to lift her T-shirt. "It's not like I haven't seen what you have already."

"Bye, Max." She swung the door open, struggling to fight back tears.

He was about to say something when he stopped and realized she was crying. "Hey, why are you doing that?"

Toya tried to turn away.

He gently pulled her chin back to face him. "Hey, baby girl, what's wrong?"

She sniffed. "Max, I'm going through some things, and I just need the money. I don't need drama, I don't need any strings attached—I just need the money."

"Is your dad really that sick?"

She nodded. "I told you that."

He looked shocked. "I thought you were just saying that to get me over here."

The man had some nerve. As if she'd have to make up a story to get him to come over.

"No, I haven't seen him in years, and he may be dying. I'm just trying to get to Detroit to see him."

Max then surprised Toya when he reached in his wallet and

pulled out three hundred-dollar bills. "Here, babe. I'm sorry. Here's the money for the door, plus some. It's all I have on me. I really thought you were messing around."

"I'm not," she assured him as she took the money.

"Is there anything I can do?"

Toya was shocked. She rarely saw this side of Max. "No, you've done more than enough," she said, pulling the money to her chest.

They stood in awkward silence for a few moments. Then he said, "You go handle your business. Hope your dad gets better. And call me when you get back." He leaned in and gently kissed her on the forehead.

Toya couldn't help but smile—not only because Max was being so generous but also because she knew in her heart that her conviction to leave him alone was still as strong as ever.

# Tomiko

It had been a hell of a week. The highlight, of course, had been reconnecting with her father. That video meeting was followed by a call from her publisher advising her that they had sold the foreign publishing rights to her most recent novel to Taiwan, Portugal, France, and Spain. The conversation she'd had with Amos had sparked her creative energy, and after she'd spoken to him, Tomiko had sat down and pounded out five pages. A few days later Greg Miller called. The stars, it seemed, had finally aligned.

Greg chose the place. Nothing fancy. A deli that served the best corned-beef sandwiches he'd ever tasted. "Do you like corned beef?"

She'd said yes.

The place was packed and the chatter was deafening. Given the swarm of people, Tomiko thought that they would have to wait nearly an hour before they got a table. They were eighth and ninth in a line that stretched out the door. Greg didn't seem to mind. He made small talk about the weather, the Tea Party, and Donald Trump's absurd behavior.

"Does he really think the American people will vote for him?"

Tomiko shrugged her shoulders. "I think quite a few will."

A short, stout man with flyaway red hair came out from behind the lunch counter. Spreading his arms like wings, he boomed "Greg!" in a thick Irish brogue. The two men embraced and slapped each other heartily on the back.

"It's been too long," the man said.

"Yes, it has." Greg laughed and then turned to Tomiko. "This is Ryan MacDougal. Ryan, Tomiko Davis."

"Ah, such a beautiful woman and such a beautiful name!" Ryan said as he pumped Tomiko's hand.

"This place has been in Ryan's family for more than thirty years."

"Thirty-five years, to be exact!" Ryan laughed. "Come with me, a booth just opened up."

The people who were waiting ahead of Tomiko and Greg grumbled. Tomiko averted her eyes as she followed Ryan to the empty booth.

"The usual?" he asked.

Greg nodded. "But I think my friend here might like to take a look at the menu."

"No, that's okay," she put in. "I'll have what he's having."

Ryan winked at Greg. "She trusts your judgment. I like her already."

Minutes later, Ryan set down two platters holding towering sandwiches: three slices of bread, thick cuts of meat, Swiss cheese, coleslaw, and a side of white sauce that Greg pointed a finger at and announced, "That there is the secret ingredient."

Tomiko studied the monstrosity. "This is enough food for a small village. I'll never be able to finish it all."

"That's good," Greg said as he brought one half of his sandwich to his mouth. "It tastes even better the next day."

"Oh, like stew?"

"Yep!"

It was true, Tomiko thought as she bit into the sandwich and savored the flavor. It was the best corned-beef sandwich she had ever had. After a few bites, Greg dragged a napkin across his lips and asked, "So where did you grow up?"

"Detroit."

"Ahh, Motor City," Greg crooned.

"Have you ever been there?"

"Twice. It's a great city."

"*Was* a great city," Tomiko stressed.

"Yeah, it's taken some hard knocks."

"That's an understatement. The city is broke, and the crime is out of control."

"Do you still have people there?"

She was glad he said people and not parents. She didn't want to talk about her broken home because then she would have to talk about Amos and she didn't want to talk about him. She turned the question around to Greg.

"And you, where did you grow up?"

Greg picked up a French fry and bit off the crusted tip. "Well, I was born in Texas. My parents were in the military, so I grew up all around the world." He took another bite of the fry, chewed, and swallowed. "Japan, Korea, Hawaii, a stint in Kenya, Argentina."

"That must have been great."

"Yes, in retrospect, I guess it was. But at the time it was difficult."

"Difficult?"

"Yeah, it seemed like as soon as I was settled in—new school, new friends—it was time to pack up and leave."

Tomiko nodded. "I guess that would be hard on a kid."

"So I know you don't have any children, but do you have any siblings?"

Tomiko grimaced. "Uhm, yeah, I have two brothers."

"Younger or older?"

"Younger."

"And are they still in Detroit?"

Tomiko squirmed in her chair and managed a quick "yep."

Greg was about to ask another question, a question Tomiko suspected would delve deeper into her personal life, and so she cut his off with her own, "And do you have siblings?"

"Three sisters. All older. One lives in Texas, one is here in New York, and the youngest is living in London, pursuing a singing career."

"Singing career? Why London?"

Greg chuckled. "Well, to tell the truth"—he leaned in and whispered conspiratorially—"she's *really* pursuing a guy named Nathan."

Tomiko's eyes popped.

"But"—Greg raised his hands—"in her defense, she does sing."

"Wow, London is a long way to go for love."

A look of surprise spread across Greg's face. "You think so? I would go to the ends of the earth for love if I had to."

The statement stunned Tomiko. She couldn't remember ever hearing a man say that.

She was stuck for so long that he filled in the silence with another question. "So how did you get into writing?"

She launched into her stock response, the one that she'd

been using since the first book of the Li'l Amos series had been published. The response that carefully stepped around the fact that the books were the direct result of a mournful longing that ran wide and deep.

Two hours later, she and Greg were back on the street. It was nearly nine thirty. Dark clouds were rolling in from the west, and the air had turned crisp.

"Looks like snow," Greg said as they navigated through the stream of people pursuing their determined paths on the sidewalk.

Tomiko tilted her head toward the sky. "Yes, it does." Their gait quickened. "I'm parked over there in that lot."

When they reached the corner, Greg took hold of her elbow and guided her across the intersection. She was thrilled to feel his touch again. And even though the material of her coat prevented skin-to-skin contact, his warmth emanated through the cottony fabric.

Inside the garage, Tomiko opened her purse, retrieved the ticket, and handed it to the cashier. She was about to fish her wallet out of her purse when Greg slid his credit card to the cashier.

"Oh, no, you don't have to do that."

"I know I don't. But I want to."

Outside, snow began to float from the sky and pedestrians began to scatter.

"Wow," Greg whispered as he watched the downfall. "It always amazes me how quickly the weather can change. Just like that," he said, and snapped his fingers.

The attendant rolled Tomiko's cherry-red Jeep Wrangler to a stop and climbed out.

"This is you?"

"Yep."

"I love Jeeps. I have the same one in black."

"I didn't take you for a Jeep man."

"No? What did you take me for?"

Tomiko pressed the pad of her index finger against her chin. "Hmmm, Jaguar?"

"Well"—Greg blushed—"I have one of those as well."

Tomiko arched her eyebrows.

"It's an old one. A very old one. I like to restore cars. But my everyday car is my Jeep."

"Where are you parked? Can I give you a lift to your car?"

"Oh, I didn't drive down. I took a cab."

"Well then, can I give you a lift home?"

"Oh, no, that's okay. I'll just hail a taxi."

Tomiko trained her finger at the opening to the garage. "It's freezing out there, and all you have on is a sport coat. Come on, jump in."

Greg shook his head. "Really, I'm fine."

"Are you sure?"

"Yes."

Tomiko shrugged her shoulders and climbed into her Jeep. Greg closed the door and leaned his head into the open window. "This was nice."

"Yes, it was."

"I hope we can do it again."

"I hope so, too."

"So I'll call you?"

"You better," Tomiko cooed.

Greg didn't venture a kiss. He just thumped the Jeep's hard-top and waved.

Looking back, Tomiko barely remembered the drive home. She was on autopilot, and when she finally came to, she was turning into her driveway. When she walked into her house, her assistant, Annie, was seated at the kitchen table, jabbing angrily at a green salad.

"What are you so happy about?"

Tomiko stammered, "Huh?"

"You've got a huge smile on your face," Annie said, and then dropped her fork and asked, "Oh my God, did Oprah call?"

Tomiko hadn't realized she was smiling. She brought her hands to her mouth, and sure enough, she was. That was another part of her post-Greg daze.

"No, Oprah did not call." Tomiko laughed as she floated off to her bedroom.

She stripped off her street clothes and slipped into a pair of sweatpants and a loose T-shirt. She answered a soft knocking on her door with "Come in."

Annie stepped just inside the doorway and eyed her suspiciously. "Soooo," she sang, "what's up?"

"What do you mean?"

"Why are you so happy?"

Tomiko smirked. "I'm always happy. What are you talking about?"

"Uh-huh," Annie hummed.

"Annie, what did I tell you about working so late?"

Annie gave Tomiko one last, long curious look and then backed out of the bedroom and closed the door.

Tomiko plopped down on the bed. Okay, so she had had a great time with a great guy. It happened. It always happened. And maybe the two of them would see each other again, and maybe again. Maybe they'd become a couple and even exclaim the *L* word to each other someday. But then what? Tomiko was a serial runaway girlfriend, never having the courage to venture into actual wifedom. Why was that? Was it really because of issues she had with her father? Amos had always known the right thing to say and how to say it to make her love him feel brand new. A lot of men she'd known had been good at that. But in the back of her mind was a dark and foreboding fear she'd tried to ignore for most of her life. A fear she could readily admit to now, and it had come from loving Amos.

# *Toya*

Even though the bus ride to Detroit took less than three hours, it felt like an eternity. Toya's heart had raced at the idea that each mile traveled put her closer to her father—but could he even be deemed that? They had shared no trips to the park, no father-daughter dances, no birthday outings. Nothing. She once had thought she remembered his buying her a teddy bear, but then later, after her mother had turned on Amos, Melba Jean had revealed that she was the one who had bought the bear and had lied when she said it had come from Amos.

What would Toya say when she came face-to-face with him? Would she hug him? Would he take her into his arms? Would he beg for her forgiveness? Would he even know who she was?

Toya edged into the nursing home. "Hi, I'm here to see Amos Davis."

The woman sitting at the desk looked up, irritated. But as her eyes met Toya's, a huge smile crossed her face. "Lawd, have mercy. You've got to be his daughter. You look just like him, except prettier." She cackled.

It had never dawned on Toya that she bore any resemblance to her father, but then again, why would it?

"You got that smooth chocolate skin just like him. Well, go

on back. He's in Room 213. You lucky you caught him on a good day," she added with a conspiratorial wink, "because he's a handful."

Toya nodded, then made her way down the long hallway. Her heart beat faster with every tap of her heels. When she reached his door, she took a deep breath and said a silent prayer that she wouldn't end up regretting coming. She almost changed her mind and walked away. She still felt like she was betraying her mother, but this was something she had to do. She had to face her father. Misty was right. That was the missing piece from the puzzle that was her life. Besides that, she wanted answers from Amos. No, she *needed* answers from Amos.

"Knock, knock," she said, lightly tapping on the door.

"What?" Amos called out. "Don't come bringin' me no more pills. I'm sick of pills."

Toya slowly pushed the door open and eased inside the room. "It's not the nurse, Mr. Davis." She didn't know what to call him. "Amos" seemed disrespectful, and she sure wasn't about to call him Daddy.

"Umm, how are you?" she stammered as she stood over him.

He stared at her like he was studying her. Then he said, "Who are you?"

That tore at Toya's soul. Part of her had hoped that he would take one look at her, then burst into tears as he pulled her into his arms. But once again, Amos Davis broke her heart.

"Ummm, my name is, um, Toya."

"Don't know no Toya," he snapped. "Everybody always comin' in here messin' with me. I just wanna watch TV."

Toya fought back the tears welling behind her eyelids. "Well, I just wanted to come see you."

"Now you see me, now you go."

"Don't you even want to know who I am?"

"So many meddlesome people in this place, I just figured you were one of them."

"No, I'm not a meddlesome person." She paused and inhaled. "I'm your daughter."

His head snapped around, and he stared at her again. For a minute, she thought he was going to say "Which one?" Toya had no idea how many kids he even had. She knew about the two daughters, but maybe he had left a long trail.

"Toya—LaToya McCann. Melba Jean's girl."

His expression softened. "Melba Jean?" The words were a whisper from his mouth. Then he smiled real big. "Umph, I love me some Melba Jean."

Toya stared at him in disbelief. How dare he fix his lips to talk about loving anybody? "Really? Because I don't think she could tell." The words left her mouth before she even realized it.

"Who did you say you were again?"

Toya could no longer hold back her tears. "I'm your daughter!" she yelled. "You know, the one you just up and left one day years ago. The one you've never bothered to get in touch with since then. No letter, no call, nothing."

Amos looked ashamed. "I . . ."

"They say you've got Alzheimer's," she said, unsympathetically.

Amos turned away and looked out the window. "Everybody's got somethin'," he said softly.

"You're my father, Amos." Was he having an Alzheimer's moment, or did he really just not know who in the hell she was?

Amos sat there, staring at nothing and quietly carving out her heart.

"I made a mistake," he muttered, but she heard him. He wasn't the only one. *She'd* made a mistake by coming here.

"A mistake," she asked incredulously. "A mistake? That's what you call walking out on me? A mistake is forgetting to sign your income tax form. A mistake is making a left turn instead of a right. A mistake is *not* forgetting you have a kid!"

Amos kept his back to her. Silence filled the air. Then, finally, he looked at her. "I-I made a mistake."

Toya couldn't believe this. She took a deep breath, trying to calm herself down. "You know what else was a mistake? My coming here. I won't bother you again." With that, she spun around and walked out of the room. Her heart sank even more because Amos didn't call out to stop her.

Toya couldn't get out of Amos's room fast enough. She had to duck into the bathroom to have a good cry. Her mother had been right; she never should've come here. And she was sorry to admit that Melba Jean had been right on the money for all these years. Amos Davis was a bona fide asshole.

Toya sniffed, then looked in the mirror to dry her eyes. The bathroom door opened, and a full-figured, pretty, brown-skinned woman walked in.

"Hi," she said cheerfully before stopping and staring at Toya.

"You got a problem?" Toya said.

"No, it's just . . . wow." She shook her head and stared at Toya as if she was seeing a ghost. "You wouldn't happen to be Toya, would you?"

"Who?"

"Toya?" the woman quickly said.

"Yeah, I'm Toya. Why, who are you?"

"Umm, I'm Cass. Cassandra—you know, we talked on the phone."

"Oh" was all Toya managed to say. She extended her hand to shake Cass's. "Nice to meet you."

"When did you get here?" Cass asked.

Toya shifted uncomfortably. "This morning, but I'm about to leave."

"Leave?" Cass asked, bewildered. "Did you see your fath—? Umm, did you see Amos?"

Toya stiffened at the mention of his name. "Yeah, I saw the man responsible for my creation."

Cass let out a sigh. "I take it things didn't go too well?"

"You'd take it right," Toya said, turning and dabbing at her eyes again.

Cass stumbled, looking for the right words to say. "You'll have to excuse him. He's sick, and he's not handling it well."

Toya wasn't feeling too tolerant about the old man's medical issues. "Am I supposed to feel sympathy for him?" She waited for Cass to give her an answer. When Cass remained silent, Toya continued. "I came just like you asked, and he did what he always did—shunned me. So I'm good. I'm catching the first thing smokin' back to Flint." She tucked her purse under her arm.

"You can't leave yet," Cass pleaded.

"Oh, yeah? Watch me."

"He really needs you."

"I think it's more like you need me," Toya said bitterly. "You need me to pick up the pieces of that old man so that you don't have to. I think you made that clear over the phone." Cass wasn't fooling anybody. It was obvious that Amos would need someone to take care of him. Cass didn't want to be straddled with that old fool, so she called Toya to come do it.

"I'm just asking you to give him a shot," Cass pleaded.

Toya was not willing to submit to any more indignities. "Look, I've been doing just fine without Amos Davis all these years. He hasn't needed me all this time, so he doesn't need me now. So whatever is going on with that man is not my problem."

"But he's your father."

Toya cocked her head. "Really? Because I can't tell. So you and *your* father have a good life." Toya headed toward the door.

"He's not my father," Cass said, stopping Toya in her tracks. That painful statement tore at her soul.

"Did he take care of you?" Toya asked. "Did he ever read you a bedtime story? Did he ever take you to the park? Well, he never did any of those things for me. He never even acknowledged me. So I couldn't care less what happens to him."

"You don't mean that."

"You don't know me, so you don't know *what* I mean," Toya said matter-of-factly.

Cass shook her head slightly, like that wasn't what she meant. "I know if you meant that, you wouldn't be here."

"Well, I just came because I had some unfinished business. It's finished now."

"If you'll just take a moment to talk to him—"

"I did."

"No, all of us need to talk to him."

*"Us?"* Toya repeated.

"Yeah, Amos has two daughters."

"That you know of," Toya quipped.

"You're right, that I know of," Cass said. "But I think that's all."

Something inside Toya stirred. She did want to know more about her other sister. "Who is the other one?"

"I'm not sure," Cass said, sheepishly. "I was hoping that you'd know her name and maybe how to get in contact with her."

Toya's mind quickly raced back to that awful day in her living room. The day she and her friends had watched Amos on TV and he'd proclaimed his love for his baby girl . . . Tomiko. Toya had never forgotten that name. She remembered thinking what a dumb name it was. And she remembered wishing she could trade places with Tomiko. Then maybe Amos would dedicate a song to her.

Toya snapped herself out of her thoughts. "Tomiko," Toya finally admitted. "Her name is Tomiko."

"Do you know where she is?" Cass asked.

"No. Never gave much thought into finding her."

Cass sighed. "Well, at least now I have a first name and that'll help. Maybe she'll come to see him too."

"Well, whatever. That's between you, Amos, and Tomiko. I'm outta here."

"Don't," Cass said, gently grasping Toya's arm. "Just stay, if for no other reason than I'd like to get to know you better."

Toya looked down at Cass's hand on her forearm. Normally, she would've gotten upset at someone grabbing her like that, but, oddly, she felt a connection with Cass. She couldn't explain it. Then suddenly a new prospect dawned on her. Maybe she couldn't get answers from Amos, but maybe she *could* get them from Cass.

"That's too long of a ride for you to make just to turn around and go right back," Cass continued, as if she knew she was getting through to Toya. "At least stay the night."

Toya looked at Cass in her fancy clothes and couldn't help but feel a twinge of resentment. The only reason she was able to dress nicely was because she used to get a discount on her clothes. Cass looked like she'd grown up with the best of everything. "Look, I'm sure Amos set you up well."

"No," Cass said with unexpected sharpness, "I take care of my own self."

"Regardless, I can't rub two nickels together. I had to borrow the money just to make this trip, so I don't have any money for a hotel. I was just going to spend the night in the bus station and leave on the first bus in the morning."

Cass looked appalled. "First of all, you're not staying in any hotel. Second, no family of mine is sleeping in a bus station."

Toya wanted to tell her she wasn't her family, not really. But the connection that loomed in the air, the promise of family, kept her from saying anything.

"So seriously, come back to my house, let's talk. I would like it if you and I could finally get to know each other. We can pop open a bottle of wine, pick up some wings, and talk, Toya. I mean, you took the time to come here," Cass said apologetically. "Unless you've got family to get back to?"

"So you just want to go back to your place so we can bond, huh?" Toya said sarcastically. Inside, though, she felt a small flutter at the idea of spending time getting to know Cass. Maybe, just maybe, they'd really connect. She shook off that thought. Her family was back in Flint, mad as hell at her betrayal. No, Amos had destroyed any hopes she had of a real family, and sitting around chatting with this woman about how perfect her life had been with her stepdaddy wasn't something Toya looked forward to doing.

"I think it's time. Don't you? I think it's past time."

Toya eyed her skeptically.

"If you don't want wings, I make a mean shrimp alfredo," Cass offered. "I could whip us up some, crack open a bottle of Moscato, and we could just chill."

Cass had a look of desperation in her eyes. Like she couldn't endure taking care of Amos alone anymore. Toya nodded. She'd stay. Maybe not for Amos. But she'd stay to see what would come of this new arrangement.

# Tomiko

New York City was abuzz as usual. The streets swarmed with tourists. Above them, the night sky was cloudless. A quarter moon followed them all the way to the red door of what looked to be a warehouse. A tall dark man wearing a white T-shirt and a skullcap nodded at Greg and opened the door.

Tomiko stepped inside and was immediately struck by the elegance of the place. Dozens of round tables draped in white tablecloths and holding towering crystal vases dripping with colorful flowers filled the dimly lit space.

"What is this place?" Tomiko asked as the maître d' guided them toward a table.

"Heaven."

Tomiko laughed. "No, really?"

"I'm not joking, it's called Heaven."

In the center of the room sat a high box-shaped stage made of glass.

"Dinner and a show?"

"Why of course!"

The maître d' pulled out Tomiko's chair, and she sat down. He placed the menus down before both of them and then proceeded to unfold their cloth napkins and lay them across their laps. Tomiko perused the menu—all top-notch dishes, many of which she'd never heard of and many more of which she could not pronounce.

Greg peeked over the top of his menu and said, "Do you see anything you like?"

"I see many, many things."

Just as she was about to rattle off what she found interesting, the musicians filed onto the stage. Four older gentlemen. All black except one, who was Asian. They began playing a tune by B. B. King and then sailed off to other blues standards that Tomiko recognized from her childhood. The music unearthed a host of memories—some sweet, many others not so sweet. She almost felt as if she had left her body and was back in Detroit. She was a little girl seated on the couch, dressed in her pajamas, clutching a battered but beloved doll. Across the room, her father had his fingers curled over the row of black-and-white piano keys, a cigarette dangling from between his lips.

Tomiko was so lost in her memories that she didn't hear the waiter ask if she'd decided what she would be having for dinner. After a moment, Greg waved the waiter away, closed his menu, and leaned back into his chair. He watched as a range of emotions rippled across Tomiko's face and wondered if something other than the music was pulling at her heartstrings.

After dinner and two glasses of wine, Greg took Tomiko's hand and led her out to the dance floor. A woman had joined the band, a songstress with an angelic voice. Tomiko hadn't slow-danced in years. She felt nervous, but the trepidation melted away as soon as Greg pressed himself against her. They slowly swirled to the music. He led, and she followed as easily

as if they'd been dancing together for a decade. So close to
him, she could smell the light scent of his cologne and feel his
lean muscled body. She wanted to close her eyes and surrender
to the moment, but she couldn't. The band was a distraction,
even a nuisance. Their music had reached into her memory
banks and pulled out every single melody her father had ever
pounded out on his beloved piano.

Greg could feel Tomiko's body tensing and relaxing, as if
she was warring with herself. Instead of asking if everything
was okay, he pulled her closer, held her tighter.

Back at the table, they ordered and consumed their dessert
in comfortable silence. Tomiko glanced at her watch and realized it was nearly midnight. She was both glad and sad that the
evening was inching to a close. She didn't want to leave Greg,
but she was desperate to escape the memories the music continued to uncover.

The bandleader called, "Last set." And the musicians
launched into "Moody's Mood for Love."

Lost in her thoughts, Tomiko forgot where she was and
began to croon along to the song. Greg looked up from his
dessert and gazed at her in wonder.

"So you're a writer *and* a singer, huh?"

Tomiko's head snapped up.

"You have a really beautiful voice."

Tomiko blushed. "Thank you."

Greg's eyes sparkled. "So what else are you keeping from
me?"

Outside, the night air had taken on a bite, and Tomiko
wrapped her arms around herself and shivered.

"Here," Greg said as he shrugged off his jacket and draped it over her shoulders. "Better?"

"Yes, thank you."

They strolled in silence for a block. "Did you like the restaurant, the food, the music?" Greg asked.

Tomiko nodded. "Yes, it was all very lovely. Thank you so much for bringing me."

"My pleasure. I suspect, though, that either your most favorite part or your least favorite part was the music."

Tomiko stopped and turned to him. "Why is that?"

"Well," Greg began carefully, "I was watching you listen to the music, and sometimes it seemed as if you wanted to smile and other times . . . well, I thought you might break into tears."

It was Tomiko's turn to be amazed. "You gleaned all of that just from watching me?"

"You have a very expressive face."

This was true. Tomiko began walking again.

"I grew up listening to that type of music." She spoke to the pavement. "My father was a musician."

"Ahhh, the elusive father," Greg whispered. "I did notice every time I mention your family you shy away from the subject."

"Yeah, well, I didn't exactly come from a happy home."

Even as she spoke, Tomiko could not believe that she was sharing this with a man who was still, by all accounts, a stranger to her.

"My father just picked up and left one day, and that was that." Tomiko threw her hands up into the air.

"I guess it still hurts, huh?"

"Yeah, sometimes more than others—"

"Like tonight?"

"It was a little painful."

"Sorry."

"Nothing to be sorry about. I'm the screwed-up one."

Greg caught her by the shoulders and spun her slowly around to face him. "Why would you say something like that?"

"I-I don't know." She huffed and then said, "All the statistics say that kids from broken homes often end being a little . . . let's say 'off-center.'" She laughed to cover up the embarrassment she was feeling.

Greg's eyes bored into hers. "I know you don't believe that."

She did, and she didn't. But really, why else was she unable to maintain a relationship? Here she was, well into her thirties, and she was still terrified of the prospect of marriage.

"Sometimes I do believe it."

Maybe it was her melancholy, the magic of the evening, or a natural attraction to the pathetic . . . but whatever it was compelled Greg to lean in and kiss her. It was a passionate and provocative kiss that left Tomiko breathless.

"I'm sorry, I-I don't know what came over me," Greg stammered stupidly.

Tomiko smiled. "It's okay, I enjoyed it." After a moment she added, "It was sweet."

They gazed at each other, their passion igniting again, and then they turned awkwardly around and started down the street. His hand reached for hers, and their fingers entwined. Her Jeep was parked just ahead of his. Greg opened her driver's-side door, and Tomiko climbed in.

"Will you call me when you get home?"

"Of course," Tomiko said as she slid the key into the ignition.

Greg gently pushed the door closed. "So for our next date I'm going to come to your side of the world."

The engine turned over, and Tomiko stretched the safety belt over her chest. "And when, pray tell, will that be?"

Greg rolled his eyes up to the dark sky and scratched his chin.

"Hmmm," he sounded. "How does tomorrow sound?"

"What?" Tomiko laughed.

"Breakfast?"

Tomiko glanced at the digital clock embedded in the dashboard. The numbers glowed: 12:45 a.m.

"Well, it's already tomorrow."

Greg looked at his watch. "So it is," he said, and walked away.

Tomiko was puzzled. She leaned out of the window as Greg climbed into his Jeep. "Hey," she yelled, "what's going on?"

He slammed his car door, and then the engine of his Jeep roared to life. The headlights came on, and Tomiko used her hand to protect her eyes.

"What the—" she whispered to herself as her cell phone began to ring. It was Greg. "H-hello?"

"Well, what are you waiting for?"

"What?"

"You know, you say 'What?' entirely too often."

Tomiko began to giggle.

"I'm going to make you breakfast."

"Where?"

"On your side of the world. Just drive."

Tomiko still wasn't sure exactly what was going on, but she shifted the car into drive, glanced in her side- and rear-view mirrors, and slowly pulled away from the curb. Greg kept close as they convoyed down the West Side Highway and then through the Holland Tunnel. Tomiko was so giddy with excitement that she'd totally forgotten her hard-and-fast rule about allowing strangers—even strangers she was really, truly falling for—know where she lived. A slither of panic crept through her as she maneuvered the car onto Route 22 and pointed the nose of the Jeep toward home.

"Stop it, girl," she chastised herself aloud. "The man isn't a serial killer." The statement and the tone sounded more like her mother's than it did her own. Tomiko's leg began to bounce with excitement.

As she turned into the driveway, the motion lights surrounding the house came on, washing the house and the three acres of land around it in bright white light. The garage door rolled up, and Tomiko pulled inside. The garage was large enough for three cars, so Greg pulled his Jeep alongside hers.

Greg climbed out and surveyed the surroundings. "All of this from writing children's books?"

"Yep."

"Nice. Very nice."

They exited the garage through a simple doorway, which opened into a spacious kitchen. Tomiko flicked on the lights, and Greg let off a shrill whistle.

"Now this is a kitchen!"

The kitchen resembled something out of *Gourmet* magazine with its red-tiled backsplash, granite countertops, and stainless steel appliances.

Greg rolled up his sleeves and moved to the sink, where he

proceeded to wash and dry his hands. Tomiko watched with amusement as he opened the refrigerator and gazed inside.

"Make yourself at home, why don't you!"

"Thanks, I will," Greg said over his shoulder.

Tomiko settled herself in one of the four tall chairs that surrounded the island. "Maybe I can help you find what you're looking for."

"Nope, I'm fine," Greg said as he began to haul out items of food.

"So we're going to have breakfast right now at"—Tomiko looked down at her wristwatch—"one thirty in the morning?"

"Yep."

"Greg, we just had dinner and dessert a few hours ago!"

Greg walked from one cabinet to the next until he found the one that held the bottled seasonings. He examined a few and then grinned at her. "You like to cook, don't you?"

"Yes, I do. I find it therapeutic."

This seemed to make him extremely happy, and his grin widened.

"Believe me," he said as he pulled a bowl from beneath the island and set it in the sink, "by the time I'm done cooking, you'll be more than ready to eat again."

As always, the conversation moved easily. When Tomiko turned the radio on, both sang to each and every song that was played. At one point, they sought to reinvent the seventies and did the bump all the way into the family room.

The voice in the back of her mind pestered her: This is too perfect—something's wrong!

Tomiko turned the volume up on the radio and drowned it out. She wasn't going to worry about tomorrow or the what-ifs. Right now she was happy, and that's all that mattered.

Spinach frittata, turkey sausage, roasted fingerling potatoes, and two cups of steaming hot coffee. Tomiko leaned back in her chair and patted her belly. "I think I'm going to burst!"

Outside, the sky was beginning to move from a deep purple to a pale blue. "Let's go out and watch the sun rise," he said as he extended his hand to her.

They had a perfect view from the deck. Greg stood behind Tomiko and curled his arms around her shoulders. She could feel his heart thumping against her back.

"So what do you think about all of this?"

"This . . . this?" Tomiko laughed.

"Yeah."

"Well, I don't know. Marjorie says I overthink things, so I'm not thinking at all. Just relishing."

Greg laughed and squeezed her. "Are you religious, Tomiko?"

Tomiko had to think about it. "I would say spiritual."

"Me, too. And I think there was something profound about our meeting where we did."

"At the hospital?"

"Yeah, but more specifically, over the new baby."

"I don't think I follow," Tomiko said, twisting her head around so she could see his face. His eyes were bloodshot from lack of sleep. He wore a serious expression on his face.

"We met over Marjorie and Dwight's newborn baby."

Tomiko still wasn't following. Greg's eyes found hers.

"I think she was the catalyst for us."

Tomiko went warm all over. "That is really beautiful, Greg."

Greg blushed. "Well . . ."

Tomiko pecked him on his chin. "You are some kind of sweet."

"Look, look," Greg spouted with excitement, "here it comes!"

The yellow crown of the sun peeked over the horizon. Tomiko had seen many sunrises, but this one was the most beautiful of them all.

"Tomiko Davis," Greg whispered in her ear. "I think I want to know every single thing about you."

Tomiko beamed and thought, Oh man, wait till I tell Marjorie!

# Amos

"Come on, Amos! You can do it! You've got to do this!"
Amos grunted in pain as he struggled to move that leg at the hip. But anytime he put any weight on it, it hurt like hell. "I'm trying!"

"I know it's not easy," said Jill, the physical therapist. "I know it hurts, but you've got to—"

He stopped walking and yelled over his shoulder, "Don't keep telling me what I've got to do! I know what to do, dammit!"

Amos was at war with himself. His mind wanted his body to do something that his body couldn't do and it frustrated the hell out of him. The pain of trying to walk again after his accident had been nothing short of torture. Amos had been in therapy for over a month and he still wasn't able to walk like he used to. This damn hip of his just wasn't the same, and he was beginning to doubt that he'd ever be able to walk again with his old swagger.

An hour later, his hip throbbed so badly that it made him want to cuss out everybody who looked at him. One of the nurses wheeled him into the cafeteria, propped him behind a table, and then came back a few minutes later with what was supposed to have been pork chops, mashed potatoes, gravy, and green beans. Amos rolled his eyes at it, knowing instinctively that it would have about as much flavor as a paper napkin.

"Can I get some salt please?" he called out to no one in particular. He waited, but when no one came to him with any salt, he scanned the room and saw some on one of the tables across the room. Amos pressed a button on his wheelchair and started toward it when one of his wheels caught against a nearby chair leg.

"Watch it!" an old man complained, then muttered, "Bastard."

"Who you calling a bastard, you motha'—"

"Amos!" Iris called to him from across the room. Amos continued over to get the salt, then turned his chair around and motored back to his table.

Moments later, Iris showed up with a woman. "You've got a visitor."

Amos liberally applied salt to his food. He didn't even bother to look up. "I'm eating," he said, gruffly.

Iris pulled the chair on the other side of the table for the person to sit in. Amos wasn't in no damn mood for Iris.

"Amos," Iris said again. "Put your fork down. You've got company."

Amos dropped the fork, huffed, and stared across the table at a face that looked too much like his own not to know who she was.

Toya looked like she was seeing a ghost.

Jesus! Why now, Toya? he wanted to say. Amos's hip was kicking his behind. He was starving for some real food. He was tired, and all he wanted was for somebody to take his ass home!

She started crying even before he words came. "I guess

you're still not happy to see me." Toya swallowed, picked up a paper napkin, and wiped her eyes with it.

He didn't need this. Not now. This was not the time for Toya to show up here crying.

"I didn't mean to cry," she said. "I didn't think I would."

"I'll leave you two alone," Iris said, turning to walk away.

Amos caught her. "I need something for my hip." He looked helplessly at Iris. "I'm in a lot of pain, and I need something for my hip."

"I'll get you something later," Iris told him, glancing at Toya. "Nice to meet you."

She nodded.

Amos could hardly take his eyes off of her. That last time he'd seen this girl she'd been . . . young.

Toya looked as reluctant to be here as he felt to have her here. He found it hard to catch his breath.

"How have you been?" she asked politely.

He grimaced at the pain shooting through his body. He felt sick to his stomach, that's how he felt. He felt like if Toya was going to come here, then she should've come a long time ago or not at all, but she definitely shouldn't have come today.

"I've been better," he said, bluntly.

She sat there. Dammit! If Toya was going to come here, then she could've at least had something to say.

"Cass called me," she finally offered. "Said you'd been in an accident and that you weren't doing too well."

"She was right," he shot back impatiently.

"It was her idea for me to come—Amos."

*Amos?*

"Cass don't come around too often, so I don't know what kinda ideas she's got in her head."

"She thought you might need someone to take care of you."

All of a sudden, Amos knew what she was doing. Now he understood why'd she'd come here. "I ain't coming back," he snapped.

The woman had the nerve to look hurt, but he knew better. Melba Jean was about as hurt as a rock. "You think I don't know what you up to, Melba Jean? You think I'm not smart enough to see what you doing?"

"What?"

"You too damn much, woman! Too desperate—won't even let a man breathe, but I told you—I'm *through* with you. I was through a long time ago."

She was as sneaky as a snake and just as mean as one, too, if you weren't careful. Melba Jean tricked him, made him lose every bit of common sense he'd had, long enough to try to get him to believe she loved him.

"You got no idea what love is," he continued. "Go ahead! Cry, Melba Jean! Go on and cry, because I ain't falling for it this time! You not dragging me into this mess!"

"What's wrong with you?"

"You what's wrong with me!" He slammed his fists down on the table. "I'm tired of it! I'm tired of your mess—of your nonsense! And I'm sure as hell tired of you! I ain't walking away from my music! Every last one of y'all is the same! But I ain't doing it!"

"Amos!"

Women pushed and pulled and pulled and pushed! Women staked claim to him and tried to turn him into something he wasn't! They tried to turn him against the only thing he ever gave a damn about, and Amos was sick and damn tired of every last one of them!

"What happened? What did I do?" She stood up.

"That's right! Leave! Get the hell out of my house! I don't want you! I never did, Melba Jean! Get out of my damn—"

"Miss! You should leave."

"Out of the way, miss! Step back!" one of the nurses said, gently pushing her aside. "Oh my God! Code Blue! He's going into cardiac arrest!"

# Cass

She had no idea how Alma had pulled this off, but in a matter of days, since she'd last spoken to the woman, Cass was getting ready to go to a black-tie event of Chrysler's new coming-out extravaganza called New Beginnings.

"It's some of *what* you know, but it's most definitely who you know," Alma had bragged when she'd called to tell Cass about the event. "Everybody who's anybody will be at this thing, Cass, and it's going to be our opportunity to come out and let all of Detroit know that C&A Event Planning is out in force!" Alma had some of that rah-rah-sis-boom-bah in her voice, and it had rubbed off on Cass.

"Bring your business cards, girl, wear your best dress, get your hair done, nails, toes, go all out for this, Cass. Spare no expense. If we want to be a big deal, then we've got to look like a big deal!"

Cass's heart raced with excitement. "Is uh . . . Darryl going to be there?" She had to ask. Cass had to know. Darryl had agreed to be a part of this with Cass and Alma, and since their last meeting at that old warehouse, he was all Cass could think about.

Alma laughed. "Of course," she promised. "You just make sure you give him an eyeful of all those unspoken promises you've got tucked away for him, and let nature take its course."

The night of the event, Cass stood in her bedroom admiring her reflection in the full-length mirror on her closet door.

Long, dark strands of hair she'd paid good money for now hung loosely down to just below her shoulder blades. Tonight, Cass had bangs and the kind of hair she had only ever dreamed about. To her, *weave* had always been a dirty word, but now she loved every single strand. The way it looked on her took her breath away.

Cass had spent every free minute shopping for the perfect dress. She'd even had her makeup done at one of those makeup counters in the mall right after she'd gotten her hair done. She had taken Alma's advice, too. Her first inclination had been to wear black. Black was slimming and hid things that needed hiding. But while she was shopping, Alma's influence lured her away from black and toward colors that were bright and vivid and full of life.

Spanx was her new best friend, and the satin-silk gown she slipped over her head fell like a waterfall cascading past her curves to the floor. Red. Cass looked like a beautiful black china doll, and she felt like Cinderella on her way to the ball to meet her prince. Life was too short, and she'd let too much of hers slip away. Tonight, though, Cass was going to step up and take what she wanted from it.

Cass showed up about twenty minutes after the start of the event. For another twenty minutes she sifted through the crowd looking for Alma and, more importantly, Darryl.

"Cass?"

The sound of Darryl's voice caused her stomach to flutter. He walked over, looking her up and down and staring wide-eyed with something that looked a lot like admiration on his face.

"Whoa!" he exclaimed, holding out both hands to take hold of hers. "You look amazing!" Darryl tugged on her hands and kissed her cheek.

Cass giggled. "Thank you."

"My goodness!" he said, his eyes trailing up and down the length of her. "Wow!"

"You look pretty amazing yourself," she said, admiring him in his black suit and pristine white button-down shirt. Darryl was classy. That was just one of the things she loved about him.

"Tonight's our big night, sweetheart," he said excitedly. "We're going to book every major gig from here to Indiana by the time this is all said and done."

"It all happened so fast," she said, taking a deep breath. "Alma was right. This is definitely the place to be tonight. I don't think Detroit has ever seen a party like this," she laughed. "Did you bring business cards?"

He smiled. "Hundreds."

This working relationship was going to be heaven, and any other relationship that may develop between Cass and this man was going to be the icing on that heavenly cake.

"I'm going to have to remember to thank Alma all over again." Cass smiled. Her BFF was an angel.

"Is she here?" Darryl asked.

Cass shook her head. "Not yet, but she called and said she was on her way." Her cell phone rang, and without bothering to see who was calling, Cass answered. "Alma?" she asked before the person even had a chance to say hello.

"Ms. Edwards?" a woman asked.

Not Alma.

"Yes," Cass said irritably.

"Ms. Edwards, this is Sunnyview Assisted Living Center. Your father has been taken to the hospital."

Cass's heart dropped into her stomach. "What?"

"He's had a heart attack, ma'am. He's being rushed into surgery as we speak. He's been taken to—"

Before she could finish telling Cass what hospital Amos had been rushed to, Cass hung up, and was then stunned by what she'd just done. It hadn't been intentional. She hadn't meant to do it, but—

"Can I buy you a drink, Ms. Edwards?" Darryl magically appeared by her side and held out a glass of champagne. Cass was speechless.

"Here's to us," he said, smiling and locking his gaze with hers. "May we have a long, prosperous, and beautiful future together." Darryl clinked his glass with hers, raised it to his lips, and took a sip.

Cass stood there like a statue.

"Oh, God!" she muttered. Amos had had a heart attack, was on his way into surgery, and she'd hung up on the nurse who'd called with the news? What had she just done?

"Oooh! Hot momma!" Alma's voice pierced through Cass's disbelief.

Alma smiled. "I am so loving it!" she squealed. "The hair, the dress! You look oh so sexy, girl! Dang!"

"You look gorgeous yourself, Alma." She managed to smile.

Alma folded her in a long, excited hug. "It's going to be a fabulous night, Cass! We are going to start leaving our mark on this town tonight, girl!"

Cass nodded. Yes, Amos had made his own bed. He had burned too many bridges and broken too many hearts in his lifetime. He had lived like a king when he was younger, doing whatever he wanted, however he wanted, and to whomever he wanted. The fact that he now was an old man, alone, was his own fault.

She didn't need to go. She had done what she was supposed to do. She'd put him in that nursing home and she'd found at least one of his biological children to be there for him now. Cass had no reason to feel guilty. None.

All that and more she kept telling herself as the long night wore on. Until a very short time ago she hadn't even known Amos was still alive. She hadn't wanted to visit him. She had no obligation to visit. She had even been cooking greens for him. She didn't have to do that. She had done more for him than anyone could have expected. So why, on a night so full of hope, did she feel so guilty?


It was nearly two in the morning when the party ended. The three of them stood outside in the parking lot leaning against Alma's car.

"Looks like we're going to be busy over the next couple of months," Alma said, scrolling through her BlackBerry. "We managed to book three events tonight." She looked at her partner. "First thing tomorrow, Miss Cass—we start looking for some help for you."

"I'll take it," Cass said without protest.

"No argument this time?" Alma asked, surprised.

"Not one, girl."

"Good." Alma sighed and picked up her purse. "I'm exhausted, and it's time to go."

As soon as she started to leave, Darryl blocked her path. "Uh, how about a cup of coffee?" he asked Alma.

"Oh, no, but you two go right ahead," she said, indicating Cass.

Darryl wasn't looking at Cass, though. As a matter of fact, he couldn't take his eyes off Alma.

"Just a quick cup, Alma?" He glanced at Cass. "I'm sure Cass is probably ready to go home."

All of a sudden, Cass felt destroyed. She stared back and forth between Darryl and Alma, unwilling to believe that he was actually trying to get rid of her.

"Just a quick stop," he said to Alma. "My treat."

Alma looked at Cass, but Cass had received the unspoken message.

"You two go ahead," Cass finally said, her heart plummeting into her stomach like a rock. "My feet are killing me."

And besides, Amos was in the hospital. For all she knew, this was karma coming back to bite her in the ass. The man was having heart surgery, for crying out loud. Her stomach twisted in knots at how she'd acted when she got that call. Cass hurried off without saying another word, and praying with every ounce of energy that she had left that Amos was still alive.

# Toya

She'd spent the last two nights at Cass's place "to talk and to get to know one another" like Cass had asked, but Cass had been the one to do all the talking. Toya just listened, sipped wine, and nibbled on the woman's shrimp alfredo. Mostly, she stayed in her room and tried to figure out what to do next. Seeing Amos had crushed her. But then, that's the effect he'd always had on Toya. The staff at the nursing home had said that he was having an "episode," but it didn't matter. He was still Amos and she was still no more than an afterthought in his life.

Toya stood outside the door to Amos's hospital room. Her heart ached in anticipation. She hated her father, but she wasn't ready for him to die. She took a deep breath and eased open the door to his room. She froze at the sight of the frail old man, tubes coming from every part of his body, looking like he was peeking his head through death's door.

Tears welled up in Toya's eyes. He looked like he'd deteriorated overnight. She was amazed at the pain she felt in her heart and saddened that the vibrant memory she had of the good-looking, charismatic man would be replaced with this.

"You've got to be his daughter," said an attractive chocolate brotha who came up alongside her.

Toya slowly nodded. "I'm . . . I'm Toya. How is he?" she asked, looking back at Amos.

The man sighed. "He's hanging in there. The old man is tougher than he looks. I'm not his doctor, but they said it was pretty bad."

Toya's heart jumped.

"I'm Mark," the man said. "You plan on staying a little while? I haven't known Amos long, but I do know that his eyes light up when he talks about his music and his daughters. That's the only time I see that grumpy old man show any kind of joy."

His daughters? The concept sounded out of place in context with Amos. A familiar twinge of jealousy stirred age-old insecurities that seemed impossible to get rid of. "He doesn't need me here. Cass should be on her way. The nurse at the front desk called her."

"He needs you. He doesn't know that he needs you, but he does."

*He* needed *her*? How ironic. Amos had never been there when *she* needed *him*.

Mark must have been reading her mind because he gently patted Toya's arm. "I don't know your history, but that man right there loves you."

Toya turned to him, startled, and the man nodded gravely. "How would you know that? Has he ever asked about me? Has he ever even mentioned my name—Toya?"

From the look on his face, Toya knew that this Mark had never even heard of her until she showed up here.

"He's not perfect, and he knows it. He's made plenty of mistakes, and he knows that, too." He shrugged. "And sometimes, forgiveness is the best way out of heartbreak."

"No amount of forgiveness in the world could heal the damage done to my heart by my father," she tearfully admitted. "Do you know why I came?" She continued without waiting for an answer. "To see if he'd changed, if I'd changed. I came here to see if any of this mattered anymore to me and to look him in the face and to be able to finally say to him, you're dismissed Amos Davis. And I don't miss you anymore."

He stood there looking dumfounded because what could he possibly have to say now? Singing Amos's praises to her was wasted effort. And Toya knew that one way or another, this visit here now, would be the last one she ever paid to her father.

Mark left Toya alone in the room, and she reluctantly made her way over to Amos's bed. She didn't know whether to take his hand or just stand there, gawking. All of a sudden, Amos slowly began to open his eyes, turned his head slightly, and looked over at Toya. She froze, expecting him to go off on her again, accusing her of being her mother or reminding her of just how little Toya, his daughter, had ever actually meant to him.

"I'm sorry, Toya." Amos swallowed.

She stood there like a statue.

"I hurt you. Of all of them." His voice cracked and a single tear slid down the side of his face. "I hurt you the most."

That's all he said before closing his eyes again. If not for the steady beat of the machine, she would've thought that he'd up and died. Toya fought back the tears. She'd been waiting a lifetime for him to acknowledge her. And now that he had them, they released a river of tears. Was it really that simple? Amos said he was sorry and Toya felt the dam of relief burst inside her. "You should be sorry," she said, not knowing if he could even hear her. "You should be sorry for the rest of your miserable-ass life, Amos!" Toya cupped her mouth with her hand and ran out of the room.

Afterward, she waited outside the ICU. The only other place left for her to go now was back to Flint. She had done what she needed to do. Toya had come here, she'd seen him, and she'd gotten an apology from him. And it was over. Amos might live or he might die, but it didn't matter.

The next bus didn't leave until two in the afternoon, and it was just now three in the morning. She'd left a mess back home. Toya realized now that she'd grown complacent living in messy places and it was time for her to make some serious changes, beginning with herself. She'd never wanted to admit that her lack of self respect had come as a result of Amos's abandonment, but shit. She'd allowed herself to accept less than, to be less than, because she'd been shown that she was. His apology to her wasn't the end, but it was a beginning; deathbed confession or not, she'd take it. Yes. He was sorry. Yes. He should've been sorry. Yes. He'd hurt her. And yes. She was ready to move on.

Like mother like daughter? "Not anymore," she said, wiping her eyes. Melba Jean could take that crap to the grave with her if she wanted to. Toya wasn't having it.

"Toya?"

Cass appeared out of nowhere and stood over Toya, wearing a fire-red strapless dress with long dark tresses flowing down her shoulders.

Cass sat down next to her. "How's he doing?"

Really? Toya looked at this woman as if she'd lost her mind. "Didn't they call you when it happened?" Toya asked bitterly.

Cass looked away.

"You were a princess back then, and you're a princess now." Toya shook her head in disgust.

"What?" Cass turned back to Toya. "What are you talking about?"

"They called you when it happened, Cass. I was there. I heard the nurse at the front desk of that nursing home call you when they were taking him to the hospital. And you just now getting here?" She looked Cass up and down. "Was the party that damn good that you couldn't get here to see about him before now?"

"I've been here for him, Toya," Cass argued, trying to keep her voice down. "I've been here since they pulled him out of that car he'd wrapped around that pole. Where've you been?"

"Does it matter?" Toya asked angrily. "You his number one girl, Cass. Amos chose you and your momma over me and mine a long time ago, so to me"—she shrugged—"it makes sense that you should be his go-to girl in all of this."

"Really? Thirty damn years later and you still harping on that? We were kids, Toya. What Amos did, who he sup- posedly chose, had nothing to do with either one of us. You a grown woman now. We both are. Amos is your father. Not mine."

"That's not what he'd say," Toya shot back smugly. What was it about her that made her so much better than Toya? What made him want to claim her as his own and not claim Toya? "Amos was my sperm donor, and that's all he was. He didn't take care of me. He didn't take me to school or sit me on his lap and bounce me on his knee. I told you I'd come to see him, and I did. But Amos ain't my responsibility. Just like I've never been his."

Toya had no idea where she would go. She had enough money to catch a cab to the bus station, but that was it. Thankfully, she'd bought a round-trip ticket to get her home, but she wasn't sitting here another minute. That was Cass's job.

"Toya." Mark was stepping off the elevator as she was getting ready to walk in. "Where you going?"

"Home," she said, trying to keep from crying.

"Did you talk to your father? How's he doing? How're you doing?"

Toya felt herself start to unravel. She was so tired. All she wanted to do was to curl up in her own bed, pull the covers over her head, and go to sleep.

"I don't know," she said, frustrated. "I'm tired, okay. I need to— I need to get out of here."

"You got a hotel? You got a room?"

She shook her head. "I'll be fine."

Cass must've heard them, because she came right over. "Mark? What are you doing here?"

He dug her. Toya could see it on his face as soon as he laid eyes on the woman. Of course! Leave it to the princess to pull a nice-looking brotha like this.

"I uh . . . I've been here for awhile. Just went down to get a cup of coffee." He left Toya standing there and walked over to Cass. "Have you seen him? How's he doing?"

Cass looked at Toya. "I just got here. Toya's been here the whole time."

"Yeah, I know. Toya?" Mark held the doors open and turned to her. "Can I give you a ride?"

She couldn't help it. Toya was exhausted, and Amos had crushed her again. She suddenly broke down crying, sobbing like a baby in front of both of them.

"Toya," she heard Cass say. The woman had nerve to come over to her and put her hands on her.

Toya lashed out. "Get your hands off me!"

"She was just trying to help," Mark said, stepping up to them.

"Stay away from me!" she warned them both. Toya had done her part. She'd come here and looked that old fool in the eyes.

"I'll take you home, Toya," Cass begged. "Back to my place. You can get some rest."

Toya pushed Cass. "Leave me alone. I'm through, Cass. I've done what I needed to do. He's not my problem anymore. He's yours."

"Cass, he had an episode," Mark chimed in.

"You don't need to go sit in some bus station all night. Come home with me, take a shower, get some rest, and I'll take you to the bus station after you wake up."

Toya desperately craved a shower, but not enough to go home with Cass.

"It's the least I can do, Toya. You came all this way, girl. Just . . . I know you don't want to leave like this."

"It's a good idea, Toya," Mark said. "In fact, why don't both of you go home, and I'll hang out here with the old man. I'll give you a call if his condition changes."

Merciful God, Cass kept her mouth shut in the ride home. Toya could hardly keep her eyes open. By the time they made it to Cass's place, Toya was practically sleepwalking.

"What time does your bus leave?" she asked Toya.

"There's one leaving at two o'clock," Toya said groggily.

"I'll get you there before two," Cass said, leaving Toya.

The warm shower was like a sedative. Toya finished, slipped into her nightgown, fell into the bed, and drifted off into a weighted sleep.

# Tomiko

Tomiko was dreaming about feathers. Hundreds and hundreds of feathers raining down from the sky. She was laughing, but her laughter sounded like the chime of her telephone.

When she finally broke free of her dream and opened her eyes, she realized it *was* the phone.

She couldn't place where she was. Her gaze searched through the early morning gray that filled the hotel room. As she fumbled for the phone, she tried to recall the previous day's events. She remembered leaving her New Jersey home, climbing into a limo, and being whisked off to Newark Airport, where she'd boarded a flight.

She pressed the phone to her ear. "Yeah?"

"Miko?"

It was her mother.

"Yes?"

"Where are you?"

Tomiko rubbed her eyes and yawned. The past day's sequence was all coming back to her now. She'd received a phone call from Mark Sheridan, the nurse who had contacted her about Amos.

*"Tomiko, Amos had a heart attack," the nurse had explained. "He's in surgery right now."*

*It was just after seven in the evening her time. "Oh my God! Is he going to be all right?"*

*Mark sighed. "I don't have all the details, but it's pretty serious. You might want to think about trying to get here."*

*"Yeah! Of course, Mark. I'll be there as soon as I can."*

*Several hours later, she had called Mark as soon as her plane landed to get the name and address of the hospital where Amos had been admitted. "I should be there within the hour," she promised.*

*"Actually, it's late, and he's resting comfortably at the moment," Mark assured her. "He came through the surgery like a champ. Why don't you get some rest, Tomiko. Come by in the morning. I can call you if anything changes."*

*"Are you sure?"*

*"Yeah. Your sisters will be here, too, by then. It'll be one big family reunion," he laughed.*

*Her sisters?*


Mere hours later, Tomiko sat up in bed, looked around her hotel room with bleary eyes, and answered the phone. "Detroit," she whispered, reminding herself, "I'm in Detroit."

"What? You said you were going to call me when you got in," her mother fussed from the other end of the phone.

"Didn't I call?"

"No, you didn't."

Tomiko tilted her head toward the nightstand. The digital clock told her it was just after seven in the morning. "Why are you calling me so early?"

Tomiko could hear her mother suck in air.

"Because you are my child and I love you, and you didn't call to say you'd arrived."

"Sorry," Tomiko muttered. "There was a delay with my flight. I didn't get into town until after two a.m., so I just got a hotel room and crashed."

"Do you want to come over for breakfast?"

Tomiko balanced herself onto one elbow. "I can't, Mom." She took a deep breath. "I have to get to the hospital to check on my . . . to check on Amos."

Ruby responded with a timid "Amos?"

She'd told her mother that she was coming to town, but she hadn't told her why. "He had a heart attack. He's in ICU."

Her mother was quiet on the other end of the phone. "You've been in touch with him?" she eventually asked.

"I've spoken to him once." Tomiko could feel the tension seeping through the phone.

"How's he been?" Ruby reluctantly asked.

The relationship between Tomiko's mother and father had ended violently. Blows were thrown, blood had been shed, and when the smoke had cleared, Ruby had lost what little she had left of her dignity, and Amos had been gone.

"He's getting old, mom," Tomiko explained. Amos was nearly twenty years older than her mother. "He's been living in a nursing home. Daddy's got Alzheimer's."

"I'm so sorry to hear that, Miko," she said sincerely. "I mean that."

"Thanks, Mom." Miko smiled.

Whatever bitterness Ruby had once had for Amos had disappeared through the years. After they split up, Ruby eventually did make it to cosmetology school and got a job working with her aunt in her salon. She even managed to fall in love again and get married, which is how Tomiko ended up with two younger brothers who had made her life hell, growing up. But she wouldn't have traded them for the world.

"Will you call me and let me know how he's doing?"

Tomiko suddenly felt all right about being here. If Ruby could forgive him, shouldn't Tomiko be able to let go of the past and forgive him, too?

"I will, Mom. I'll call as soon as I can."

Tomiko hurried to get dressed, then went down the el-evator to the basement parking lot, where her rental car was parked in a dark bay. She rushed to the hospital.

Mark was gone by the time Tomiko arrived at the hospital, and if she did have any sisters there, she wouldn't have known them if they'd walked up and slapped her upside the head. A nurse showed her to Amos's room. He was asleep.

"Is he sedated?" she asked, concerned.

The nurse shook her head. "Just sleeping," the nurse assured her.

"Can I talk to him?"

"Yes," the woman smiled. "I think he'd like that."

She left, and Tomiko pulled a chair up next to his bed. Hot tears stung her eyes. She had been a little girl the last time she was this close to her father. It was one thing to see him on a computer screen, but something else actually to see him up close like this. Amos was real to her again, and all of a sudden, she remembered how much this man had meant to her grow-ing up—when he was in her life, and when he wasn't.

Tomiko leaned in close to him. "Daddy?" she whispered. "It's me. It's Miko," she said tearfully.

She stared long and hard at him, past the deep lines on his face, past the gray beard and hair, looking for the man who used to sing her songs and make up stories to tell her. He had seemed so perfect to her back then, but Tomiko wasn't a child anymore, and she understood that there was no such thing as perfection in anyone.

Amos had been guilty of his share of trespasses, but he had been there for the things that mattered, and it was those things that stayed with her all these years. He had broken her heart, but looking at him now, she could see that he had also broken his own. Amos had suffered losses in his life, too. He'd been hurt, he'd died a little inside like most people, and he'd pushed through long days of searching for that elusive dream of his that refused to be caught.

"Sittin' in the evenin' sun . . ." she began to sing to him, the way he'd sung to her. "I'll be sittin' till the evenin's done. . ."

He didn't leave her because he didn't love her. Amos left because he couldn't stop loving music. He couldn't stop running to it when it called to him. Tomiko was an artist, too. She'd inherited that from him, and to ignore her muse would've been impossible, so she understood. But his had been cruel. It had tortured him, and after it used him up, it had left behind a lonely old man with nothing but pain.

His eyes started to flutter; then they opened. Tomiko kept singing.

Amos blinked, and then he swallowed. He slowly turned his head to face her and looked into her eyes.

"I'm just sittin' on the dock of the bay," she continued. "Watchin' the tide roll away . . ."

# Cass

It was nine o'clock in the morning when Cass walked back into that hospital. She was surprised to see that Mark was still there, sleeping in the waiting area. He looked so peace-ful—he looked pretty good, as a matter of fact. She didn't want to wake him, so she crept by him on the way to the nurse's station.

"Hi. I'm Amos Davis's . . . daughter," she said. "He was brought here last night. Is he all right?"

"Amos is doing fine, all things considered," the woman said, smiling. "Your sister came in earlier to sit with him. We allow only one visitor at a time in the room, so if you'll take a seat in the waiting area, I'll let her know you're here."

Her sister? Cass nodded and went back to the area where she found Mark. Cass opted to sit across from him rather than next to him. He looked like that was some pretty good sleep he was getting, which made Cass a bit envious. She'd spent five hours tossing and turning and wrestling with her bedsheets. The last several hours had been nothing short of agonizing.

Cass had made a fool of herself over Darryl. She'd loved Darryl from afar, while he had been busy loving Alma, and last night it became all too clear to her that Cass had never stood a chance with that man. She wanted to cry, but she hadn't even had time to cry. Hearing that Amos had had a heart attack, and her response to the news—Cass shook her head in disgust at herself. She couldn't believe what she'd done when she got that call last night about his being rushed to the hospital. She knew better, her mother had raised her better than that, but Cass had convinced herself that since Amos never gave a damn about her, she didn't need to give a damn about him. *God hates ugly!* Her mother's warning came rushing back to her. Maybe if she'd gotten her act together and had told Darryl and Alma what was going on and then rushed to the hospital to be here for Amos, things would've worked out differently and Darryl would've realized that she was truly the woman for him after all. And then there was Toya. Period. She hated Cass *and* she hated Amos, and Cass was going to have to face that woman again to get her back to the bus station in time to catch that next bus out of Detroit.

"Hey."

She looked up at Mark to see him staring back at her. Cass was glad he was awake. "Hey."

"He made it through the night all right."

"You've been here the whole time?" she asked, stunned by his dedication to Amos.

Mark rubbed sleep from his eyes. "I left long enough to take a shower and grab a bite to eat, but yeah." He smiled.

Cass stared at him in awe. He really did care about that old man. She and Toya had grown up knowing Amos; they had loved Amos. But Mark barely knew the man. "Why?"

He looked surprised that she'd even asked. "He's my friend."

This dude was obviously running on only one cylinder. "Amos is your friend? How can Amos possibly be your friend, Mark? The two of you are not only decades apart in age, but you're as different as night and day."

He laughed. "We like the same music. We both love your cooking. He hates getting enemas. I hate giving enemas."

Cass laughed.

"We have a lot in common."

She just shook her head. If he wanted to use enemas as the basis for a friendship with Amos, then who was she to question it?

"How's Toya?" he asked, concerned.

Cass shrugged. "Pissed. I guess. I don't know. Toya and me, our mothers, Amos."

"I think I sort of get it."

"Amos isn't my father by blood, but he is hers. But I think I got more of him than she ever did," she explained, suddenly feeling more guilty about it than she had expected to. "When he and my mom split up, I was devastated," she explained, looking into Mark's handsome face. "I never had much to do with my real father, but that was fine because Amos was all the father I could want and need when I had him."

Maybe that's what it was about? Cass held on to the last statement she'd just made and pondered it quietly. When she had Amos, he was all the father she had ever needed. Her problems with Amos came when she no longer had him. That had been the problem for her mother, Linda, too.

"He made us fall in love with him," Cass continued, more to herself than to Mark. "More in love than we thought we could ever fall for any man, and then he took that away from us." Cass looked at Mark, realizing that he'd been witness to a very painful revelation.

"I don't think that's what he did, Cass," he explained tenderly. "I think he left the love he gave you, but he took himself away. And I think that's why it hurts."

Cass tried swallowing the lump swelling in the back of her throat, willing herself not to cry. She hated crying in front of people; she was not a pretty crier, and she definitely didn't want to cry in front of Mark, because she wanted him to think she was as pretty now as he'd thought she'd been last night.

"Amos has got demons. You understand that, don't you?" Mark went on to say. "I've seen them in that nursing home when he takes one of his trips back down memory lane. Amos's demon was his music, Cass. It took me a while to catch on, but in his memories, he's always afraid that somebody's going to try to take it from him, or take him away from it."

"He loved his music more than he could've possibly loved any of us."

"I don't believe that. I believe that he was tortured by his music, by his dreams of becoming something he was never able to become."

"Amos was a selfish, womanizing, manipulative user who took advantage of the people around him," she said calmly. "He used us until he was through with us, and then he left us."

He laughed. "Selfish, womanizing, and manipulative? Yeah. I

can see that. But there had to have been something good about him, Cass. You wouldn't have been so hurt over his leaving if there wasn't something good about him."

Cass had never really thought about it like that. What was good about Amos were those things that made her love him.

"Toya called you a princess last night. Is that how he made you feel?

She didn't answer, but she didn't need to. The look on her face must've said it for her.

"The old man's not perfect," Mark said, sighing. "I don't know anybody who is. But he's old, and he's not going to live forever. I'm not saying you should take him home with you and set him up in a room in your house. But I think you owe it to him and to yourself to try to make the most of what time he has left. And not for his sake. For yours."

Mark stopped talking and stared over Cass's head.

Cass turned around and looked at the woman standing behind her, who looked as dumbfounded at seeing Cass as Cass was at seeing her.

"I'm Tomiko?" She cleared her throat. "Tomiko Davis."


"Tomiko?" So that was her name. "I meant to write to you about Amos, but with everything going on, I—" Cass shrugged. "I'm sorry."

Tomiko was petite, with soft, natural curls pinned back away from her face. She had Amos's smile.

"I was surprised when I got Mark's e-mail, though, and he told me about Daddy. I had no idea that he had other children."

"Knowing Amos," Cass blurted out, "we're just the tip of

the iceberg." She regretted the words as soon as they were out of her mouth and wished with everything in her that she could take them back. "He's not my biological father, though. Amos and my mother got together when I was two. He's Toya's father."

"Toya?"

Cass nodded. "Yeah."

"Is she here in Detroit, too? Will she be coming to the hospital?"

"Sort of, and no. Toya is in Detroit, but she's leaving in a few hours to go back home to Flint. And no, she won't be coming back here."

Tomiko was no dummy. She sat there studying Cass's words like puzzle pieces.

"She doesn't want to see him."

"She tried seeing him before he had his heart attack, Tomiko. It didn't go well." Cass saw no reason to hold anything back now. For all she knew this could be the last time she ever laid eyes on Amos's daughter. "She and Amos have never been close. I think that was hard on her when she was a little girl, and she just hasn't gotten over it." There. She'd said it. She'd put Toya's business out there on the street for her half sister to see.

Tomiko's next words caught Cass off guard in a big way. "Have any of us?"

Cass wondered if she looked as shocked by that question as she felt.

"Until today, I hadn't seen my father since I was six, maybe seven. And until recently, I hadn't realized how much I hated him for that. I hadn't realized how much of an effect losing

Daddy had had on me even as a grown woman. Isn't that crazy?"

"No. No, it's not crazy at all."

Tomiko smiled. "He was awake when I left his room, Cass. Maybe you should go in and say hi to him."

# Toya

"Hello?" Toya answered the phone groggily. She'd slept so hard that she'd barely heard it ringing.

"Hey, baby. How you doing?" It was Max.

Toya's first instinct was to hang up on him, but right now, she welcomed the sound of his voice. "Tired."

"How's your father doing?" he asked, sounding genuinely concerned.

Toya pushed herself up in bed and leaned back against the headboard. "He's fine, I guess."

"You guess? You don't know?"

She sighed. "I don't care. How about that?"

"I don't get it, baby. What's up?"

If she had any tears left, Toya would've started to cry right, but she was running on empty. "What's up is that my father never gave a damn about me. And if I didn't know it before I took this trip, I certainly know it now."

"Toya," he said, scolding. "I know that can't be true."

"Why can't it be true, Max? You don't give a damn about me. No man I've ever been with has ever given a damn about me! So tell me why that can't be true?"

Max was silent on the other end of the phone.

"What else?" she asked abruptly. "What else do you want? Why'd you call?"

"I called to let you know that I give a damn about you, Toya. That's it."

"All right," she said definitively. "All right then, if that's true, Max, if you really do care about me, you'll lose my number. You'll stop calling me, stop trying to see me, and you'll keep that pit bull of a wife of yours off my behind! Do you understand me? At least do that much for me if you care! At least care enough to let me go!" This time, Toya did hang up on him.

After hanging up, Toya looked at the time on her phone. "Shit!"

She jumped out of bed and left the room to look for Cass. "Cass?" she called out, stomping through the house in her shirt and panties. "Cass!"

That heffa had let her sleep too late! Toya's bus had left for Flint twenty minutes ago and Cass was nowhere to be found! Toya was livid. The next bus didn't leave until two the next day! What the hell was she going to do for another whole day in Detroit? Toya had no money, no friends, no car! She was stranded in this town! Damn! She'd hung up on Max too soon. If she'd have known this would happen, she'd have demanded that he prove he cared about her by driving out here to get her!

The sound of keys turning in the front door lock got her attention, and lo and behold, Cass walked in with some other chick, who looked like her trusty sidekick.

"You up?" Cass sang out, looking as happy as a pig in slop.

"Yes, I'm up!" Toya shot back, driving her fist into her hip. "And I missed my damn bus, thanks to you!"

Cass's expression changed. "I'm sorry, Toya. You were sleeping when I left, and I didn't want to wake you. I didn't expect to be gone so long, but—"

"But nothing, Cass! Now I've got to wait until tomorrow to catch the next bus home! What the hell am I going to do until then? Hang out with *you*?"

"You know," Cass said, and tossed her purse down on the sofa, "I'm pretty damn tired of you talking to me any old way! I took you in, Toya, offered you a shower and a bed to sleep in! I'm sorry you missed your bus, but there'll be other buses!"

"So what you do you want? A trophy?" Toya was appalled. "Thank you for nothing, girl! Now I gotta be stuck here with you!"

"It could be worse, Toya! You could be on a bus right now headed back to— What did you say you got at home that's so important for you to get back to? Oh! That's right! Nothing! No job! No man! No nothing!"

"Will you two please stop!" Cass's little buddy stepped up and chimed in.

"Who the hell are you?" Toya blurted out indignantly.

"She's Amos's daughter! And your sister, fool!" Cass blurted.

"Cass!" the girl yelled.

"Her name is Tomiko!" Cass continued, unabated. "And so yeah! If you wanna be mad at me because Amos left you and your momma, then you can just go ahead and be mad at her, too, because he skipped over Melba Jean to get to her momma!"

"Cass!" Tomiko yelled again. "Stop it!"

Toya was shocked. So, this was Amos's precious little girl, Tomiko? This is the one whose name he uttered when Toya and her friends watched him perform live on television and he pretty much dissed the mess out of Toya live and in living color.

"Toya." Tomiko forced a smile and walked over toward Toya. "I had no idea that I had a . . . that Amos had other children. I mean, I suspected, but I didn't know."

Toya looked that woman up and down, wrinkling up her nose like she smelled like something foul.

"Put your hands on her, Toya, and it's me and you," Cass warned from across the room.

"Cass, will you please be quiet?" Tomiko demanded. "We're trying to work this out."

"We ain't trying to work out *nothing*," Toya shot back. "The two of you can hang around and play dress up, do each other's hair and nails if you want to." Toya turned and headed back upstairs. "I'm out."

She had forty dollars in her purse, which was hopefully enough to get a cab to the bus station. Toya was over this nonsense. She was going to go back to Flint, wash all this drama off of her, and work on getting something going for herself that didn't include Max—or any other married man—Cass, Tomiko, or Amos! She'd let that man define her for too long, and Toya was over it. He could live or he could die in that hospital, but the truth was, Amos Davis had died a long time ago in her heart.

Toya was so angry that she didn't even hear Tomiko come into the room. "He asked about you."

The sound of her voice startled Toya. "Leave me alone, Tomiko!" she said, shoving clothes into her small overnight bag.

Tomiko closed the door behind her. "He wants to see you, Toya."

Was this chick for real? "I'm not trying to see him," she grunted.

Tomiko sat down on the side of the bed. "You're not the only one he hurt, Toya," she explained tenderly. "He didn't just break your heart."

Toya stopped. "He was my father! And he refused to claim me, Tomiko! Oh, I knew all about Cass. I knew about you. I knew that he'd rather call both of you his daughter than me!" Toya glared at that woman. "I promise you, Amos couldn't have possibly hurt you the way he hurt me! I promise you that. I'm the one he didn't want. He made sure I knew it, too!"

Tomiko sat quietly for a few moments. Toya wished she'd just leave.

"When I was really little, Daddy used to make up stories for me," she started to say.

Toya cringed at the way that woman said the word *daddy*, like it was sweet, creamy butter melting on her tongue.

"He made them up because he couldn't read all that well."

Toya hadn't known that about him. But then again, there were a lot of things she didn't know about Amos.

"I used to think he was making up the names, but now I know better. He told me a story once about a little bird, and the bird was named Toya."

Toya stopped packing and looked at Tomiko.

"The bird had hurt its wing and it couldn't fly. He called it the prettiest bird he'd ever seen, and it was a sad story because all that the little boy in the story wanted to do was to fix that bird's wing." Tomiko shrugged. "But he couldn't because he couldn't reach it."

Toya wished Amos had considered her like that. She wished

that what Tomiko was telling her was true, but after what she'd seen with Amos the other day, she wasn't convinced.

"The boy loved that bird," Tomiko continued, mimicking Amos's southern drawl and deep voice. "One day, he found a way to get to it. He jumped over a fence and ran over to the bird and then he picked it up. The boy thought he was being careful, but he was clumsy, and as soon as he touched it, he knew he'd hurt it even more. So all he could was to put it down and leave it where it was and walk away."

Of course Toya was choked up. But she wasn't about to let Tomiko see it in her.

"That supposed to make me go see him?"

"I hope so."

She thought back to their encounter at the nursing home before his heart attack. Toya could see as clear as day that he didn't want her there. But she had stayed anyway, and she had tried to reach out to him, and, just like he always did, Amos shot her down.

"I can't keep letting him hurt me like he does, Tomiko." Now she was crying. Toya sat down on the bed next to Tomiko. "I've got to get over Amos and move on with my life so that I can do better. I deserve better," she sobbed. "Just when I think I can do it, somebody or something always comes back to drag me back down, and it's because of him! It's because of the way he's always made me feel! Like I'm less than! Like nobody's ever going to want me because my own father didn't even want me!"

"Then tell him that, girl!" Cass stood in the doorway of the room.

"He needs to hear it! Bad heart or not, Amos needs to know what he did to you and how it made you feel, and if you don't tell him now, then you might not ever get the chance again!"

"If I tell him what's on my mind now, Cass, then it really could kill him!"

"Well." Cass sat down on the other side of Toya. "Then maybe you should tell him gently. Cuss him out, but in a whisper."

Toya surprised herself and laughed.

"The point is," Tomiko continued, "you have to do this for you. Not him. If you deserve anything, Toya, you deserve this, and he owes it to you to listen."

"He told me he was sorry," she said, softly to Tomiko. "He woke up for a minute after his surgery and said that he was sorry for ever hurting me."

"Was that enough?" Tomiko asked, gently.

Toya shrugged. "It should be."

"But is it?"

Toya just stared at her.

# Cass

Toya had agreed, reluctantly, to go back to the hospital with Tomiko to see Amos. Cass had opted to sit this one out and to try and get some rest. She lay across her bed staring up at the ceiling fan and willing her eyes to close and to stay that way for at least a few hours, but she was in a whirlwind with what was happening with Amos, meeting Tomiko, dealing with Toya, and, of course, thinking about Darryl and last night.

In retrospect, the signs had been there all along. Darryl hadn't been interested in Cass. He'd never been interested in her because Alma was the one he'd always wanted. Cass thought back to the times the three of them had been together. Alma was the one he'd always tried to sit closest to. She was the one he stared at when she spoke. She was the one he got nervous around, like a schoolboy with a crush. And he always seemed disappointed when he found out that Alma was running late, or that she had canceled for one of their meetings at the last minute. Cass felt like a fool for not seeing it all before, or maybe she had seen it but had chosen to ignore it.

Just as she reached that very conclusion in her mind, someone started to pound on Cass's front door.

"C'mon, Cass!" Alma shouted. "I know you're home! And you know I've been calling!"

Cass rolled her eyes and sighed in misery. If a meteor fell out of the sky and landed on Alma's head right now, Cass might feel a little bit better.

Alma knocked again. "I'm not leaving! Open the door, or I'll knock all day!"

Cass found the strength to pick up her cell phone and hit Alma's number. She could hear the other woman's phone ringing outside her door.

"Go away," she said dismally when Alma answered. Cass hung up before Alma could respond.

"You're being silly, Cass!" Alma yelled. "Open the damn door! We're grown women! I know we can do business better than this!"

Cass had taken such a chance, a huge chance with Darryl. She'd set her heart on the possibility that the two of them could somehow end up together, maybe even get married, and maybe even get a dog together. She'd believed it was possible. Cass had put herself on the line, gotten her hair and makeup done, and for what? For that fool to show his true colors all over her best friend and right in Cass's face.

Alma's knocking was starting to give Cass a headache. Cass had made up her mind not to let anything or anyone—not even Amos or his bad heart—come between her and Darryl. What in the world would she have done if she had found out that Amos didn't make it? Cass felt like curling up and crawling under a rock to die. She deserved it.

"Cass?" Alma called, sounding as if she was growing tired of pounding on Cass's door. "We didn't go out for coffee. You know I'm not interested in Darryl, right?" she said, begging for pity. "I know how you feel about him. I'm your girl, Cass. I would never do you like that. You know that, right?"

Finally, Cass relented. It was true that Alma had never led him on. She saw in Darryl a business partner who could help expand the business. Cass crawled out of bed, shuffled to the front door, and let her come inside.

"Darryl's not the only man out there, Cass," Alma said, rushing into the living room.

Cass had to come to terms with the fact that it wasn't Alma's fault that men found her beauty irresistible, and that Darryl was just one of those men.

"I've never been interested in Darryl, and you know it," she informed Cass. "Even if I was, you're my girl, and I am not skanky like that."

"I don't think I can work with him," Cass said, discouraged.

"It's okay." Alma shrugged. "We don't have to work with him if you don't want to."

Cass studied Alma, whom she'd known for a very long time. Alma, the real one, would've put up more of a fight. She'd have argued and tried to tell Cass how unreasonable she was being.

"He backed out?" Cass asked.

"It's not a big deal, Cass. We don't need him, and if we ever do decide to find another band, shit, we have our pick of them."

"He *did* back out. How come, Alma? He was all excited about this, just as excited as you and me. What's up?" she asked.

"Just said it wasn't for him, Cass."

"Why not?" Cass challenged.

Alma took her time answering, but Cass knew where this was headed. "Because I told him I wasn't interested in him. That's all. Like I said, we don't need him."

"He wanted you that badly?" Cass asked, feeling herself start to break down again.

"Don't go there, Cass, c'mon," Alma said, exasperated. "It's not a big deal."

A lump swelled in her throat, and Cass felt her whole pathetic world crashing around her all over again. Not only did he *not* want Cass, but he wanted Alma so badly that if he couldn't have her, then he wanted no part of the business. The whole situation had turned out as awfully as it could have.

"I'm through with men," Cass finally said.

"No, you're not," Alma argued.

"Yes, I am," Cass insisted. "I'm single. I'll always be single, and I'm good at it, Alma," she said sorrowfully. "I just need to accept the fact that I'm going to grow old by myself because that's my destiny."

"Oh, Lord!" Alma gasped. "Will you stop? Cass, it's not that serious. Darryl was one man!"

"Darryl was the man I wanted!" Cass argued. "He was the only one!"

"Do you hear yourself? Really? I mean, *really*. You're being dumb."

"No. Dumb was thinking that I could get with a man like that, that he could want me. That's dumb."

"And how many other men besides Darryl have you obsessed over since you've been widowed? Think about it. How many other dudes have you gone out with, Cass? How many have you slept with? How many times have you given out your number?"

Cass stared wide-eyed at that woman, waiting for her to make her point.

"You've made it up in your mind that you can never have anybody, Cass. Why? You're a beautiful woman."

"He didn't think so."

"So?"

Cass shook her head. "I knew you wouldn't understand."

Alma was not going to let her off the hook that easily. "No, I get it. I get that you set yourself up for failure. You make it so that no man will want you. You don't go out. You don't show off that cute little figure of yours. I've seen men checking you out, only to have you turn away like they're invisible."

"I don't do that," Cass shot back.

Alma rolled her eyes. "Please! That's *exactly* what you do, and then when you do decide to woman-up and step out of your comfort zone just a little bit, take a chance and get shot down, it proves your point and you go back into that turtle shell you live in. Why is that, Cass?"

Cass had no answer for that.

"You're afraid to be with anybody, because you're afraid of him letting you down. That's all it is. I can see it even if you can't." Alma picked up her purse to leave. "But it's not my fault. And I'm not going to let you blame me because you don't have the nerve to admit the truth to yourself."

Leave it to Alma's know-it-all ass to have all the answers. Cass watched her walk out the door without bothering to try to stop her. The woman was tall, slim, gorgeous, and smart, and that really wasn't fair. Not fair at all. But the longer Cass sat there, the more of what Alma had said to her started to tattoo itself onto her brain, and the more she started to wonder just how much of what her friend had told her was true.

Cass finally scrolled through the missed calls on her phone. Alma had called seventeen times. As she listened through each message, Cass sighed, unexpectedly relieved at the sound of another voice. "It's Mark. Just thought you'd be interested to know that he made it through and is resting comfortably."

Mark had called earlier that morning from the hospital, ending the last one with a request for her to call him when she was rested and on her way back to the hospital.

She liked Mark. He wasn't *GQ* model cute like Darryl, but he was nice to her and to Amos's mean behind. Cass felt foolish for even thinking of him like that, for thinking of herself and her pathetic love life at a time when Amos was as sick as he was. But Alma hadn't been completely wrong. Cass had had men in her face, nice guys, who'd wanted to get to know her better, and she'd come up with every excuse in the book to shoot them down. Lately, Darryl had been that excuse. Darryl had been her piano man fantasy, capable of singing women out of their panties, smooth, suave, debonair. Cass suddenly felt a bit sick to her stomach. Darryl had been Amos!

"Jesus!" she gasped in horror.

It was as if a light had gone off over her head. Of course it made sense now. He had been Amos thirty years ago, and she'd been pining over him like some kind of crazy groupie! And here she was thinking that Toya was the one with issues! How long had her life been stalled like this? Cass had been in a holding pattern since, well, since Ricky had committed suicide. And even before that, if she sat and thought long and hard enough, she was sure she could pick out moments, bits and pieces of her life that reflected back to that old man lying in the ICU right now.

"Dammit, Amos!" she said with a grimace.

Cass hadn't been any different than her mother when it came to that man. Just like Toya hadn't been any different from hers. The thought made her skin crawl, but the truth had a way of making that happen sometimes.

"He's the first man any of us ever loved," Tomiko had told her earlier at the hospital. "And I don't know about you, but I loved him pretty damn hard."

So had Cass. And so, in her own way, had Toya.

Cass sat there shaking her head when her phone rang. It was Mark. Her heart raced at seeing his name on her phone and the first thought that came to mind was of Amos.

"Mark!" she said, breathless. "Is he all right? Did something happen?"

Mark laughed. "No, Cass. As a matter of fact, they've moved Amos out of ICU. Looks like he's doing fine."

Cass breathed a sigh of relief. "Thank goodness."

"I was calling for a different reason, though," he said.

"What reason?" she asked, curious.

"Well, I was calling about that red dress you had on last night."

Cass was confused. "My red dress?"

"So, my fraternity is having a ball next weekend at Harrol's," he explained.

Harrol's was one of the most lavish event centers in all of Michigan.

"And I was wondering if you'd be interested in wearing that dress again and accompanying me as my date."

Naturally, Cass was stunned by the invitation. "Your date?"

"Yes. My date."

Cass was not prepared for this. After all, she had just come to terms that the man of her dreams wasn't so dreamy, and Cass had just begun the process of nursing a broken heart. It was entirely too soon even to begin thinking about seeing anybody else. She needed time, time to mend and heal her broken heart.

"Well, I . . ."

"Saturday, at seven? I can pick you up at six thirty."

What in the world did she have to lose? "Sure." She felt herself smiling. "I'll be ready at six thirty."

Actually, she was probably going to be ready by six, but he didn't need to know that.

# Toya

Toya and Tomiko had been sitting with Amos all morning, mostly watching him sleep. Every now and then he'd
open his eyes, turn his head and see the two of them, then drift
back off to sleep. Hours later, he finally spoke.

"Hello, ladies." His voice was raspy and weak. Tomiko hurried to his bedside with a cup of water and patiently waited for
him to drink.

"Hey, old man," Tomiko said tenderly.

Toya didn't realize that she was holding her breath, until
Amos turned his head toward her.

"Damn, if you don't look like your momma," he said.

Was that a good thing? "Most people say I look like you,"
Toya countered.

"But prettier," he finished.

"So you remember me?" she finally got the courage to ask.

"More than you give me credit for," he admitted.

"I'm going to leave you two alone," Tomiko whispered in
Toya's ear before leaving.

Amos just stared at her, his expression the same as he'd
worn when they'd first seen each other at Sunnyview, like
she was a fool for coming and he wished she hadn't. But both
Tomiko and Cass had been right. Toya couldn't go home

without doing this, without her saying what she had to say, heart attack or no heart attack. After today, she'd made up her mind that she'd never see this man again. But before she got on that bus to head home, she would say all the things on her mind and then leave it at that.

She stood at the foot of his bed, remembering how handsome he had been when he was younger. Amos had strutted in and out of her mother's life like a peacock, proud and fancy. Now he just looked old and vulnerable. Toya almost felt sorry for him and for the man he'd become.

"Did you ever think about me?" she asked aloud, even though she wasn't necessarily asking him that question.

Amos just lay there, staring at her.

Toya had nothing left inside. She was emotionally empty now, except for the need to say her piece and leave. Amos meant nothing to her. He was a scar inside her that hadn't healed, but it had scabbed over and it had closed.

"All I ever wanted was for you to want me, Amos," she finally said. Hearing it out loud somehow changed the power of it. Saying it, in that moment, almost seemed to set her free. But there was so much more that she needed to say. And in a way, she was happy that he was lying here in this hospital like this, unable to argue or defend himself. Amos was forced to hear her this time. He was going to have to listen, and he was going to have to own whatever she decided to give him.

"I know you and Momma had problems," she said, rolling her eyes. "I saw them each and every time the two of you were in the same room together." Toya pursed her lips together to keep from crying. She was finished crying over him or anybody else. "She wasn't the easiest person to get along with," she said with a shrug. "Still isn't, but that had nothing to do with me."

Amos blinked. Was he listening? Or was he off somewhere in la-la land thinking she was Gladys Knight or whoever? It didn't matter.

"I worshipped you, Amos. But you acted like I wasn't even alive, like I never mattered. You paid more attention to Cass than you did to me, and Tomiko? Boy!" A rogue tear escaped down her cheek. Toya hurried to brush it away. "You made sure the whole world knew about your precious baby girl, Tomiko! I know! I saw you on television exclaiming her name to the whole city of Detroit when that man on television asked you if you had any kids! You said her name, Amos, and you never mentioned mine!"

Toya was crying like a fool! That's not what she'd wanted to do. It's not what she wanted him to see. She turned away from him and faced the window.

"I'm sorry that I was Melba Jean's daughter," she said. "I'm sorry that you hated her, but you didn't have to hate me, too. I didn't choose you, Amos. But you chose her, and you made a kid with her. It was your job to step up and be there for that kid, and you weren't because you couldn't stand my momma! But that wasn't my fault!" She turned to face him once more. To hell with him. Toya had spent a lifetime putting this man up on a pedestal and he had never deserved it. For the first time, looking at him now, she realized that.

"I don't need you now," she said softly. "I don't even want you, Amos." Toya picked up her purse and started to leave. She'd said what she had to say, and he'd had no choice but to listen. Whether he got it or not wasn't her problem. But she'd gotten rid of it.

"Toya."

She stopped at the sound of his voice, scratchy and hoarse. Toya refused to meet his eyes.

"Toya . . . baby."

Why'd he have to go and call her that? A knot the size of a basketball swelled in her stomach. Toya turned around to Amos's outstretched hand. Tears slid down the sides of his face. Her feet tried to stay cemented to the floor, but Toya tore them away and went to him, taking hold of his hand.

"I missed you," he finally said. "I thought about you. I regretted you, but only because I knew that I could never be what you needed."

Toya burned her face against his shoulder and cried. "I needed my father."

"I am so very sorry," he began to sob. "But I never knew how to be one. I knew how to woo women, how to charm them, and love them for a time, but then music would get in the way. It was my joy and my curse and it cost me. It cost me everything, even you."

"And now it's too late," she said, dismally, brushing off his excuses.

"Is it?" Amos held out his hand for her to take. "I'm still breathing. You're still breathing. And breath is everything."

# Amos

*The* eight-track was already in the deck, and all he had to do was push a button and wait. Not until he heard the first lick from the guitar did he even bother to turn the key in the ignition. There wasn't a sweeter sound in the world than that opening guitar riff on Stevie Wonder's "Superstition." Amos Davis slowly pulled his black '76 Camaro away from the curb and headed for Chicago. Linda wasn't happy about his leaving, but then again, Linda didn't know what it felt like to chase a dream. She had, after all, given up her dream in exchange for him.

He followed the lure of the next gig like a bee follows the trail to the honey hive. It was just instinct.

"We need you to sit in for Gus next weekend, man. Gus got problems, or problems got Gus, but whatever it is, he ain't gonna be able to play at Izzy's." Amos had no idea how this brotha got his number. His name was Wayne Brown and he headed up a blues band in Milwaukee called Chi-Town Five. He'd called a week ago, asking Amos if he could do him the honor of performing with them at the Blues Festival at Izzy's in Chicago. A week later, Amos was on his way.

Izzy's was a dive about a hundred miles out of his way, but that was all right. Amos was just answering his calling, that's all. They needed a piano player, somebody who could pick up where Gus left off, and Amos needed to get his hands on a keyboard. Besides, they called Amos because they knew that if anybody could come through for them, he could.

The Chi-Town Five should've been his band all along. Driving down the tree-lined single-lane highway from Detroit, Amos remembered the night when it all came together, everyone sitting there in Brown's living room in his small South Side Chicago home, five men high on gin and weed, grooving to jams they made up on the spot. They were soul and funk, rhythm and blues, jazz and boogaloo all rolled up into a sound that even the angels couldn't help but dance to. People had gathered outside the door, and before they knew it, there was a party going on in Brown's front yard.

When all was said and done, the five of them exchanged glances, nodding because they all had been sharing the same consciousness, using one soul, blending into one sound, and had all reached the same conclusion.

Amos said it first. "I think we got somethin' here."

That was all that needed to be said, and from that point on, they were in business. The Chi-Town Five was born. That was six years ago. They were as good, if not better, than any group out there: Earth, Wind & Fire; the Ohio Players; Junior Walker and the All-Stars. Hell, Amos could run down a list of a hundred groups who'd signed on with the big record labels that the Chi-Town Five could play under the table. The others had just gotten lucky. That's all. That was the only difference between playing in sold-out stadiums and playing in dives like Izzy's, as far as Amos was concerned. Talent didn't mean shit these days, but luck was a whole other kind of vibe.

He left the group because Linda didn't want him playing in clubs every night, which he found ironic because he'd met her in a club. Amos was sitting up onstage, beating blood from those piano keys, his voice hoarse from singing too damn much, and there she was, standing *on his side of the stage, twisting plump hips into perfect figure eights. How'd she know he had a thing for hips? To this day, he wondered.*

*A pretty dark-skinned girl with big brown eyes and a pretty mouth, Linda put a spell on Amos, all right, one that made it hard to be home with anybody who wasn't her. One thing led to another, and Linda had welcomed him home with open arms.*

*Linda had something about her that just didn't seem real sometimes. Love never had nothing to do with how he felt about Linda, but he couldn't deny the power she'd held over him these last couple of years, either. So when she said, you need to quit gigging and stay home with me or else . . . Well, he didn't even want to think about what "else" could possibly mean. Amos told the group he had to be there for his woman. They were disappointed, but they'd all seen Linda. They understood where he was coming from.*

*A long time ago some fool had had the nerve to ask him once if he knew how to read music.*

*He might as well have asked Amos if he could jump up and touch the moon because he couldn't do that, either.*

*"Read music?" Amos asked, shocked. "Naw, I don't read no damn music, and if you was a real musician, you wouldn't be readin' it, neither."*

*The man looked like Amos had just said something bad about his momma.*

*"Music comes from the soul, son," Amos explained earnestly. "It ain't dots and lines on a piece of paper. Music is somethin' you feel. You breathe and taste it. You listen for it, and if it looks like anythin' at all, it looks like the curves on a beautiful woman, the light in a child's eyes. Music, good music, looks like a big, thick, juicy steak."*

*The man laughed, but Amos was serious. The best kind of music came from the heart, and it didn't have nothing to do with no pen and paper.*

*"Sing it, man!" One boisterous voice caught his attention as he played alongside his bandmates on Izzy's stage.*

*Amos sang lead on the Temptations' "Ain't Too Proud to Beg," as good as David Ruffin on his best day, only he did it with more soul. Amos sang that song from that place inside him that had put him on his knees many nights, beseeching some woman in his life for forgiveness, and he didn't need a sparkly blue two-piece suit or fancy dance steps to make sure every person on that dance floor heard him loud and clear.*

*Linda had thrown a fit when he told her that the band needed him to sit in for a night. He'd left her standing in the kitchen with her mouth poked out and fire in her eyes, and he knew there'd be hell to pay when he made it home. But right here and now, he didn't give a damn. Amos had been born to be up onstage, singing and playing the piano. Factory work kept the bills paid, but it didn't do nothing to satisfy his soul.*

*That dark, smoke-filled room, smelling like whiskey and sweat, was home sweet home for . . .*

His eyes were playing tricks on him. Amos faltered, blinking his eyes to try to focus on what couldn't possibly be real coming into view beyond the gyrating bodies swaying in front of him. "Miko?" he whispered in awe. Amos raised his hand to touch her face. Was she real? Was she standing there in front of him?

"Yes, Daddy." She smiled. "It's me. It's Tomiko."

Amos was confused. What was she doing here?

"Does yo' momma know you in here? Did you sneak out?" he smiled.

She smiled back. "I followed you here. I came to hear you play."

She was his heart. Tomiko was the perfect part of him. "Can you sing with daddy?"

"Of course I can."


The piano in front of him wasn't real, but Amos positioned his fingers on air, and played the melody circling in his dream and hummed. Tomiko resisted the urge to be afraid because he was living in the past and present at the same time, but there was something beautiful about this moment. He was having his cake and eating it too, living in that world where he was king and sharing it with her believing that she was six years old.

He looked up at her as his fingers moved on invisible piano keys. "You remember the words to this?"

Tomiko's eyes glazed over with tears as she bobbed her head. "You go first, Daddy. I'll sing the chorus."

Amos laughed.

# Amos

## Three Months Later

Amos could hardly move fast enough, shuffling down that hallway at the speed of molasses freezing in the winter. Jennie V. looped her arm in his and walked with him toward the nurses' station. She called herself his girlfriend, but that mess wasn't even remotely true.

"Looking good, old man," Mark said.

"They here yet?" Amos asked excitedly.

"Not yet."

"Good." He looked at Jennie V., who was smiling up at him.

"You could just be ready for 'em when they get here." She grinned.

He was nervous sitting in front of that piano. Most of the residents filled the room, waiting eagerly for him to start, but he wasn't about to begin until the girls got here. Amos took several deep breaths to calm his nerves, closed his eyes, and remembered those memories most clear in his mind. He thought back to the musky smell of cigarettes and whiskey, of perfume mixing with cologne.

*He saw the lights bouncing back and reflecting off shoes polished like glass, and tapped his fingers to the rhythm Boss Man Jones plucked on his guitar to help calm his nerves before they played. Brotha Luke finished tuning his bass, while Ike Preston waited patiently holding his drumsticks, watching the room fill up with pretty girls who worshipped the ground he walked on. Making music was the only kind of magic Amos knew, and he clung to those times in his life, whether in his right mind or not.*

He opened his eyes in time to see Cass coming through the door first, and not long after her came Toya, still looking apprehensive and pensive, still needing to be convinced. And finally, looking as sweet as ever, Miko came in, trailing behind the other two, and took her seat right next to them.

Mark came in like he promised, sat down next to Cass, and kissed her like he meant it. Jennie V. sat in the middle of the front row the way she always did, smiling like every word to come out of his mouth was supposed to be gospel and meant for her. Maybe she was right. Maybe today, every word was hers.

The entire crowd stirred as two older men strode into the room. Amos blinked several times, not sure if what was happening sprang from his diseased mind or if he really was seeing two of his longtime band mates swaggering their way toward him. Boss Man Jones and Ike Preston still looked mighty dapper, even if their faces were craggy and their hair was white.

Chortling at the huge look of surprise on Amos's face, Mark came forward as the three old friends shook hands. "Man, you need to tell your friends where you're at," Mark told him. "As soon as I called them, they both said they wanted to come see you."

"And here we be, you old son of a gun," said Boss Man. "What, you can't pick up a phone?"

The three men laughed together, and when the uproar died

down, Amos announced, "You know something? I've been doing some new writing these days. I got a new song I want to play for you." He looked past them and pointed at his three daughters. "And especially for them. Because the song's about the new start in life that they've given to a lonely old man."

Amos had come to realize that he got more than he deserved. His girls might never forgive him for everything he did wrong, but they forgave him enough to be here now. Cass caught his eye and winked at him. Toya gave him as much of a smile as she could muster, and Miko stared at him the way she used to when she was a small girl, sitting on his lap and singing right along with him.

His girls had become his inspiration. Instead of his music pulling him away from them, he was going to sing a song he'd written for them:

> *Wish there was a way to turn back time*
> *Wish there was a way to right past wrongs*
> *But there are no do-overs in life and so I sing this song*
> *To tell you what I feel in my heart is true*
> *To tell you that I love you, really I do.*

# Acknowledgments

FROM J. D. MASON

My dad inspired the idea for this story. He passed away some years ago and, along with him, some unresolved issues between the two of us passed away, too. I loved him more than I think he knew, and he loved me more than I believed he could. I miss him. The last message he left me on my phone before he died he said, "Hey, J.D. This is J.P. Call me. I got something to tell you." I didn't get a chance to call him back. Despite his shortcomings, he was the first man I ever loved. His smile was infectious, he told the best jokes, and boy could he sing!

# Reading Group Guide
## *Finding Amos*

### Introduction

When Amos Davis finds himself in a nursing home after a car accident, he is saddled with the news that he suffers from Alzheimer's disease—and the chilling realization that there is no one to care for him. Alone, the once-famous musician must confront the consequences of his years spent womanizing. His only hope for a family is in the three daughters—by three different women—that he abandoned years ago.

Up until now, Cass, Toya, and Tomiko were only connected by the heartbreak caused by their absent father. Now, they must reconcile their painful pasts with their present opportunities to connect and forgive—in the hope of rebuilding the family they never thought they'd have.

### Discussion Questions

1. The novel opens with Amos daydreaming about the past. In the memory, his father tells him he is not a "real man" because "a real man works. A real man's hands got calluses. A real man's got a crooked back from being bent over all the damn time workin' in them fields" (page 2). Do you think that Amos ever considers himself a "real man"? In the end, how might Amos redefine what a real man is?

2. Discuss the structure of the novel. Do the changing points of view make this story equally about all of the characters—Amos and his three daughters? Or does

this story seem to belong to one character more than another?

3. On pages 109 and 110, Max's wife, Jewel, confronts Toya in her home, and Toya is reminded of scenes from her childhood between Melba Jean and Amos. "Like mother, like daughter" (page 109), she thinks to herself. Do you think Toya is likely to suffer the same fate as her mother? Is confronting her estranged father the remedy she needs to overcome the cycle of self-abuse? In your response, consider how Amos's other two daughters, Cass and Tomiko, are like or unlike their mothers.

4. Examine as a group Toya and Max's relationship. Is Toya in love with Max, or with the *idea* of Max? What does he represent to her? Do you think that their relationship could ever work? Why or why not?

5. What do Cass, Toya and Tomiko have in common? Do you think their shattered relationship with their father has made it difficult for these three women to find love? Is one more successful in love, or life in general, than the others? Is one the most damaged?

6. "If you go see that man, don't expect any miracles from him, Toya . . . he can make you believe in 'em, but Amos ain't never been good at deliverin' on 'em" (page 152), Melba Jean tells her daughter. Do you think that the ability to change—or the inability to change—is a theme of *Finding Amos*? In the end, does Amos change? Does Toya? Do Cass and Tomiko?

7. What symbolism can you glean from the title *Finding Amos*? Who is finding Amos? Is this person or persons seeking Amos physically, mentally, or both? Do you think the title might also refer to Amos finding himself? Why or why not?

8. "You can't disappear into a kitchen or lurk around in the corner of a room for the rest of your life" (pages 161-2), Alma tells Cass. What does Alma represent in Cass's life? Do you think of her as a help or a hindrance to Cass's growth as a character?

9. Revisit the scene, beginning on page 170, when Tomiko FaceTimes with Amos. How does she feel about seeing her father again after so many years? In your opinion, does it make sense that Tomiko wonders why "that love was nowhere to be found" (page 171)? Do you think it's possible to love someone even when they don't deserve it? Why or why not?

10. Consider the role of gender in *Finding Amos*. How do the women function in relation to the men in the novel? Is it notable that Amos has only daughters? Consider the bond of female relationships in your response, particularly between mothers/daughters, and the daughters and their close female friends.

11. Discuss Mark's character. Do you think of him as a kind of guardian angel for Amos? Without Mark, do you think that Amos's daughters would have been reconciled with their father and with one another?

12. On page 230, Amos admits to Toya, "I hurt you. Of all of them, I hurt you the most." Does this confession change the hardness of Toya's heart toward her father? Do you think this moment is a catalyst for the change that comes at the end of the book, both for Toya and all the characters? Why or why not?

13. In the end, Amos's music brings him closer to his daughters. "Instead of his music pulling him away from them, he was going to sing a song he'd written for them" (page 274). Do you agree that the book's message might be that the very thing that keeps you from opening your heart might be the very thing in the end that enables you to love? Do you think art has the power to heal? Consider Amos and Tomiko in your response.

## Additional Activities:
## Ways of Enhancing Your Book Club

1. *Finding Amos* is unique in that it is co-written by three very influential writers: J. D. Mason, ReShonda Tate Billingsley, and Bernice L. McFadden. Read a book by each of these authors, such as *Crazy, Sexy, Revenge* (Mason), *The Secret She Kept* (Billingsley), and *Gathering of Waters* (McFadden). Discuss with your group the signature styles you find in each of these novels. Can you pinpoint what each writer brought to *Finding Amos*? Do any characters in *Finding Amos* remind you of characters from the other novels?

2. Initially, Cass is only able to demonstrate her love for her father through food. At Mark's urging, she brings Amos collard greens, corn bread and cakes to supplement the unappetizing hospital food. Arguably, it is through cooking for her estranged father that Cass is able to slowly open her heart back up to Amos. For Cass, food has healing power, and enables a dialogue to take place between father and daughter that otherwise may not have been possible. Host a potluck with your book club, and in the spirit of openness, bring your favorite signature dish from childhood. Over the meal, share with your book club how the food reminds you about who you are or where you came from. Share stories, memories, pictures and tidbits about how you connect certain dishes with certain events in your life.

3. Music is the defining motif of *Finding Amos*—it is music that is responsible for Amos's wayward lifestyle and the thing that ultimately unites the family together in the end. Listen to Amos's genre of music—folksy blues—with your book club, or, if possible, attend a local venue that features live blues music. Consider how you feel listening to the melodies, and imagine being the abandoned daughter of the singer. What is it about music in general, and this type of music in particular, that causes one to have a strong emotional reaction? Is there a song from your childhood that evokes a particular emotional reaction? Start by listening to "(Sittin' on) The Dock of the Bay" by Otis Redding to begin your discussion.